Good Times

As they say in *New Orleans*, let the *good times* roll.

JIFFY KATE

Books by Jiffy Kate

Finding Focus Series
Finding Focus
Chasing Castles
Fighting Fire
Taming Trouble

French Quarter Collection
Turn of Fate
Blue Bayou
Come Again
Neutral Grounds
Good Times
Ever After (coming Winter 2020)

Table 10 Novella Series
Table 10 part 1
Table 10 part 2
Table 10 part 3

New Orleans Revelers
The Rookie and The Rockstar
TVATV (coming Fall 2020)

Smartypants Romance
Stud Muffin (Donner Bakery, book 2)
Beef Cake (Donner Bakery, book 4)

Standalones
Watch and See
No Strings Attached

Finley

"Happy New Year!" I hear someone yell, or slur rather, as I lock up the door in the narrow back alley behind Neutral Grounds. Shaking my head, I chuckle to myself. In the short time I've lived here, I've become accustomed to the liveliness of the city. It's not just a New Year's Eve thing, it's a New Orleans thing.

This city is like a living, breathing creature, more vibrant than any city I've ever been in.

And who would've thought I'd be here?

On New Year's Eve, no less?

Not me, that's for damn sure. I've never been one to plan out my life or look too far into the future, taking each day as it comes and rolling with each punch life has given me. But if you would've asked me last year on New Year's Eve where I saw myself in a year, I probably would've said right where I was—at a bar in downtown Dallas—living what I thought was my best life.

But that was before Shep planted the seed of starting fresh in New Orleans.

And then Maggie went to live with her sister.

The stars aligned, and here I am.

As I walk past a group of musicians pounding out a rhythmic soundtrack to the evening, I toss a few dollars in the upturned bucket. Being a musician myself, and a street musician at that, I know every little bit helps. It's impossible for me to pass a bucket or open instrument case and not drop in whatever change is in my pocket. If I didn't, I'm afraid some bad juju would jump right on me and I don't need any of that.

"Thanks, man," one of the guys calls out, giving me a nod of his head as he continues to beat the side of a five-gallon bucket, sounding better than a drummer with a high-dollar set of drums.

Every night here in New Orleans is electric, but tonight is even more so. There's a very distinct hum, an intense charge, I can feel deep down to my bones as I make my way through the French Quarter.

When CeCe offered to let me stay in the apartment above her coffee shop, I had no idea how perfect the location would be. Honestly, I was just happy to have a clean and safe place to stay. And the super cheap rent was something I couldn't afford to pass up either.

Once I realized how close I was to the heart of New Orleans, with all of the eclectic people and musicians roaming around, I knew I'd found a place to call home.

That's exactly what it feels like, too.

Home.

With my saxophone case in hand and equipment bag over my shoulder, I walk quickly toward Lagniappe, a popular restaurant here in the Quarter. I haven't been yet, but it's owned by Micah Landry, a friend of Shep and CeCe, and has a reputation for good food, as well as good times, so I've been looking forward to this gig for weeks.

In the few months since I moved down here, I've quickly made a name for myself as a local musician and I've made some great connections, thanks to CeCe, Shep, and their friends. At times, it almost feels too good to be true, especially with the way I've been able to fit in with the locals. Back home in Dallas, I had a few trusted people I liked to work with, but I never truly felt like I belonged. It was like I was always trying to prove myself. Don't get me wrong, I have to prove myself here, too, but it's with a more creative vibe rather than a competitive one.

I walk into the building and have to admit I'm impressed. At first glance, it definitely lives up to the hype. Hardwood floors, leather seating, and warm lighting give the place a really cool vibe.

"Hey, Finley," someone calls out, catching my attention.

Turning, I see Micah Landry walking toward me with a huge-ass grin on his face. I've only met him once, to set up this gig, but I'm a fairly good judge of character and I know he's a nice, genuine guy. I've had to deal with some shady fuckers in the past so it's a relief to work with someone with Micah's reputation and good nature to back it up.

"Hey," I reply, walking toward him and offering my hand for him to shake. "Thanks, again, for hooking me up with this gig tonight." It is, after all, New Year's Eve in New Orleans, and though it's not the biggest holiday for the city, it's still a busy, high-demand kind of night and I appreciate the opportunity.

Instead of shaking my hand, he uses it to pull me into a sturdy hug, beating my back for good measure. "Don't mention it." Releasing me, he grabs the equipment bag from my shoulder and takes off toward the back corner. "Come on, let's get you set up. Then, we'll get you some food and I'll introduce you to some people."

"Now, that's an offer I can't refuse," I say, allowing my nose to entertain the amazing aroma filling the restaurant.

Micah laughs. "I'd hope not. My brother basically took over the kitchen and made our family's New Year's Eve favorites—jambalaya, fresh oysters, and crème brûlée."

My mouth is watering at the mere mention of jambalaya. I've had it a few times since I've been in the city and each time it's been a little different, but every time it's been some of the best food I've ever put in my mouth.

Before I can even get my amp and stand set up, Micah is pulling me away from the stage and shoving a plate of food in my hands as he walks me around the room, introducing me, not as tonight's entertainment, but as *his friend*, Finley Lawson.

It makes me feel like more than the hired help and I try not to let that affect me, but it does.

Once I've finished my plate, I excuse myself and head to the stage. Regardless of how at home I feel, I was hired to do a job and it just so happens to be something I love doing. Even though I'm getting paid to be here, there's nowhere else I'd rather be.

Not tonight.

Tonight, I'm here, in an amazing restaurant in the middle of New Orleans, playing for a group of people who make me feel like I belong.

After my first set, I take a short break and make my way around the room mingling and grabbing a drink as I take in the crowd. Most of the people I've been introduced to so far are family members of Micah or are friends or local business acquaintances.

One thing I've noticed is the people around here treat each other like family and are very close knit, looking out for one another. It's different from any other place I've ever lived or worked before, and I love it.

Glancing across the room, I spot Shep standing in a corner with his best friend and business partner, Maverick Kensington. Maverick and Shep have always been thick as thieves, the three of us go way back. My grandmother, Maggie, was the housekeeper for Shep's family. After she took me in, Shep took me under his wing, which was more than most of the people in my life had attempted.

If it weren't for Maggie and Shep, no telling where I'd be today—probably living on the streets or following in my parents' footsteps with drugs and violence.

Shep is basically the big brother I never had.

He took a chance on a kid from the wrong side of the tracks and never looked down on me for where I came from. Shit, he bought me my first saxophone, and through the years, has paid for lessons and helped me find gigs, never judging me for my choices in education or employment.

So, sitting in this room tonight, with him and his friends, it feels like the best way to ring in the New Year.

The possibilities feel endless and within reach.

It's a heady feeling and I try not to let my mind get too carried away. I still have a gig to play and people to entertain. Speaking of, everyone seems to be having a great time and it makes me happy to know I've helped create this atmosphere, if only a little; it means I'm doing my job. But even more than that, it's fun. I fucking love what I do, which is why, even when the pay is shit, I continue to follow my passion.

There's a special high a performer gets when the music they create is enjoyed by others, even on a smaller level like this. I can only imagine what it must feel like to experience the high multi-million-dollar performers out there get, selling out stadiums night after night. I don't really have those aspirations, personally, but I can certainly appreciate the appeal.

Right now, at this moment, this is enough.

"Dude! I've never seen anyone wail on a sax like that before," a guy with sandy-blond hair says, walking up and clapping me on the shoulder. "And using looper pedals? Genius!"

His enthusiasm is contagious, and I instantly smile, recognizing a fellow musician when I see one. No one else gets this geeked out by looper pedals. "Thanks, man."

Just as I'm getting ready to ask what he plays, Deacon Landry, Micah's brother and the creator of the amazing food I ate earlier, walks up and chimes in. "I told you, Tucker, this dude is the real deal!" He laughs, giving me a wink. "Finn, this is my brother-in-law, Tucker Benoit. He *used* to be a well-known guitarist around these parts back in the day."

"What the hell, man," Tucker says, obviously taking offense to Deacon's ribbing. "I can still play. In fact, I think Finley and I should play together sometime. Whatcha think, Finn?" Tucker asks.

My eyes grow wide at the thought. I love any type of collaboration. "Absolutely," I tell him, nodding. "I'd be down. Just say when and where."

Tucker taps my beer with his own, like we've just sealed a deal. "Awesome," he says finishing off his glass. "So, where are you from and how am I just now hearing about you?"

"Originally from Dallas," I say, nodding as I run a hand through my hair. "But I've been down here for about four months. Shep," I say, pointing over to where he and Maverick are still standing around talking, like two old biddies, but now have Carys and CeCe keeping them company. "He told me I should move down here and give the New Orleans life a shot, so I took him up on it for a change of scenery and better opportunities."

"You remember CeCe's husband, Shep," Deacon says, turning to Tucker who nods his head in acknowledgment, and then back to me. "CeCe is old friends with my wife, Cami, who just happens to be Tucker's sister."

I shake my head, amused at how everyone is so connected. "Damn, did I just move into a soap opera?"

Tucker laughs, shaking his head. "It's a small fucking world. Nola might be a big city, but it functions like a small town where everyone knows everything about everyone else's business. There's never a dull moment, that's for sure."

Deacon claps my shoulder, tipping up his beer before adding, "Don't worry about all that, Finn. You keep doing what you're doing and you'll be just fine." His eyes trail off across the room and I watch as his entire face lights up. "Oh, speaking of, there's my beautiful wife." Stepping out of our circle, he calls out, "Cami, love, come and meet Finley."

I watch as a petite, blonde woman walks our way, smiling and waving at various people until she stops and tucks herself into Deacon's side. He immediately kisses the top of her head before introducing us properly.

"This is Finley," he says, nothing but love for the woman at his side as he gazes down at her. "Finley, the one and only, Camille Benoit-Landry."

Quirking an eyebrow, I offer her my hand. It's obvious how much Deacon adores his wife, but there's something else there too—pride... awe.

"Nice to meet you, Finley," she finally says, giving her husband a slight eye roll. When she smiles at me, I can see the resemblance between her and Tucker but there's something else familiar about her. "I'm sorry I missed your set; this baby is draining all my energy lately. Will you be playing again?" She rubs her belly, and it's then I notice the quite pronounced basketball under her dress.

"No worries," I say with a smile. "I'll start my second set soon, and I'm taking requests. Would you like to sit down? I'm sure I can find you a chair."

"Aren't you a sweet potato?" she gushes. "Thank you, but I'm fine. I just got out of the car, so I need to stretch my legs a bit. I'll be sitting soon enough."

Deacon gives her a stern look. "You didn't drive, did you? I thought the new girl was going to bring you?"

Cami looks at me and rolls her eyes again, this time not so subtly. "I'm perfectly fine to run my own art gallery, but drive myself at night? Forget it."

"Well, if I had my way, you wouldn't be working right now either. Is it so wrong for a man to worry about his wife?" Deacon asks.

Cami looks like she's about to tell him off, so I interrupt and redirect the conversation. "Did you say you own an art gallery? Here in the Quarter?"

Tucker chuckles as he turns his back to our small group, murmuring under his breath in my direction, "Nice job. You're gonna fit in perfectly."

"Yes, I own 303 Royal Street Art Gallery," Cami says sweetly, the glare she had on Deacon morphing into a smile. "We just recently opened. I'm planning on having a party soon, something low-key. I'll make sure you're on the invite list. Oh, you should bring your sax! We'd love for you to play for us, if you're interested."

"That's where I know you from," I say, hoping I don't sound like a stalker. "I set up and play on the corner of Royal Street, close to your gallery."

Her face lights up. "I think I've seen you there!"

"I guess that kind of makes us pseudo neighbors," I say, smiling. "And I'd be happy to play for you." I'm always up for something out of the ordinary. And just like tonight, you never know who you'll meet. One opportunity can very well open the door for your next, and so on and so on. That's pretty much how it's always been for me.

"Wonderful," she says, eyes darting around the restaurant. "Let me introduce you to the gallery's new manager. She's here somewhere… you know, since *she drove me*," she says, taking the opportunity to get a dig in at Deacon while nailing him with a glare.

I'm guessing this is a sore subject around the Benoit-Landry household right now. Their easy banter makes me chuckle.

I watch as Cami continues to scan the crowd behind her before calling out to someone across the restaurant. With all the people mingling and chatting, it's hard to hear much outside our small group.

"Here she comes," she says, her smile beaming. "She just flew in this morning and I've already put her to work, poor thing. She's probably already reconsidering taking the job." Cami reaches for someone, bringing them into the center of our little circle. "Georgette, this is Finley."

In an instant, my world freezes.

That *small, small* world Tucker was speaking of only moments prior comes to a startling halt.

She's here… in New Orleans.

How?

Why?

My mind is spinning as my eyes drink her in. It's been five years—five long damn years—since she walked away from me, never looking back.

"Jette?" I ask, the nickname I gave her when we were teenagers slipping out of my mouth on a whisper.

Recognition dawns on her and causes her to gasp as a checklist of emotions flashes across her face—shock, confusion, embarrassment—but she never once acknowledges me. She doesn't even say my name.

I'm not the masochistic kid I once was, so I don't wait for her next move. If it's anything like her last one, she'll be gone without a trace… no forwarding address, no phone number… no email.

Just fucking… *gone*.

Quickly, I excuse myself and head back to my saxophone, the burn of Georgette's abandonment from five years ago still stinging like it was yesterday. On autopilot, I look over my playlist, refusing to search the crowd for her—the last person I ever thought I'd see in New Orleans.

I'm a professional and well-versed in picking up the pieces left behind by Georgette Taylor. As they say in the industry, the show must go on. But a few minutes into my set, I can't help but notice her.

Those blonde curls I've dreamt about for so long are hard to miss. And I catch sight of them just as she walks out the front door, not looking back.

Georgette

I'M NOT SURE WHY I RUN, BUT I DO, ALL THE WAY TO THE
hotel I'm currently staying at. As I approach the front door, a man
dressed in a suit greets me with a tip of his head and a smile. "Good
evening, Miss."

"Hi," I breathe out, still panting from the unexpected physical exertion.

"Are you here for a party?" he asks, holding the door open for me as I
stand there with my hands on my knees, trying to catch my breath, like
a dimwit.

In or out, Georgette, make up your mind.

"Uh, no," I reply, shaking my head as I walk past him into the lobby.
I *was* at a party, a perfectly lovely party with delicious food and festive
drinks and nice people… and Finley Lawson.

Finley. Lawson.

In New Orleans.

How is that possible?

Of all the places in all the world.

"Spending New Year's Eve alone?" he asks, a kind smile on his face.

"Seems that way." I shrug, trying to blow it off, but inside I'm still reeling. I should've stayed at Lagniappe, but there's no going back now. Besides, what would I say?

Sorry for running out on you... again?

The doorman resumes his post but not before tipping his head once more, sending me on my way with a polite greeting. "Have a good evening." That's pretty much been my experience thus far in New Orleans—so many nice people.

"You too," I tell him, digging in my sparkly bag for my key card. "And Happy New Year."

"Yes, Happy New Year."

After a morning of flying, followed by a meeting with my new boss, and then an evening of meeting new people, I'm actually exhausted. So, it's not a horrible thing to be back in my room before midnight. I'll need the extra sleep to be ready for my first week on the job. According to Cami, I'll be hitting the ground running.

The gallery is newly opened. She's been doing everything herself while searching for the right person to hand it all over to while she has her baby... *me*. I'm that person.

Well, at least, she *thinks* I'm that person. I pray I'm that person. Up until now, I've held several positions at various galleries in New York, including my last job as an assistant buyer at Sotheby's.

But I've never managed an entire gallery. *By myself.*

Cami knows that, though. I didn't hold anything back from her in my multiple interviews. We spoke about everything from my education, which includes a degree in art management, to my internships. But what she seemed most interested in is my love of art.

And that's what I ended up loving the most about her... and 303 Royal Street.

More than anything, I want to work with people who love art as much as I do. I want to be in a city that loves what I love, and that's what made New Orleans feel like home the second I stepped out of the Uber and onto the sidewalk in front of the hotel that sits next door to the gallery.

Everything about this city screams creativity wrapped in culture.

Trevor, my boyfriend, said this was a step backward. I've been at Sotheby's for the last two years, since I graduated from NYU. According to him, I should've stayed at Sotheby's and worked my way up.

But that's Trevor, he's ambitious and driven. Those are two of the qualities that drew me to him, that and his stunning smile and ash-blond hair. He was handsome and he filled a gaping hole at the time. When we first started dating, I didn't even want a relationship, so we were friends, which is how my two most important relationships have started—friendships that turned into more. But unlike my feelings for Finley, which came fast and furious, my feelings for Trevor were slow and subtle. Eventually, he was what was comfortable. He made me feel like I had a place to call mine. In a huge city, like New York City, that says something.

Staying at Sotheby's and following Trevor's advice was always a possibility. I could've done that. I probably would've been happy… or something close to it.

But one lonely night, when Trevor was working late, which had become more of a norm than an occasional thing, I felt something call to me. It was like a wild echo on the wind, something that reached deep down into my soul.

For the past couple of years, we've been at an impasse with our relationship. My job at Sotheby's was growing stagnant. It felt like the world was turning around me and I was stuck in the middle, going nowhere.

That night, I got to daydreaming, one search leading to another, and before I knew it, I was on a website with listings of job opportunities. As

I narrowed down the search to art manager and director positions, 303 Royal Street Art Gallery was the first listing.

Artist-owned and operated.

New Orleans, French Quarter.

Competitive salary.

And there was a personal note from the owner.

Hello,

I'm Camille Benoit-Landry and I've been an artist since I was five. There's a good chance my blood has been replaced with paint. It's all I've ever wanted to do, except for having a family. Which brings me to why I'm looking for a special person to help run my gallery. Just after the new year, I'll be welcoming my third baby into the world, and my husband insists on me taking some time off. So, for a couple of months, I'll be handing over the day-to-day duties of 303 Royal Street to someone else...

The note itself was out of the ordinary. Typically, you wouldn't get that much insider information about a job opening, which is what caught my interest and attention. The rest of Cami's personal message went on to describe the dynamic of the gallery, which is still in the newborn stage itself. Everything she described spoke to my soul—open to local artists, flexible hours, collaborative opportunities. It sounded fresh and bursting with possibilities.

Everything my life was not.

Plus, she assured me that after she returns to work, she'll want me to stay. With three children, a husband, and an art studio in the small town she lives in, there's no way she can keep up with it all.

My official title should actually be *Camille Benoit-Landry's right-hand woman*, because I basically signed on to do anything she needs me to do. Just on my first day alone, I've been her stylist, confidant, and chauffeur.

But one thing she didn't mention is during my first twelve hours I'd come face to face with Finley Lawson... the boy I loved... the boy I left behind.

I haven't seen him in over five years, but that doesn't mean I haven't thought about him. However, I wasn't prepared for how my heart would feel when he called out my name…

Jette.

He's the only one who's ever called me that.

The only person who's ever truly understood me.

He holds so many of my firsts, so many of my memories.

Seeing him tonight had my heart skipping into overdrive and my mind spinning.

He's so much the same, but also changed. No longer is he the boy I fell in love with—awkward and still finding himself. Now, he's *all man.* The softer edges have been replaced with hard lines and well-defined features. But those mesmerizing gray eyes haven't changed, they still pulled me in and made me forget to breathe.

That's why I had to run.

I needed some space, some time to think.

I have no doubt Finley and I will cross paths again; I feel it in my bones, but next time I see him, I'll be more prepared. He won't catch me off guard and push me off my feet with one word.

As I let myself into my hotel, I kick off my black pumps and exhale. Leaning my back against the door, I allow the coolness to seep into my heated skin. My mind wants to chalk it up to the warmer weather or the run, but my heart knows the truth… it's Finley.

It's always been Finley.

3

Finley

I'VE BEEN LOOKING FOR GEORGETTE IN EVERY PERSON I pass on the street.

That's not really a new thing. I've had her on my mind for the past five years. Any time I saw a petite frame with unruly blonde curls, I'd do a double-take, making sure it wasn't her, but that was back in Dallas, somewhere I'd expect to see her.

Not New Orleans.

Never in a million years did I expect her to be in a dimly-lit restaurant in the heart of the French Quarter on a random New Year's Eve. But there she was, looking as beautiful as ever, and as caught off guard as I was.

She's different, but the same. Her hair is shorter and more tamed, but there's still a hint of the wild nature begging to be set free. That was always Jette in a nutshell.

Her family has a lot of money and always expected her to fall in line—be the perfect daughter with perfect grades who chooses the perfect university and gets the perfect degree.

They also wanted her to choose the perfect boyfriend, who in turn would become the perfect husband to complete their perfect family.

That wasn't me.

Jette and I first met when I got into a magnet school for fine arts. Most of the students were from the neighborhood where I lived with my grandmother, Maggie, who worked for the Rhys-Jones family. But just because I lived in the same neighborhood as many of my classmates didn't mean I fit in. It was obvious I wasn't one of them.

I didn't dress like them.

I didn't talk like them.

I didn't go to Aspen for Christmas or the Hamptons for summer vacation like them.

My parents didn't work in one of the high-rise buildings downtown like theirs.

And for some reason, Georgette saw past all of our differences, down to the core of who I was—a kid who loved music and art and just wanted to be better than the people who brought him into the world.

Before my grandmother took me in, I didn't know where my next meal was coming from or if I'd be sleeping in a bed or a cardboard box. Going to school on a regular basis was a foreign concept. But then my mother was arrested on drug charges, and for the first time in my life, they stuck. She went to jail and I went to Dallas.

A few years later, I met Jette.

She was my first true friend.

My first girlfriend.

My first date.

My first kiss.

My first... *everything*.

She made me believe I was more than my upbringing—more than my past or where I came from. It didn't matter that my mom was in prison and my dad didn't know I existed. According to her, I could do anything I wanted, be anything I wanted, and have anything I wanted.

I started to believe it.

But then we graduated, and two months later she moved to New York. Since we were no longer in school, I had no way to contact her… no email, no phone… no *Jette*. She just left, taking with her the thing I wanted the most in this world—*her*.

A piece of my heart followed her bouncing blonde curls and contagious personality all the way to New York. I can't say I've really forgiven her for that. Typically, I'm a let-bygones-be-bygones kind of person, water under the bridge and all that, but when someone steals a piece of your heart, it's hard to let that shit go.

Sure, I've had relationships in the last five years, but nothing serious. It's kind of hard to commit yourself to someone when they're only getting half your heart.

As I approach the corner I play at a few days a week, my eyes scan the sidewalk across the street, landing on the door to what I now know is Cami Benoit-Landry's art gallery, 303 Royal Street, and also where that aforementioned missing piece of my heart now works.

I can't help the smile pulling at my lips as I set my saxophone case at my feet and start to set up. Scratching my head, I wonder about all the unanswered questions floating through my mind over the past few days:

How long is she here for?

What has she been up to for the last five years?

Has she thought about me?

Does she have someone… a boyfriend? Someone waiting for her back in New York?

Did she use her last dime to fly halfway across the country to look for me only to catch a glimpse and realize she didn't have a place there and nothing to offer, so she got back on that plane and flew back, resolved to be happy that I was happy?

No, wait.

I'm the one who saved up for months and flew across the country only to have my heart crushed.

That was me.

I did that.

Needing a distraction from the incessant thoughts of Georgette, I quickly get to work setting up my amp and looper pedals. Basically, when I need to be, I'm a one-man-band. Sure, I like to play with other musicians, and nothing beats the feel and vibe of Good Times, the club I play at on the regular. But I enjoy this too, just me and my sax and the streets of New Orleans.

Warming up, I play a few notes, letting them waft into the air and blend with the morning chill.

For New Orleans, this is a cold morning. My weather app said we'd reach the mid-sixties today, but for now, it's a balmy forty degrees and my cold hands take a little longer to limber up, so I take it easy, working my way through a few melodies I could play in my sleep.

A little Ella Fitzgerald.

A little Nat King Cole.

And then, before I know it, I'm playing *her* song.

Unforgettable.

That's truly what she is. I meant it the first time I ever played it for her and I mean it this morning, standing across the street from the art studio she now works at, in a new city, with years of history behind us and an uncertain future in front of us.

Forever and a day, Georgette Taylor will always be the epitome of this song.

Regardless of the city.

Regardless of the state of our relationship, or lack thereof.

The time for me to forget her passed a long damn time ago. Besides that, I don't want to forget her. She's part of me, who I am. And I'll always be thankful for the years when she was often my only friend.

When I see her wild blonde curls peek out the door of 303 Royal Street, I almost falter, missing a note, but then recover when I see her eyes roam the sidewalk before landing on me.

Something tells me Jette hasn't been able to forget me either.

And for now, that's enough.

She stands at the door for the entire song. There is a moment, when she pushes more of her body out the door, I think she's going to come across the street, but then, the song is over and she retreats back inside.

Taking a moment to catch my breath and smile at a few people passing by on the sidewalk, one tossing a five into my open case, I let my eyes drift across to the closed door and wonder how long it would be before we'd come face to face again.

I really hope it's not five more years.

4

Georgette

I SHOULDN'T HAVE OPENED THE DOOR, AND I MOST certainly should not have stuck my head out for a better listen. But, dammit, he was playing our song—our freaking song—and I had no choice but to go toward the music.

Like a moth to a flame.

He knew what he was doing, too, the big jerk. He was baiting me, testing me, and I fell for it like it was my job. The only upside to our interaction, if you can even call it that, was his very brief almost slip-up. I'm sure no one else noticed how he missed a note, but I did. I know that song as well as he does and I'm sure he was mentally kicking himself something fierce. Meanwhile, I was able to revel in the fact that I'd made Finley Lawson falter, even after all these years.

I didn't gloat for long, though. The look he gave me, once I allowed myself to focus on his eyes, heated my body in ways I wasn't prepared for. The blush on my cheeks was from allowing myself to be caught in his trap so easily, but the warmth I felt everywhere else—*and I do mean everywhere*—was a flashback I wasn't expecting.

Finley always had this effect on me, even if he was clueless to it, and today was no exception… on both accounts. So, I did what any respectable adult woman would do: I quickly stepped back inside the gallery and slammed the door, hiding out of Finley's view.

"Who are we hiding from?"

Covering my mouth to stifle a scream, I whirl around to see an amused Cami standing so close I can't believe I didn't hear her, which makes my cheeks turn pink.

Damn Finley and his saxophone, already wreaking havoc. Some things never change.

"Sorry," Cami says, holding her round belly while laughing at my expense. "I thought you heard me come in from the back."

Stepping away from the door, I try to play it off, but inwardly, my heart is still racing. "It's fine… I thought I… uh, saw something." Searching for a lie, I busy myself with a stack of papers—shuffling and tapping them on the desk.

"Finley, perhaps?" Cami questions, lifting an eyebrow. "He's out there a few days a week. I've been listening to him and his sax for a while now. Come to think of it, I'm really going to miss it when I take off to have the baby. Oh, you know what would be great?" she asks, but doesn't give me time to get a word in. "A lullaby album. Can you even imagine? I wonder if he has anything recorded?"

When she finally takes a breath and turns to look at me, I think my face probably says everything I can't.

Yes, I can imagine.

I've often wanted something similar over the years.

No, I don't know if he has recorded anything.

That would require us to be in touch, which we haven't been.

The mere thought of Finley playing lullabies makes my ovaries ache, which is crazy because I'm only twenty-three and not nearly old enough to feel my biological clock ticking. It must be the pregnancy hormones oozing off Cami.

That's it.

Moving right along.

Nothing to see here.

When I don't verbally respond, afraid my inner monologue will come spilling out, she adds, "You should go talk to him."

"I should," I tell her. I've been berating myself over the past few days for running out of the restaurant. I was caught off guard, jet-lagged, and exhausted. That's my story and I'm sticking to it. But now he's here, well, across the street, and I'm no longer any of those things. So, why can't I just walk across the street and say hello?

When I don't continue, Cami gently pushes for more. "So, y'all were friends?"

"Yeah, best friends, actually," I say, wincing. It's the first time I've talked about Finley out loud in a very long time and I wasn't expecting it to hurt, but it does.

She quirks a knowing eyebrow. "I get the feeling there's more to this story, but I'm going to ignore that fact, for now. If you two were so close, I'm sure he's thrilled to see you. Get out there. Go catch up. Do something besides running from the building like it's on fire."

"You're right," I say with a long sigh. "There's a story, but it's a long one." Rubbing my chest, I try to quell the tight squeeze behind my rib cage, remembering. "I doubt he's *thrilled to see me*, and unfortunately, it's all my fault. The truth is I feel terrible about how things ended between us and I want to apologize, I'm just struggling with pulling up my big girl panties and doing it. Seeing him here… it's the last thing I expected."

Cami wraps her arm around my shoulders and pulls me to her—as close as she can, considering she's very pregnant—hugging me tightly. "Oh, sweetie, it sounds like fate to me."

Her voice is soft and soothing and I find myself giving in to her hug. It's equal parts motherly and sisterly, both something I've never really had. My mother was more of a delegator, even when it came to her only child. I had a closer relationship with my nanny than her.

"Sometimes it's easier if you don't think too much about it," Cami encourages. "Just do it. I have faith in you. And remember, you're in New Orleans now. If you need some liquid courage, there's always a daiquiri shop around the corner. And I'm always looking for someone to live vicariously through these days."

She gives me a wink before walking off, leaving me to decide my next step alone.

For the next hour, I look through portfolios from potential local artists, but my heart and mind aren't in it. They're both across the street with the boy I fell in love with so long ago. Stopping to think and do the math, I realize it's been, what? Nine years? Has it really been that long since Finley Lawson walked into a crowded cafeteria looking so unsure of himself and out of place among the spoiled rich brats we went to school with, myself included?

Walking over to the door, I peek out and see he's still out there. When he finishes a song, he stops to talk to onlookers, smiling and being… Finn.

God, I've missed him.

And he's definitely not the boy I fell in love with, but I can still see pieces of him.

That smile.

Those eyes.

Everything else about him has been honed and refined—sharper jawline, broader shoulders, even longer legs. What else is different? It's been five years since I've seen him.

Our last day together was a hard one, probably the hardest of my life.

We'd just graduated and for the better part of that last summer we spent together, I'd been indecisive about my future.

My parents wanted me to go to a reputable university and earn a degree that would allow me to work for my father. Finley wanted me to go somewhere close so we could stay together. In the end, all I wanted was to be my own person.

Shifting my body, I lean against the door and watch Finley from the safety of the gallery.

I also wanted *him*, but even in my immaturity, I realized I couldn't have my cake and eat it too. If I would've stayed in Dallas, my parents would've continued to run my life, holding me down under their thumbs until I succumbed to the pressure and submitted to their demands.

Just thinking back on it makes me feel claustrophobic and I have to step away from the door and walk over to the desk, distracting myself with a stack of prints. The ache in my chest now feels more like an elephant has taken up residence.

Setting the prints back down on the desk, I rub at the ache as my mind drifts back to the day I jumped on a plane, on a whim. It was the second time I rebelled against my parents.

The first was Finley.

He was my first everything.

My first love.

My first date.

My first time.

And my first heartbreak.

And now, all these years later, he's back and he's right across the street.

When my phone rings from the desk nearby, I trip and knock the portfolio sitting on the edge of the desk flying across the floor. On my hands and knees, I grab the phone and answer, pressing it to my ear as I multitask. Gathering the prints, I breathe out, "Hello?"

"Georgette?"

Pausing, I sit back on my heels and swipe errant curls out of my face. "Trevor?"

I haven't heard from him in a few days, not since our quick phone call when I let him know I'd made it safely and he had to let me go due to a meeting.

"Are you okay?" he asks, the noises of New York in the background. "You sound... out of breath."

Chuckling, I take a breath, realizing he's right. "Yeah, fine. I was just... distracted and then you called and it startled me and I dropped a stack of—"

"That's my Georgette, always a scatterbrain."

My brows draw together in defense. I hate when he does that.

When I don't respond, he finally asks, "Are you settling into the new job?"

"Yeah, everything here is great."

Glancing around the gallery, I feel my heart swell, knowing this is where I'm supposed to be and proud of myself for following my gut on this one.

"Well, you just let me know when you're sick of the south and ready to come back home," Trevor says teasingly, but it makes my hackles rise. "I'm running to a meeting so I can't talk long. Just wanted to check-in."

And see if it's too soon to say I told you so, that's the part he leaves out.

Well, Trevor, don't hold your breath... or maybe...

"Talk later," he says abruptly and then the call ends. I glance at the phone and scowl, tempted to dial him back and give him a piece of my mind, but I know it's futile.

Standing, I tap the portfolio on the desk to straighten its contents, as my mind drifts back to one of our arguments before I left New York.

"You need to stay at Sotheby's and see this through," Trevor says, pacing

his pristine office on the fortieth floor with windows on two sides of the room and the city lit up behind him. "If you're always flitting about from one job to another, how will anyone reputable take you seriously?"

When did I start dating my father? Because that is exactly something George Taylor would say. "This is a reputable gallery... a reputable job. It hurts my feelings that you refuse to take it seriously... take me seriously!"

By the time I'm finished with that statement, my voice has risen to an unacceptable octave. I can tell by the way Trevor cocks his head and lifts his eyebrows, as if to ask me if I'm finished with my tantrum, he's annoyed by my outburst.

But it's not a tantrum, it's a plea for him to respect me and my decisions.

"It's a start-up gallery in New Orleans." He winces like the words taste bad on his tongue.

"Reputable is Sotheby's. Reputable is somewhere you can have a future and build a career. Reputable is a gallery that will allow you to be seen and known, let everyone know who Georgette Taylor is and why they should want you and value you."

See, this is where Trevor and my father typically differ. Where my father just throws down the law of George Taylor and expects everyone to submit, Trevor usually knows exactly what to say to smooth things over. He's good at turning the tables, making his case sound sugary sweet.

But not this time.

"I'm going to New Orleans."

Unbuttoning his suit jacket, his tell of frustration, he braces his hands on his hips. "Is this about the proposal?"

I think what he means to say is lack of proposal.

Trevor and I have been together for over four years and I'm tired of being someone's girlfriend. I want to move on with my life. For as long as I can remember, I've had five goals in a very particular order:

1. Get a degree.
2. See the world.
3. Get a job.
4. Get married.
5. Have babies.

I've done the first three and I'm ready for the last two. It might sound crazy to most people. I know Trevor thinks I've lost my mind. But I can't help what I want. The way I see it, if I don't accomplish number four, I'll never get to number five. Because more than anything, I want to right all my parents' wrongs.

I want love.

I want a home and not just a house.

I want to take my children to school and cook them dinner.

I want to hug them and kiss them and put Band-Aids on booboos.

And I want all of that with a husband at my side.

There are probably feminists out there rolling their eyes at me, but isn't that what feminism is all about—women getting what they want in life and not being told what they need. Don't get me wrong, I still want my career, but again, I want it on my terms. I want to have a job I believe in at a place I feel connected to.

For me, that's not Sotheby's.

I want more.

I thought Trevor was the one… I still think Trevor *could be* the one. Even with his flaws, which we all have, he's still a good fit for my life. My parents love him. He and my father have a better relationship than the two of us ever dreamed of having. My mother even speaks highly of him, which is rare.

But the Trevor of today is different from the Trevor I met during my first week in New York. That Trevor was supportive and fun-loving. We had similar dreams and desires. He made me feel safe and well-cared-for. When we went out, he always placed his hand at the small of my back and guided me through a room, putting me first. I felt treasured and valued.

Now, I often feel like a second thought. His meetings and business obligations seem to take precedent. But occasionally, I get a glimpse of the man I fell in love with, *my Trevor*, and I still feel hope for our future. Every relationship goes through trials and tribulations.

Hopefully, that's all this is.

When the door of the gallery chimes, I shake off the memory and thoughts of Trevor, forcing a smile on my face. "Welcome to 303 Royal," I call out, stepping around the desk, but stopping short as I come face to face once again with Finley Lawson.

"Finn."

His name comes out like a grand discovery, much too breathy for my taste, but it's too late. It's already out of my mouth and I can't take it back.

A familiar smirk takes over his chiseled face, those amazing eyes putting me in a trance, like they always have. "Kinda thought you might've forgotten my name."

I laugh, partially to release the tension that's taken up residence in my chest and partially because that's so Finn. He's always been the one to rescue me from my awkwardness, embracing my quirkiness, unlike Trevor.

"I was just packing up for the day and wanted to stop by and say hi. New Year's Eve was…" He pauses, running a hand through his hair that's still perfectly imperfect—rich chocolate brown with unruly curls.

We've always had that in common, the unruly curls.

And so many other things, I reminisce, as I momentarily lose myself in those gray eyes.

"New Year's Eve was a surprise," I finish for him, chuckling as I smooth down the front of my skirt. "I mean… New Orleans of all places." To stop myself from fidgeting nervously as I wait for his wrath or anger over how we parted, I twist my fingers together behind my back.

"What are the odds," he says, sounding more amazed and caught off guard than anything else.

I nod, unsure of where to take this conversation, but once again, Finn to the rescue.

"I have to go, but I'd love to catch up… maybe have a drink."

Now, there's a difference. The only drink Finn and I shared in the past was a bottle of wine we'd pilfered from my parents' cellar on our graduation night. "Uh, yeah… a drink would be great."

A drink between old friends. That's okay, right?

"I play most nights at Gia's Good Times," Finn says, grabbing a pen and one of the gallery's business cards from the desk beside me. "It's on Frenchmen. My set tonight is early. I should be finished by nine. We can have a drink afterward, if you'd like."

I'd like. I'd like that very much.

"Sure," I say, taking the card and reading over the address, although I have no clue where it's at. I've only been in my new city for a few days and most of that time has been spent here at the gallery and next door at the hotel I'm staying at. "I… I'll see you there."

Finn nods, his expression shifting as he takes me in and there's an elongated pause in our conversation. I'm waiting, still, for him to say something, anything, about the past. And I'm pretty sure he's thinking about it with questions on the tip of his tongue, but then he turns on his heel and walks toward the door.

But just when I think our conversation is over, he turns. "Don't walk there," Finn says, hesitantly. "It's not safe for…" He starts, then stops. "It would be better if you take an Uber or something. I'll make sure you get back safely, okay?"

And that's the Finn I've always known. It's like a warm, soothing balm. Regardless of our past, he still cares, always looking out for me.

"Okay."

5

Finley

"Okay, listen up," Gia says, standing on a wooden box in the middle of the dimly-lit backroom. "For all you newbies, Mardi Gras season is upon us and shit's about to get real."

A smartass from the back stands up and yells, "Come on! This is New Orleans; shit is always real." Various hoots and hollers follow, as well as, boisterous laughter.

"That may be true, y'all, but Mardi Gras is a whole other beast. We got two full months of parties, parades, wild tourists, and even wilder locals, so we have to be prepared to work harder than ever. It's a damn good thing we work at the best jazz club in the city, am I right? We get paid to party so let's make sure it's the best one every night!"

A bottle of Jack is passed around, like it is on most nights, and I take my obligatory swig. Wiping the back of my hand over my mouth, I feel someone slide a hand around my torso, inching down to the button of my jeans.

Smirking, I turn skillfully out of the advance. "Gia." It's half greeting and half warning. I try to play it safe, because she's my boss, but she also has a thing for the young talent she brings in. I've seen her slip off into a dark corner with several of the musicians who play at her bar.

I'm not interested in being a notch on her bedpost, but I do love my job.

I love this bar.

I love the people I play with.

Most of them became friends after the first week I was here. All of them love music as much as me, some more. The older guys have been doing this much longer than I have, putting in years on the stage, in the streets, and dozens of bars.

"How's my favorite sax player?" she asks, coming around to face me. Her red lips are full and pouty as she closes in, her mouth hovering mere inches from mine.

"Good," I say, feeling my body tense. When I don't meet her halfway and my jaw tightens on instinct, she pulls back and pats my chest.

Giving in to her advances isn't a requirement for working at Good Times, but most of the guys are happy to oblige, except me. Which might actually make me more appealing. Some people are turned on by the chase.

"Give us a good show," she says, her hand tightening into a fist as she grabs the front of my shirt. "I'll be watching."

Her departing sentiment is delivered in a singsong with a wave over her shoulder as she saunters over to the bar, checking in with the guys stocking glasses and bottles.

Shaking my head, I take a deep breath. I think I've been holding it and could use a little air, but our first set is getting ready to start and I can't keep my eyes off the front door. Ever since I invited Jette to the bar, I've been on edge.

I want her here.

I want to see her and talk to her.

But I'm also a little worried.

New Orleans, especially New Orleans during this particular season, is a little crazy. Gia was right, shit is getting real. I've noticed the hum in the air getting louder and more intense since New Year's Eve. More and more people are flooding into the bars and clubs. Even my walk home in the wee hours of the morning is louder, with people staying out later.

I've always felt protective of Jette, even before we were friends.

The first time I saw her at school, she was standing across the cafeteria and the bitchy girls she hung out with were having fun at her expense. Apparently, someone found a picture of her from middle school when she still wore braces and posted, what they deemed unflattering images of her, on social media.

The comments were cruel.

It was obvious to an outsider like me that they were jealous. They needed to make her feel bad to make themselves feel better.

I remember watching and feeling my blood boil. Their opinions didn't matter to me, but I could tell they got to her. I wanted to do something, stand up for her—protect her—and I didn't even know her name. All I knew was she was the most beautiful girl I'd ever seen, even in the pics they'd posted of her in braces. And under her wild blonde curls, blue eyes, and button nose was a loneliness I recognized. It was the same loneliness that stared back at me in the mirror.

She made me feel helpless. My usual method of handling a situation like that was using my fists, but I couldn't hit a girl. And besides that, I was at a new school in a new city. I couldn't mess things up. My next stop would've been foster care.

So, I waited on the outskirts, staying close, just in case.

Fortunately for her, they moved on to their next victim a day or two later.

Fortunately for me, she started eating lunch outside by the fountain, which happened to be the same place I ate lunch.

Every day, she opened up a little more. First, just saying hello. Then, telling me her name. Next thing I knew, we were sharing PB&J sandwiches and homework.

And that was how it was for four years—Finn and Jette.

"Finn, man. You ready to warm up?" When I turn toward the stage, River, the bass player, is giving me a look. "What's up with you? I've been trying to get your attention and you've been staring at the damn door."

"Sorry," I say, scratching the back of my head before running a hand through my hair. I don't offer an explanation, instead, I take my seat and start getting my sax hooked up to the amp, but I still keep one eye on the door.

After we warm-up and the crowd descends, we jump right into our set.

Playing with these guys is one of the best things about moving to New Orleans. Before I came here, I mostly played solo in coffee bars and jazz clubs around Dallas, but nothing like this. Everything about Good Times is *alive*. From the first moment I walked in here, I knew it was where I belonged. I can practically feel the spirits of jazz players from days past. The old wooden tables and chairs hold music and memories most have forgotten.

My first night here, I had to force myself not to lay down on the dirty, worn floor and make snow angels. I just wanted to soak it into my bones.

Tonight, the patrons are only adding to the vibe. A few are dancing up close to the stage. Nearly every table is full and drinks are flowing. But the second she walks in, just like the first day I saw her—just like New Year's Eve when she walked back into my life—the world stands still.

Thankfully, air keeps flowing out of my lungs and my fingers work on autopilot, but my eyes are on her, watching as she excuses her way through throngs of people.

She's here.

She came.

I'm still getting used to the idea of us being in the same city again, but I can't deny how happy it makes me to see her, even if her presence does drum up old feelings and buried emotions.

Once she finds a spot to sit, her eyes find mine. If I thought the world stood on its axis when she walked in, it tilts in this moment. Her smile starts small and then grows as the tempo of the song we're playing picks up.

Her shoulders relax as she leans back into her chair, absorbing the atmosphere.

When the set is over, I place my sax on its stand and hop off the front ledge, heading toward her but then lose sight as people begin to filter in and out of the club. Approaching the table she was sitting at, I momentarily panic when her seat is empty.

"Hey," she says, her voice coming up beside me, making me jump and spin in her direction. Laughing, she tips her head back and I can't take my eyes off her. That laugh. Those blue eyes. God, she's beautiful. Not that I'd forgotten, but the effect she has on me had dulled over the years, mostly because I willed myself to let her go.

For my own sanity.

"I wasn't sure you'd come," I admit, wanting to reach out and pull her close to me, guarding her from the people as they move about, but I don't.

She's not mine, I remind myself.

Not anymore.

"And miss you play?" she asks incredulously, giving me an infamous Georgette Taylor snort. It's crazy how something so unattractive can be so endearing, but damn, I've missed it.

I've missed her.

I smile, marveling at her standing in front of me and trying not to let it show. "I'm glad you came."

"Looks like there are a couple of seats at the bar," she says, glancing back over her shoulder. She's right, a couple is vacating the two seats at the end, probably the quietest spot in this entire place. It's like the universe is also happy she's here.

On instinct, I place my hand at the small of her back as we start to make our way through the crowd. But when she glances over her shoulder, making eye contact, I can't tell if it's okay that I'm touching her in such a familiar way—a way I used to touch her all the time—so I pull it back and rake a hand through my hair to suppress the need.

"So, you play here every night?" she asks, raising her voice as the volume of the club increases.

Getting the attention of Marcus, one of the bartenders, I hold up two fingers. He knows what to pour and I know Jette will approve. We were never big partiers back in high school, but when we did break the rules and imbibe, we always drank Jack and Coke.

"Just about," I say, answering her question as I try to find my figurative footing when it comes to her. "Occasionally, Gia forces me to take a night off, but I rarely ask for one."

"Gia?" she asks, giving Marcus a smile of appreciation as he slides a napkin and a drink in front of her. "Thank you."

"She's the owner," I tell her, giving Marcus a nod of appreciation.

I hear Jette whistle as she takes her first sip and sets the drink back on her napkin. "Good ol' Jack and Coke." She cocks her head, blinking her eyes. "A nice *strong* Jack and Coke," she amends.

Laughing, I place my drink down. "Yeah, Marcus has a bit of a heavy hand."

"Not complaining," she says, taking another drink as she looks around the club. "This is a great place."

"Different from the clubs in New York?" I ask, needing to go there. At some point, we're going to have to address the elephant in the room.

Swallowing, her eyes dart from the people around us, to me, and back. "Yeah, way different. It's so… I don't know."

"Authentic?" I offer, knowing that's how I felt when I came here for the first time, like every other jazz bar I'd ever been to before paled in comparison.

"That's exactly what I was going to say," she replies, her eyes finally landing and staying on mine. "I went to some great restaurants and bars in New York, but none of them had this vibe."

For a moment, I let myself remember the girl who left Dallas. She was so young and naive. I remember being scared for her as she flew across the country to a big city like New York, afraid it was going to swallow her whole. I guess that's one of the reasons I saved my money to go there. I thought she might need to be rescued. But when I got there and she was thriving—making friends, finding her place—I had no choice but to leave her be… let her go.

I want to tell her that, but now isn't the right time.

This is basically our first real conversation in five years. I don't want to mess it up with the past.

"What'd you think of the set?" I ask, pointing to the stage.

Jette's face lights up. "So great," she says with awe. "I mean, you've always been amazing, but hearing you here, in this place, with the full band. It was… next level."

"I'm glad you liked it."

She picks up her glass and downs another good bit. "I didn't like it. I loved it. I missed it."

Yeah, but did you miss me?

"Can you stay for another set?" I ask, finishing off my drink and setting the empty glass on the other side of the bar. "I have to play one more and then I could walk you home or we could share an Uber."

Taking another sip, she nods, and I try not to focus on her lips when she licks the remnants of her drink away. "I'd love to stay."

6

Georgette

"HOLY GEEZ," I GUSH WHEN MY EYES LAND ON THE ROUND monstrosity Cami is displaying proudly.

Not her protruding stomach.

The baked goodness decorated in purple, gold, and green icing with matching strings of beads. It smells like heaven and looks like Mardi Gras threw up in the box.

"Pecan Turtle King Cake with caramel Bavarian cream and chocolate ganache," Cami says with so much seduction I feel my cheeks pink. "It's from Joe's. We'll do Randazzo's next week."

"Next week?" I mean, I love carbs just as much as the next girl, but if we're going to be eating one of these every week for the next month, I'll need to work out morning, noon, and night. Fortunately, the hotel has a great gym.

"Oh, and Gambino's," Cami continues, not paying attention to me or my question or my inner carb crisis. "Actually, maybe I can sweet talk Deacon into picking one of those up later this week. I bet his mama will be sending him or Micah over with a list."

I'm getting ready to ask her what the difference is between all of the different King Cakes, but her eyes grow wide and she gets the most excited expression, even more excited than she was the day Micah brought over leftover crawfish mac and cheese from Lagniappe.

Apparently, the baby really loves carbs.

"I just got the best idea," she exclaims. "I don't know why I didn't think of this before." She laughs, setting the cake down on the desk where it practically takes up the entire space. "Georgette, your boss is a freakin' genius! If you ask Deacon, he'll try to tell you this baby is sucking out my brain cells, but the idea that just popped into my head proves I've still got what it takes. My creativity is alive and well!"

I have no doubt she's right. In just the short amount of time I've known Camille Benoit-Landry, she's quickly become my favorite artist and one of the most creative people I've ever met. She has a vision for this gallery and her passion for local artists, giving them a platform, is commendable.

However, I'm sure the look on my face comes closest to expressing *whatthehellareyoutalkingabout* instead of *yesyouareafreakingenius*. I try to cover it up with a smile, but I can feel the awkwardness of it. "So," I hedge, "what's the, uh, idea?"

This is the equivalent of a parent asking a child to tell them about their artwork.

"A King Cake Party," she says, her eyes grow even wider and her smile stretches to match them as bright white teeth blind me. Her excitement is so contagious I can't help my giggle.

"King Cake Party," I repeat. "That sounds… delicious."

"Right?" she asks, buzzing around the gallery like a woman on a mission.

Well, because she *is* a woman on a mission.

Last week she barely had the energy to drive into the city and stay for a couple of hours.

Now, she's Martha Stewart on steroids, rambling off details of this King Cake Party that we're apparently now hosting here at the gallery.

"Annie will help us," Cami continues as I pick up a notepad and begin to follow her around taking notes. "She loves stuff like this. We'll invite everybody—Micah, Dani, Tucker, Piper, CeCe, Shep, Carys, Mav… Shaw, Avery… oh, Jules, of course. And Mary and George. Oh, and Deacon." She laughs like she almost forgot about her husband and I bite back one of my own.

Maybe I should call him?

He gave me his cell phone number and all the numbers to the restaurants he and Micah own, giving me strict instructions to call him if Cami shows any signs of distress.

I wonder if spontaneous party planning counts?

"We can't forget my father-in-law," she continues. "He recently retired and he's driving my mother-in-law batshit crazy. Don't write that down." Stopping abruptly, she peers over at my notes, like I'd seriously write that down.

"Your secret is safe with me," I tell her in all sincerity. I met Sam and Annie at the New Year's Eve party. He seemed really nice and he and Annie seemed ridiculously happy. So, it does surprise me that he's driving her *batshit crazy*, but I keep that to myself.

"Everyone can bring their favorite King Cake… or bake their own, if they're into that sort of thing." Finally taking a break and placing her hand on her stomach, she inhales and exhales and I watch her, looking for any signs of labor.

Is delirium a sign?

After a few seconds, she looks up at me. "Oh, don't forget to invite Finley. Maybe he could play for us. I know my brother is itching to get him in the studio, but maybe they could have a jam session at the party?"

Finley.

He's been on my mind a lot lately.

I went from thinking about him occasionally—when I heard great jazz, walked into a coffee bar, watched a musical on Broadway... ate a peanut butter and jelly sandwich—to thinking about him hourly, sometimes by the minute.

As friends, of course.

Watching him play at the club a few nights ago was like going back in time, but better.

He's better, somehow. I never thought that was possible, but he so is. The man version of Finn is stronger, surer of himself, settled, but not in a bad way. It's more of an air of contentment, being happy in the place he's in. I appreciate that he doesn't try to make apologies for who he is and how he's living his life. He just lives it.

And don't even get me started on his physical features.

I'd be here all day.

When he invited me to come hear him play, I was hesitant. I know we need to talk about me leaving and us losing touch and so many things in between, but I don't know if I'm ready for that yet. Thankfully, we stuck to fairly safe topics and when he walked me back to my hotel, we parted with a *see you soon.*

That felt oddly normal and... *good.*

I've missed him.

"Georgette? Did you get that?" Cami asks, licking icing from her fingers.

Did I blackout?

How the hell did she consume a piece of cake without me even noticing?

I swear, this woman and her hidden talents.

"Yeah, King Cake Party," I say, glancing down to the notepad. "And we're inviting half of New Orleans."

Cami smiles widely. "Have I told you how great you are at this job?"

"Thank you?" I'm never sure what the appropriate response is when she gets like this.

Pulling off a chunk of King Cake with her bare hands like a savage, Cami adds, "You should take a piece of this to Finley and invite him to our party."

I pretend to ignore her suggestion but inwardly, I make a mental note to do what she says. It's what a friend would do, right? And Finley and I are friends, right? We were, and despite everything, I still feel that instant connection and pull.

After we hammer out some quick details, the King Cake Party is now officially on our schedule, happening next week. Since this is Cami and Deacon's third baby, they didn't have a baby shower, so according to her, everyone owes her.

Not gifts or anything, just cake.

Later in the day, after Cami and I go over some potential new local artists, she's out of steam and Micah drops by to pick her up on his way back to French Settlement. The Landrys all live about an hour outside the city and have restaurants in New Orleans, French Settlement, and Baton Rouge. I've only been to Lagniappe, but I have plans on going on a Landry food tour soon.

My stomach growls just thinking about it, so I slice off another sliver of King Cake. Eventually, I'm going to have to add some additional nutrients to my diet, but this will have to do for now. I'm on my own until closing time, but since we don't have any appointments this afternoon, it should be relatively quiet.

As I'm licking the icing off my fingers, my eyes drift back to the cake and Cami's suggestion of taking Finley a piece and inviting him to the party. And then I glance over at the door, wondering if he's on his corner playing.

Slicing off a decent-sized piece, I place it on a paper plate, stick a plastic fork in the flaky pastry, and head for the door before I can change my mind.

It's not that I don't want to see him.

We're friends.

Old friends.

At one time, we were best friends.

But I have to admit, after Finley walked me back to my hotel, I went straight to my room and sent Trevor a text. There wasn't anything romantic about mine and Finley's time together, but somehow, I still felt guilty.

But then my text went unread for an entire day and took the edge off.

If Trevor wasn't concerned with who I'm spending my time with, why should I feel the need to assuage my guilt? Besides, Finley and I *are* just friends and there's nothing to feel guilty about.

Except there was a time when we weren't just friends.

And we never really got over that.

At least, I didn't. I just moved to New York and buried my feelings, chalking them up to that old adage—you can't have your cake and eat it too.

Back then, I couldn't have New York and Finley. It wasn't fair to either of us, so I took one for the team and left, with no forwarding address or real way for us to stay connected, because if we had, I would've run back home—back to him—the first time it got hard.

Of course, Trevor finally called this morning and apologized profusely for being *busy*, and of course, I forgave him. I even told him all about my evening at the club and he said it sounded like a very *New Orleans* thing to do. He might've meant it as a dig, but he was right. It was the most fun I've had since I've been in this city. Getting a real glimpse into the culture and nightlife was exactly what I needed and it left me craving more.

After locking the door and flipping a sign to let everyone know I'll be back in fifteen minutes, I turn toward the road and look both ways before jogging across. Finley sees me the second I step onto the opposing sidewalk and even though his lips are on the saxophone, his eyes light up with a smile.

There are a few people standing around listening, so I join the crowd and enjoy the show, losing myself in the moment, almost forgetting for a second that I'm on a sidewalk in New Orleans listening to my oldest friend play a song as old as time in a city that feels more right than anything has in a long, long time.

When the song is over, the crowd applauds and Finley dips his head in humble appreciation. They toss change and bills in an open case and I stand back, just watching.

"Is that for me?" he asks, gesturing to the cake in my hand.

He's now standing a mere few inches from me, adjusting his sax to the side, letting it hang from the strap around his neck. For some reason, my heart pounds a little faster at the sight. It reminds me of a sunny day in a public park in Dallas. Finley had invited me to come while he played. I laid under a tree on a blanket and read an assigned book for my Senior AP English class and we'd steal smiles and hot looks, letting the connection zip between us. Even though we were surrounded by people, it was like we were the only people on earth.

I miss that.

It's been so long since I've felt so wholly seen and understood.

Clearing my throat, I shake my head and bring my attention back to the present. "Yeah, I, uh… Cami's pregnant," I blurt out, like he didn't know that bit of information and it explains why I'm standing here with this piece of cake. "She has a problem. Actually, *we* have a problem because she buys at least one King Cake a day and there're only so much baked goods two women can consume in a day. So, I thought I'd bring you a piece."

Finley squints an eye, looking down at me.

Have I mentioned how tall he is?

So tall.

Taller than he was the last time we kissed.

What the heck?

Where did that thought come from?

"Thank you," he says, reaching out and accepting the plate and saving me from my inner monologue and the off chance those random thoughts come flying out of my mouth.

Crazier things have happened.

"I didn't eat breakfast or lunch, so…" He holds up the plate and offers me a wide Finley Lawson smile, full of bright, white teeth and so much charm it makes my stomach drop.

"Good," I say, smoothing my hands down the front of my skirt to dry my palms that are suddenly sweating. New Orleans, man. I'd never be sweating like this in the middle of January in New York.

Finley steps back and cuts off a bite of the flaky, sweet goodness. Popping it in his mouth, he moans his appreciation and I avert my eyes, searching for something else to distract me.

Anything.

"Oh," I say, remembering the other reason for me coming over here. "Cami wants me to invite you to our King Cake Party. It's going to be at the gallery next week and if you'd be interested, we'd love for you to play. She even mentioned something about playing with her brother, Tucker."

"Right," Finley says, nodding as he takes another bite. When he's finished chewing, he licks lingering sugar off his lips. "We talked at the New Year's Eve party. I have his number. I'll give him a call. When is the party?"

Stop, Georgette.

Stop this right now.

Of course, Finley still affects me like this. I can't help that.

I've always been attracted to him. Even when I first met him and he was lanky and awkward, I still thought he was beautiful with his caramel-colored skin, dark eyes, full lips… and that thick, wavy hair.

Most women would kill for his features.

Time hasn't changed any of that, only improved.

"Next Friday night," I tell him, swallowing down the flood of feelings. Old and new, all-consuming.

"I'll be there."

Smiling, I try to quell the flip in my stomach. "Great," I reply with a nod as I retreat a step. I need to get back to the gallery. I need to call Trevor, *my boyfriend.* And I need my old *friend*, Finley, to stop looking at me with those intense, gray eyes.

Yeah, everything is great.

Totally fine.

Nothing to see here.

I'm practically halfway across the street when I hear Finley callout after me. "Wanna meet me for coffee?"

Whipping around, I glance around to make sure I'm not about to get creamed in the crosswalk and brush rogue curls from my face. "What?"

That's a rhetorical question, I know what he asked. I'm just not sure what my answer should be.

We're friends.

We've always been friends.

Besides my boss and her family, he's the only person I know in the state of Louisiana.

Having someone to explore my new city with is ideal.

It's the safe thing to do, right?

I think even Trevor could agree with that.

"Coffee?" Finley repeats.

It's not dinner or a date, Georgette. Get a grip.

"Sure," I finally reply.

His smile lights up the entire street. "Great. Do you know where Neutral Grounds is?"

I nod. It's Cami's favorite and her friend, CeCe, owns it. And CeCe is married to Shepard Rhys-Jones, who's from Dallas. Finley's grandma worked for his family.

Small world.

I nod my response.

"Meet me there at six?" he asks. "We can talk more about the party."

Right, the party.

Good idea.

"Sounds like a d—" I almost said date and feel like smacking my forehead, but instead, I force a smile and correct myself. "Deal. I'll be there." And then I run across the street like a scared little girl, back to the safety of the gallery.

After unlocking the door and taking the sign down, I lean against the wall and let out a deep sigh. "What are you doing, Georgette?" I ask myself, closing my eyes but then opening them quickly, because behind my lids are only flashes of gray eyes, brown curly hair, and full lips.

Walking over to the desk, I pick up my phone and shoot Trevor a text.

Me: Hey, you.

Hey, you?

God, I'm an idiot, but in my defense, I'm short on things to call Trevor—besides Trevor—because he thinks every nickname is stupid. The first time I called him *babe*, he looked at me like I'd spilled milk on his alligator loafers.

"Don't call me that," he'd said. *"We're not in high school. We don't need pet names."*

Always so damn serious.

I wait a second for the three little dots to show up, but they never do. Not that I thought he'd reply right away, but I'd hoped he would. Just this once. Because I need him to. I need to get my head on straight.

Why do I have a feeling Finley is going to want to talk about more than the King Cake Party?

Am I ready for that?

Thankfully, the front door opens and a few women walk into the gallery.

"Welcome to 303 Royal," I greet, getting my mind off Finley and back onto my job. This is where I thrive, where I know my place and I'm confident in my abilities. It's like the universe knew exactly what I needed. Taking a deep, much-needed breath, I step away from the desk and square my shoulders.

Let's sell some art.

7

Finley

"**How's Maggie?**" **Jette asks, taking a sip of her coffee** as we sit by the window in the front of Neutral Grounds. I picked this spot before she got here for two reasons. One, I wanted some privacy because I'm hoping to finally broach the topics we've been evading since she walked into Lagniappe. Two, I needed somewhere to put my eyes besides Georgette Taylor, and the people watching outside this window is a good distraction.

Sometimes, I still have to ask myself if this is real life.

I've missed her so much, more than I've admitted to myself in a long time.

"She's good," I tell her, picking at the cardboard sleeve on my cup. This week has actually felt like winter here in New Orleans. The temps have finally dropped into the forties at night and mid-fifties during the day. It's nice. And CeCe is reaping the rewards.

Neutral Grounds is buzzing.

Speaking of CeCe, I catch her watching us and chuckle.

"What's funny?" Jette asks, glancing over her shoulder.

"CeCe," I say, shaking my head as she realizes she's been caught creeping and busies herself behind the counter, engaging a customer in conversation.

Jette turns her attention back to me and her cheeks are tinged with pink. She's always been so easy to embarrass; her emotions are always on display. "She's great," Jette says. "I guess she and Cami go way back. Cami told me when she was in New Orleans for college, CeCe worked here for her uncle. That painting hanging over there is one of Cami's first pieces she ever sold."

My eyes leave Jette and go to a beautiful landscape painting behind the counter. It's full of color and the images seem to be alive on the canvas. "It's beautiful."

"Yeah," Jette says wistfully. "She's so talented. I've been trying to talk her into bringing more of her own work to the gallery, but she insists the mission of the gallery is to bring attention to local, lesser-known artists."

"You two seem to be fast friends," I say before taking a sip of my coffee. *Damn, this is good.* I played in a lot of coffee bars in Dallas and none of them compared to this. CeCe is a coffee genius, which is why she's getting ready to start selling her own bulk coffee. The space next door is currently being remodeled into a roastery.

Jette smiles. "Cami feels like the sister I never had, but she's also my boss, of course. It's so different from my job in New York."

Here we go. I've been waiting on a segue and this is the closest we've come to discussing her leaving, New York, college, and the last five years, so I know it's now or never.

"Do you miss New York?" I ask, glancing down at the table and then back up at her. She bites down on her lip and then averts her eyes and I hold my breath. I'm not sure what I expect her answer to be or even want it to be, for that matter, but I need it.

Are you staying?

Is this temporary?

Will you come back into my life and let me get used to having you around again, only to leave me?

If the answer to that last question is yes, then I don't know if I can continue whatever this is we've fallen into, or back into. For me, I think it would be better to pretend she's not even here and go back to how my life was before New Year's Eve—life without Georgette. I'd finally gotten used to it and was doing just fine.

Lies.

All of it.

"This is going to sound bad, but I don't... like, nothing," she says, with a shocked laugh, like she even surprised herself with that answer.

I know she surprised me.

I thought she would at least bring up *the boyfriend.*

Yeah, I know about him.

I've done some snooping on Georgette Taylor, this version sitting across from me, the one that on one hand is so familiar, yet on the other hand, is a complete stranger. I needed to know some basic information, so I bribed CeCe into giving it to me. She asked Cami and then got back to me.

Pretty sure I already knew about Trevor, just not his name. Back when I flew to New York to find Jette and beg her to give us a chance, I think he was the guy I saw her with, the one who convinced me to let her go without even saying a word.

She was with him, it was obvious.

And she was happy.

That was enough for me, because it's all I ever really wanted.

"I thought I would miss it and that it would take me a while to adjust to a new city," she continues, her shoulders raising up as she inhales and then relaxing as she blows the breath out. "But I feel so at home here, like this city was just waiting for me."

Her smile and laughter are contagious and I find myself, once again, not wanting to ruin it with the past, but I'm not the kid I used to be. The difference between eighteen and twenty-three is that I no longer shy away from heartache or hard topics. I've learned it's better to man-up.

"How long are you planning on staying?"

That's the first question I need answered.

Jette's beautiful blue eyes go wide, but then she recovers, cocking her head and leaning back into her seat, taking her coffee with her. She seems relaxed as she answers, "As long as New Orleans will have me."

"What does that mean?" I ask, pushing.

She sighs, placing her cup back on the table. "I don't know, Finley." Her tone sounds calm with a hint of annoyance. One thing Georgette has never liked is people pushing her. She despised her father for pushing her toward a career she didn't want. She despised her mother for pushing her to be someone she wasn't. I think, at one point, she even despised me for pushing her to choose me.

"I'm here for however long Cami wants me here," she continues. "For however long I'm a good fit for the gallery. Hopefully, that's for a long time. But if Cami comes back from her maternity leave and feels like she no longer needs me, then I guess I'll move on to something else."

"Back to New York?"

She shrugs, noncommittally. "Perhaps."

Perhaps?

What the fuck kind of answer is that?

"Yes or no," I push, knowing I'm treading on thin ice.

Jette huffs, her blue eyes boring into me. "I'd go wherever I could find a job," she says, but then swallows and adds, "but I'd love to stay here, if that's what you're asking."

We sit in silence for a moment, with years of unspoken words floating around us.

"I don't even know why we're discussing the demise of my current employment status," she finally says, breaking through the tension. "I just got here and you're already trying to get rid of me."

I smirk, brushing my thumb across my bottom lip. "No, I just got you back and I'm wondering for how long."

Her expression softens and she reaches across the table, placing her hand on mine. "I missed you, you know. I missed this… us."

"Why did you leave?" I ask, the question tumbling out before I have a chance to filter my thoughts.

"Why did you not answer my calls?" she counters.

I recognize the hurt on her face. It looks a lot like how I feel.

"My phone got stolen from the coffee shop the day after you left," I tell her. "I went to your house to ask your mom to give you my new number, but she wouldn't even open the door. Shep tried to get it to you, but you never came home. I tried to call your old number, but—"

"I got a new phone when I got to New York," she says, cutting me off.

She bites down on her bottom lip as she turns her attention to the window, her blue eyes shining with emotion.

"I tried to write to you," I admit. "But I didn't know what dorm you were in, so the letters were returned." It's on the tip of my tongue to tell her about me going there, but I'm not ready for that. It feels like too much of a confession, too big of a gesture for friends.

She sighs, finally looking at me again. "I'm sorry I left without saying goodbye. I just… I knew if I saw you, it would only make it harder. I didn't know we'd go nearly five years without talking." The laugh that escapes her is sad. "When I came home, the few times I came home, I went to the coffee shop you always used to play at but you were never there. I decided it was best to…"

"Leave us in the past?" I ask.

There's so much sadness in her expression as she nods. I hate it. I've never liked seeing her sad, always wanting to do anything to make her happy. That's when I decide this is enough. For today, this is enough.

"Let's do that," I suggest.

"Do what?" Her brows pull together in confusion.

Flipping my palm over, I invite her to place her hand in mine. "Leave it in the past. Start fresh here in our new city."

When her shoulders fall in defeat, I realize she's misunderstood what I'm suggesting, I quickly amend, "as friends."

"Friends," she repeats.

I can't interpret the expression that crosses her face, but as quickly as it flashes across her features, it's gone, and in its place is a beautiful smile. I've always been able to tell when her smiles are the real deal, because it reaches her eyes and there's a small dimple in the top of her right cheek.

There's still more we need to discuss, but the rest can wait. We've covered enough of the past for one day. "We should go exploring," I suggest, switching gears to give us both a reprieve. Plus, I want to spend more time with her, in whatever capacity I'm allowed. "I've been here for a while now, but I don't get out much, except to play my gigs."

"Ever been to Bourbon Street?" Georgette asks, her eyes lighting up with excitement.

I smile, happy to have the easiness back between us. "A few times." When I first got here, I went out of sheer curiosity and then the guys from the club invited me out a few times after we've closed down. I tried playing on one of the corners down there but I felt like I was competing with the music filtering out of the bars. The corner on Royal is much more my speed and I love the atmosphere.

"I'm dying to go," Jette admits.

"Really?" I ask, a little surprised. "Bourbon doesn't seem like your scene."

Her smile grows and it's a new smile. Part of it is the same familiar one that's played over and over in my dreams these past five years but it's mixed with something new. A part of Jette I don't know, the part she's become since she left Dallas and grew her wings.

I want to know this Jette too.

"Well, I'll never know until I go," she finally says and it speaks to my soul. It's how I felt the day I left Dallas. I was so unsure of coming here and starting over in a new city, but after Maggie left and I was basically alone, I thought, fuck it, what do I have to lose?

And I'm so glad I did.

If I had stayed in Dallas, I would've completely missed this opportunity to get to know *this* Jette—my old friend, all grown up.

We part ways with a promise of getting together soon to start our explorations. Jette also mentioned needing to find a more permanent place to live, so I'm going to help her do that too.

Even though she's all grown up, it doesn't mean she doesn't need someone to look out for her. New Orleans is a great city, but all great cities have their downfalls. And like any city, there's always someone trying to take advantage of an easy target.

Georgette Taylor might've lived in New York for the past five years, but she's still the sheltered girl who grew up in one of the most affluent neighborhoods in Texas. With her blonde hair and blue eyes and bubbly personality, *target* could very well be her middle name.

After she leaves, I walk over to where CeCe is cleaning up after a recent rush of customers and grab a towel to help her.

"You don't have to do that, you know," she says while eyeing me over her shoulder.

"I know I don't but I like feeling useful around here. It's the least I can do to thank you for my low rent."

CeCe chuckles as we make quick work of the tables. "I'm just thankful you're here in New Orleans. Knowing you're living in my old apartment is a bonus and gives me and Shep peace of mind." It's basically the same thing she tells me every time I bring up my cheap-ass rent. There's not a place in the French Quarter, unless it's a cardboard box, that would be cheaper.

"Now," CeCe says, tossing her rag on the counter before turning toward me with her hands on her hips. "Enough small talk, give me all the dirt."

I should've expected this.

Since marrying Shep, CeCe has quickly become like an older sister to me, taking me under her wing without a second thought. She's also a nosy motherfucker, just like her husband.

"Come on, spill it!" I swear to God she stomps her foot and then points her finger at me. "And I'll know if you're lying."

Laughing, I mimic her stance and answer, "What? I was having coffee with a friend."

"Bullshit. Try again."

I roll my eyes at CeCe, knowing it won't do me any good to play games with her. "It's not bullshit, she really is a friend. We were best friends in high school."

"But not just friends," she hedges. "There was more there."

It's not a question; it's a statement. And it's true. We were so much more.

"Yeah, but that was years ago," I finally say, straightening a couple of chairs as I try to avoid CeCe's stare and the growing ache in my chest.

"Doesn't mean it can't be more again," CeCe says, making her way back around the counter. "Shep said you two were really close, like each other's shadows. He also mentioned he thought he was going to have to stage an intervention when she left for New York."

I sigh, glancing out the window. "It wasn't my best moment."

After a few seconds of silence, a new customer walks in and puts an end to our heart-to-heart.

"My only piece of advice is don't have regrets," CeCe says, lowering her voice. "She's obviously back in your life for a reason, take advantage of the opportunity. If nothing else, get some closure, because you, Finley Lawson, deserve to be happy."

"Thanks, CeCe." I wrap my arm around her shoulder, hugging her to me, before kissing the top of her head. "I'm gonna go take a nap before my set tonight. I'll see you later."

"Bye, Finn. Let me know if you want to bring Georgette to dinner one night. I'll need some advance notice so I can make sure Shep is on his best behavior."

"Will do," I reply, laughing as I make my way to my apartment upstairs.

8

Georgette

WALKING INTO THE GALLERY THIS MORNING, I FEEL LIKE
I'm bouncing on air. Since my talk with Finn yesterday, I feel lighter. I
guess I didn't realize how much the past was weighing me down. Clearing
the air a bit with him was the best thing I've done in a while. It was a long
time overdue, like five years overdue, and now that it's over, I feel like I
can breathe better. Regrets try to creep in when I think about being out
of touch with Finley for so long and how things ended with us, but I
push those thoughts out of my head. Finn said we should leave the past
in the past and I couldn't agree more.

We can't go back.

But we can go forward.

And having Finley back in my life is exactly what I needed. I've
missed him and his friendship so much. I actually woke up this morning
and the first thought in my head was *I wonder what Finely is doing today?*
We have plans to meet up tomorrow. It's his day off and he's going with
me to look at a few apartments.

I can't live at the hotel forever. It was fine for the first few weeks but

I'm ready to have my own space and eventually, I'd like to get the rest of my belongings from New York, what little I have, and bring them here too.

That thought brings Trevor to mind and I glance down at my phone and the text message I sent him last night that he still hasn't replied to.

What will he say to me wanting to move the rest of my things to New Orleans?

What would that mean for us?

Why hasn't he texted me back?

As I flip on the lights, I glance around the space and inhale deeply.

God, I love this place.

The pristine white floors and equally white walls are the perfect backdrop for the colorful art we're beginning to amass. There's a new artist coming in today to show some samples and I have a good feeling about him. He's a local and got his start painting in the Quarter, exactly what Cami is looking for.

Speaking of Cami, she was supposed to be here early this morning because she has a doctor's appointment later today, but I haven't seen her yet. Leaning over the desk, I check the message book and calendar to see if she left a note but there's nothing new.

I grab my phone and send her a text to check on her. This pregnancy is getting down to the wire and apparently, she's been having Braxton Hicks contractions for a while, which is why her husband, Deacon, is so worried about her all the time. Plus, I think he's just really protective of her. It's sweet. The couple times I've seen them together I do nothing but smile. But it also makes my heart ache.

I want what they have.

As I'm daydreaming about my future, my phone dings.

Cami: Sorry I'm a no call no show! Carter left his backpack at home and I had to go back and get it. Then my mother-in-law made me come in for cinnamon rolls

when I dropped Cash off.

I laugh out loud. No one makes Cami do anything, except carbs. She is weak to their demands.

Cami: Good news though, I'm bringing you one!

What I let out next is something between a moan and a groan. First, I'm sure the cinnamon roll is amazing. I've sampled Annie Landry's cooking and it's all been phenomenal. Her boys definitely got their food skills from her. Second, Cami is constantly leading me into the arms of the devil with her King Cakes and beignets, and now, cinnamon rolls.

If this baby doesn't hurry up, I'm going to be living my best six-hundred-pound life.

An hour or so later, Cami arrives at the gallery, cinnamon rolls in hand.

"What's on the agenda today?" she asks, flittering around the gallery like she's not carrying a butterball turkey under her pretty pink dress.

"A meeting in ten minutes with the new artist you booked last week," I tell her, glancing down at the calendar and then back up at her. When we hear the door chime, we both look over to see a man walking in with a large portfolio under his arm. "And that's probably him."

Of course, he'd be early, but Cami doesn't miss a beat. She smoothes down her dress over her round belly and greets him midway across the gallery, introducing herself and then me.

After a great meeting, where we end up accepting a small collection of his paintings on a trial basis, I call us in some lunch and then we spend the better part of the afternoon going over our plans for when Cami is out for maternity leave. It's still a month away, but we have quite a bit to do before it gets here, namely finding someone to help out while she's gone.

I'm more than capable of handling the gallery on my own, but there are times we need more than one person here. We have someone who comes in and packages up paintings once they sell, which is nice. Plus, there's a cleaning service that comes in twice a week to dust and tidy up the place. But occasionally, we'll have a meeting with an artist or buyer while the gallery is open, like today, and we need someone to man the desk and greet walk-ins.

Our location makes this gallery unique. If set in a city like New York, most of our clientele would be through appointments only, but in a city like New Orleans, you have so many people just wandering in off the street. It isn't always a bad thing. Just last week, I sold a painting for five grand to a woman window shopping while her husband was in a meeting at the hotel next door.

It just adds to the uniqueness of 303 Royal and I love it. I love the environment. I love the challenges. I love the art. I love the city. Everything about this place makes my heart happy and that convinces me I did the right thing in taking this job.

"Let's keep moving," Cami says, gingerly taking a seat at the desk across from me. She's been pacing and randomly adjusting things as we've been talking. According to the baby book she left on the desk last week, my guess is this is her version of nesting. "We still need to discuss tomorrow night."

Tomorrow night is the King Cake Party, but since we didn't have an official grand opening party, it's playing many roles and I want to make sure it's perfect, for Cami. She's worked so hard on this gallery and she wants to have everyone together one last time before the baby comes, and I want that for her. I also want to prove I can handle things while she's away.

We go over every fine detail of the evening. It's going to be low-key, but I still want to make sure it goes off without a hitch. With all of the Landrys in attendance, it's sure to be a fun time. Finley and Tucker are going to play to give us a nice soundtrack for the evening. We have at least a dozen King Cakes coming, and Micah offered to bring over plates, forks, and napkins from Lagniappe. CeCe is setting up a small coffee bar and Shaw O'Sullivan offered to serve a signature drink for the evening. Apparently, everyone is in the spirit these days. With Carnival in full swing, it's a party twenty-four-seven.

"So, I think we're set," Cami says, closing her planner.

I double-check my list and nod. "I think so. I'll give everyone a quick reminder email today and make sure no one needs me to do anything."

"As long as everyone is here, it'll be a success." Cami sighs and closes her eyes as she places a hand on her belly.

"Are you okay?" I ask, reaching across the desk. "Is it a contraction?"

After a deep breath, she opens her eyes and smiles. "No, I'm good, but I have to run. My doctor's appointment is in half an hour and Deacon is supposed to pick me up out front."

"Okay, you go. I've got everything handled here."

We have one more appointment on the books for this afternoon, a man and woman stopping in to look for a few new pieces of art for their house that's being remodeled in the Garden District. That's an area of New Orleans I still haven't been to yet, but I'm hoping to visit soon.

As a matter of fact, one of the apartments on my list is there. But the three I want to check out tomorrow are closer to the gallery. I'm trying to think of ease in getting to work. My trust fund is available, and I could use it to buy a car or even a house, but I try not to use it unless I need to. It's there and it's mine, but I like fending for myself.

Trevor thinks it's absurd. The topic of my trust fund has always been a sticky subject between him and me and I really can't explain it, but I like making my own money and living within my means. It makes me feel self-sufficient, like a responsible adult.

However, I wouldn't mind investing in a piece of property here if I found the right place. That seems like a good use of the money. Also, I have an in when it comes to property and investing with Shep and his best friend Maverick. They mostly buy and sell commercial property, but Shep gave me a couple of listings he thinks are a good deal and one of them isn't far from where he and CeCe live.

Having them as neighbors would be amazing and it would make this new city feel even more like home.

"ARE YOU SURE YOU'RE OKAY WITH ME MEETING FINLEY?" I ASK, FOR the second time. Cami has seemed preoccupied all day, scurrying around the studio like a squirrel on crack… or a pregnant lady on carbs. She brought beignets today, fresh from Cafe du Monde.

"I'm sure. Go," she demands, practically pushing me toward the front door. "I don't want you to live out of a suitcase forever, it makes me nervous, like you're not planning on staying. So the sooner you find a place, the better."

Rolling my eyes, I laugh her off and head for the door.

Leaving, honestly, hasn't crossed my mind since the second I stepped out of the cab and onto Royal Street.

"Call me if anything comes up or if you have any contractions. I won't be far," I tell her, shouldering my bag and reaching for the handle of the door, but before I can open it, Finley steps inside almost running right into me.

We both laugh and do an awkward half-hug. I'm not sure where the awkwardness stems from. Finley and I have always been good at being friends, but ever since our talk at Neutral Grounds, things have been good, but occasionally, well, awkward. It's like we're not quite sure how to navigate being *just* friends. Before, there were never any perimeters around our relationship.

We were just Finn and Jette.

"Ready?" he asks, glancing over my shoulder at Cami in a questioning motion.

Cami waves us both off. "Yes, she's ready. And hello, Finley, can't wait to hear you play tonight." Walking up to him, she gives him a hug that holds zero awkwardness and plants a kiss on his cheek. "Although, you know you're invited even if you don't play, right? We don't just love you for your saxophone. But my brother would be sorely disappointed if you didn't come play with him. I'm pretty sure he's been looking forward to it since New Year's Eve."

"Well, the feeling is mutual," Finley says, rubbing the back of his neck like he always does when he's uncomfortable under someone's scrutiny or praise. "And thank you."

"Of course," Cami says. "You're family, which means you're stuck with us."

Finley gives her a smile and then turns to me. "We better get going if we're going to keep you from being homeless."

"You make it sound like I'm going to be in a van down by the river," I tease, elbowing him as I duck under his arm and out the door. "Except, I don't even have a van, so it'd be more like a cardboard box."

I hear Cami chuckle as the door closes behind us before she calls out, "Have fun, you two!"

Finley and I fall into step, periodically moving to the side as large groups pass by.

"So where are we headed first?" Finley asks, putting an arm out in front of me to block a couple of guys who aren't paying attention. Already drunk from a stint on Bourbon Street, from the looks of it.

People in New Orleans take day drinking to an entirely new level.

"It's a loft apartment," I tell him, pulling out my phone and checking the address. "Just a couple more blocks up and then one over."

A few minutes later, we're making our way up a dank staircase and into an apartment the size of a closet. When the listing said loft, I think it actually meant studio and small, like smaller than most apartments in New York City. The location is great, definitely within walking distance to the gallery and only a short walk to Neutral Grounds and some of my other favorite places, but zero room. One look from me and we're back out the door and down the stairs.

"Next," Finley says as we step back out onto the sidewalk, not even bothering to ask what I thought.

"What? You didn't like that one?" I ask with a chuckle.

He scoffs, "You could hardly turn around. Besides, the stairwell is dark and I wouldn't like knowing you had to walk up it every night to get home."

Keeping my eyes trained ahead, I try not to let him see my smile. Finley's protectiveness is always something that's made my heart swell. It's different from the stifling overprotectiveness of my father, which was often misplaced and never showed up when I needed it.

It's even different from Trevor's controlling nature, which I've always tolerated and chalked up to being his own unique way of caring.

But when Finley makes comments like that, I know it comes from a place of genuine concern. He's not trying to box me in or exert control. He's simply worried about my well-being.

It's always made me feel cared for and *loved*, even.

When we go to turn the corner, I feel a hand touch my lower back and I practically lean into it before straightening, remembering who he is and what we are.

The gesture is so familiar and for a second it takes me back to when we were just Finn and Jette, two teenagers figuring out the world around us. I wouldn't say we didn't have any cares, because we did, Finley probably more than me, but we didn't let them weigh us down.

I miss those days.

But unlike those days, I'm not Finley's and he's not mine.

And Trevor would have a lot to say about Finley placing his hand on my lower back.

Wouldn't he?

Maybe my overactive brain is making more out of the gesture than necessary.

"How much further?" Finley asks, pulling me out of my thoughts and dropping his hand.

I try not to think about how I immediately miss his touch as I glance down at my phone and then back up to the street corner. "Two more blocks."

"I know this area," Finley says as the sidewalk begins to clear. Soon, it's just the two of us. "It's not far from Shep and CeCe... and Shaw and Avery."

"Shaw, the bar owner?" I ask, taking in the bright colorful houses as they come into view.

Finley nods, gesturing ahead to a beautiful two-story house with a gorgeous front porch. "That's Shaw and Avery's. Have you met them?"

"Just briefly at the New Year's Eve party, but they're going to be at the gallery tonight."

"They're great," Finley says. "I think you'll really like Avery. She and CeCe are best friends... and Carys, Maverick's wife."

"She owns the hotel, right?"

He nods, pointing to the house we're passing. "That's Shep and CeCe's place."

"Well, then that must be the townhouse," I say, pointing across the street.

"Do they have a room for rent?" Finley asks as we look both ways before crossing over to the other side.

Pulling out my phone, I look up the code the realtor gave me and punch it in on the keypad at the front door. "No, I'm thinking about buying it."

When the deadbolt disengages, I push the door open and walk through. The second I step into the foyer and catch a glimpse of the hardwood floors and expansive ceiling, I feel my heart skip a beat. As we walk into the front room, I notice the tall windows and built-in bookcases and I'm practically sold.

Doing a spin, I halt when I notice Finley's furrowed brow.

"What? You don't like this place either?" I ask, giving the space another look, expecting to find cracks in the ceiling or a nasty water leak. But everything is perfect and pristine—something old that's been made new. It's perfect.

When he doesn't reply, I jokingly add, "There aren't any dark staircases or sketchy neighbors."

Finley's expression finally shifts and he turns his eyes to the floor before he lets out a laugh and shakes his head.

"What?"

"Nothing," he says, bringing his eyes back up to meet mine. "I just forget sometimes."

"Forget what?" I ask, turning to walk into what I'm assuming is the kitchen.

And I'm right.

And it's glorious.

White subway tile adorns the walls, setting off pale gray cabinets and stainless-steel appliances. There's a large, farm-style sink and open shelves for dishes. I can visualize myself standing here making coffee on a Sunday morning as the sun filters through the window.

"I forget how different we are," Finley says quietly, stepping into the kitchen and I stiffen, my hand freezing on the cool marble counter.

Turning, our eyes meet and for a second, I don't know what to say.

It's only money.

It's not like that.

We're not different.

Everything that comes to mind sounds stupid and insensitive. We are different. Finley has struggled for everything he's ever had. Even when he moved in with Maggie, things still weren't easy. At school, everyone knew he was the grandson of the hired help at the Rhys-Jones estate. They knew he was enrolled because of who his grandmother worked for.

If I had to guess, not a lot has changed for Finley over the years. But I also know that money has never made him happy. He's always found happiness in much simpler things and I've always loved that about him.

"You're right," I finally say, wanting to clear the air on this topic instead of letting it fester. "We're different. I have a trust fund and it's been sitting untouched since I turned twenty-one." I shrug, letting out a deep sigh. "I can't change that. But I know you, Finley Lawson, and I know you don't care about money or the things it can buy."

Finn smirks and then rakes a hand through his curly hair. "You're right. I don't. And that was a stupid thing for me to say."

"Will it change your opinion of me if I buy this place with my trust fund?"

He lets out a breathy chuckle before his teeth bite down on his full lower lip and then release it. Those big, dark eyes look over at me from beneath long lashes women would kill for. "Of course not," he mutters. "I'd be happy knowing you were somewhere safe, surrounded by people who care about you."

"What is it then?"

Sighing, he shoves his hands in his back pockets and begins walking around the empty house. "I guess I just forgot about all of that. You haven't been around in so long and then you show back up here, in New Orleans. And you're the same, but different. I guess I forgot that you're Georgette Taylor, only child of Mr. and Mrs. George Taylor, and everything that entails."

"The only thing that entails is my lineage and the fact I have a trust fund my grandfather left me. That's it," I call out as I lose sight of him around the corner.

When we meet back up in the dining room, Finley's brow arches. "I'd venture to say your mother and father still wouldn't be happy you're spending time with me."

Rolling my eyes, I snort. "My mother and father no longer get to dictate who I spend my time with."

"I bet they approve of Trevor."

The statement is out before either of us can process the implications. But I see it on Finley's face the second he regrets saying it. And I feel it in my chest the second I realize he's right.

They do approve of Trevor, unlike Finley, who they never approved of.

Well, that's not entirely true. For a brief period of time, when they assumed there was no chance I'd be interested in someone like Finley, and thought we were merely study buddies, they were fine with me spending time with him. But the second they saw the spark that has always been there between us, they hated the idea of the two of us being together.

I spent four years hiding Finley from them and lying about where I was and who I was with.

"We should go," I say as I walk past him and straight for the door.

"I'm sorry," he whispers, but I don't acknowledge it.

As I lock the door behind us, I can feel the tension rolling off Finley.

"You're right," I finally say as we're walking down the sidewalk. "They do approve of Trevor."

But that's not why I'm with him.

Is it?

"And you're also right that they probably would hate to know we've reconnected," I admit. "But I meant what I said. I'm an adult now and they no longer get to dictate anything about my life. It's one of the reasons I rarely go home. I like being my own person and making my own decisions. It's also why I haven't touched my trust fund. Even though it's not their money, I've never wanted them to be able to throw it in my face and use it as a way to prove I can't handle being on my own. I can handle it. I'm doing it."

My voice might have gone up a notch, but I can't help it. I want Finley to know even though in a lot of ways I'm the same girl he once knew, I'm also different.

"You are doing it," Finley says as we approach the corner and come to a stop. He turns to me, his hand coming up to squeeze my shoulder. "You're everything I ever dreamed you would be, Jette… you're smart and ambitious. You know what you want and you're out there taking chances. I couldn't be prouder of you. I'm sorry I said anything about the money or Trevor. Neither of those are my business."

He's proud of me?

I'm not sure I can even remember the last time someone said that to me.

And it does something to me, but I try to stuff it back down and save that emotion for when I'm alone in my hotel room later. I'll definitely be coming back to this moment.

"Thank you," I finally say as we start walking again. "And don't worry, I'll still invite you over for peanut butter and jelly sandwiches."

Finley laughs and it's the best sound I've heard all day.

When he grabs my hand to keep me from getting plowed over by a horse and carriage, I let him, and it doesn't feel awkward or wrong.

It feels like everything is right in the world.

Even after all this time, we're still just Finn and Jette.

LATER, AS I'M WALKING AROUND THE EMPTY GALLERY IN MY PURPLE dress with a gold tulle overlay, I carefully arrange the plates, napkins, and forks Micah dropped off earlier.

There's a small stage set up in the back corner for Tucker and Finley.

Tall, pub-style tables are placed around the gallery for people to stand at while they eat King Cake and mingle. Each one is adorned with tealight candles, creating a warm glow against the white floors and walls.

Just as I'm making my way back up to the front, the door opens and Cami calls out, "Laissez les bon temps rouler."

Let the good times roll.

I've already learned that one in my few weeks on the job.

"I've brought part of the entertainment and three King Cakes," she announces as Deacon and Tucker walk in behind her, each carrying a boxed cake. Then a beautiful woman with long, dark hair walks in behind them. "I don't think you met my sister-in-law, Piper," Cami continues, still buzzing around, just like she's been doing for the past couple of days.

"No, I haven't," I say, walking closer. "Hi, I'm Georgette Taylor."

"Piper Gray," she says, reaching out to shake my hand.

"So nice to meet you. Cami's told me so much about you."

She gives her sister-in-law the side-eye and then turns back to me. "She's pregnant and loaded on carbs. Don't believe a word she says."

"Hey!" Cami exclaims. "I might be pregnant but I'm not deaf."

"Where would you like me to set up?" Tucker asks, coming back in from a second trip outside. He now has an amp and a guitar in tow.

I point toward the back corner as Finley walks in the open door, carrying a similar setup, but instead of a guitar case, he has his saxophone.

"Finley," Tucker greets, clapping him on the back. "Dude, I've been counting down the days."

Finn chuckles. "Me too, man. Let's do this."

I hear Tucker introduce Finley to Piper and the six of us go about getting things ready.

Soon, the entire gallery is full of people and laughter. Cami did the honors and cut the first slice of King Cake, making the announcement that this would become an annual affair and that everyone who gets a baby in their slice should be prepared to furnish the cakes next year.

"Hey," Cami says quietly, coming up beside me as we listen to the incredible musical entertainment. Tucker and Finley sound amazing together. They've covered everyone from Nat King Cole to Jay-Z. It's been perfect. The entire evening has been perfect.

"Hey," I say, clinking my glass half-full of Moscato with her sparkling water.

Cami's smile is so serene as she takes it all in. "You did so good. The evening is everything I hoped it would be and then some. That goes for the gallery, as well. I couldn't be happier with how everything is going so far and so much of that is thanks to you. Hiring you was the best thing I've done in a while."

My cheeks heat up at her praise and I hide my smile with a sip of wine. "Thank you," I finally say as I swallow the sweet liquid. "For hiring me and bringing me to this city… and into this amazing group of people."

Finley was right, I met Shaw's wife, Avery, and I love her. She's close to my age and so fun to be around. Seeing Cami with CeCe and Carys and Avery makes me smile. And then you toss in her sisters-in-law, Piper and Dani, and it's a whole tribe of women I'd love to know better.

And don't even get me started on Annie. She's everything I always wanted my mother to be—warm, caring, inviting. This isn't even her house and she's made every person feel like a part of her family. I can't imagine what it's like on their plantation, but I hope to find out one of these days.

"I have something to tell you," Cami says, keeping her voice low. "But I don't want you to freak out, because you're ready... more than ready. And I wouldn't say that if I didn't mean it because this gallery is like one of my babies and I'd never entrust it to someone I didn't think was capable."

I feel my eyes grow wide as she rambles, hoping she's not getting ready to say what I think she is.

"My doctor is putting me on bedrest. I'm not even supposed to be here tonight, but I convinced Deacon I needed this last hurrah." Her eyes travel across the room to meet up with her husband's, which haven't left her the entire evening.

Earlier, I noticed he'd been hovering more than usual, and now I know why.

"As of tomorrow, the gallery will be in your care." My eyes are still trained forward as I try to digest what she's telling me. I feel Cami's hand wrap around mine that's dangling at my side. "Dani has agreed to step in and be your extra set of hands when you need her. She's planning on making a daily appearance. If you don't need her, you can send her on her way. But if you do, she'll be here for any and everything. She's a photographer and has a great eye for art, so use her. She's also been around my studio for a while now and knows the ins and outs of things. Her schedule is flexible, and she's been hanging around the city quite a bit to be closer to Micah, since he's pretty much full-time at Lagniappe these days. It's really a win-win for everyone."

Taking a deep breath, I try to relax.

It's fine.

Everything will be fine.

And knowing Dani is going to be around does set my mind at ease a bit, but I also know there's no way to prepare for the couple months ahead.

"Sink or swim, right?" I say, half-joking, as I turn to face Cami.

She squeezes my hand tighter. "Oh, honey. You'll be soaring. I promise."

9

Finley

"GREAT SET, MAN!" ROGER PATS ME ON THE BACK WHILE I
open the door to the tiny dressing room backstage. I yell my thanks to
him before stepping inside and walking straight for the sink to wash
my face and freshen up. Once I'm done, I peel off my sweaty t-shirt and
replace it with a clean one from my duffel bag. I always work up a sweat
while playing but the added heat of stage lights is a killer for sure. I can
work through three or four shirts a night sometimes, so I know to pack
extras with me, including deodorant.

Especially the deodorant. Can't have stinky pits.

I still have one more set to go before my time is up here at Good
Times and I'm thankful for the break to walk around, stretch my legs,
and drink a cold beer. I wish Jette was here so I'd have someone to talk
to but she's been slammed at work this week, running the gallery on her
own now that Cami is on maternity leave, and has been going to bed
early. I know she's in her element and doing what she loves most but I
miss her. Taking my phone out of my pocket, I automatically open my
text conversation with Jette and look at the gif of a puppy yawning she

sent over two hours ago.

Jette: Going to bed. Kick some ass tonight!

I smile even wider than I did when I first opened her message because I did. I kicked some major ass tonight and that's not me being arrogant or conceited. Some nights are just better than others, and tonight was one of my best. That's another reason I wish Jette was here; she would've loved it. She's always been my biggest cheerleader and I want to make her proud.

"Baby, baby, baby! You are on fire tonight!" Gia saunters up to me and places her hands on top of my shoulders. "You playin' for someone special or did you just get laid? Whatever it is that has upped your game, keep it up. Oh, and," she runs a long, red fingernail down the middle of my chest, "save some sugar for me."

"Nothing's changed, Gia, I'm just having a good night." I twist my torso to place my empty beer glass on the bar behind me and to remove myself from her arms. She laughs when I succeed.

Typical Gia.

"Honey, you're having an incredible night. One might even say, tonight could be life-changing for you," she hedges.

"Oh, yeah? In what way?" I don't want to fall for any of her schemes but I'll be damned if I wasn't interested in what she has to say.

Gia's eyes light up when she sees she has my full attention. She brushes her thick, auburn hair away from her face and leans closer to me. "Let's just say, I've been in touch with a local musician… a very famous one, in fact… who's looking for new talent to do some studio work. You're a hot, young musician, Finley. I bet you play more than just the sax, right?"

"Yeah, I play drums and keys pretty well and can get by on guitar and bass. What does that have to do with being young and hot?" I spit out that last word because that is not how I see myself and I feel stupid even repeating it.

"Because you have it all. Looks, youth, and talent—it's the fucking trifecta of our industry! Even your naiveté is endearing." She says this with a laugh but too soon, her eyes darken as they take me in from my head to my toes. Gia licks her lips before continuing. "This could be a really profitable opportunity for you and I'm inclined to give my famous friend your name... if you give *me* something in return."

This is a bit different from how I've seen Gia work in the past. Normally, it's harmless flirting that ends with a laugh as soon as I turn her down. This is the first time she's propositioned me in this way and I don't like it one bit.

I step away from her completely, watching as she stumbles to regain her balance. "No, Gia. I've told you before, I don't work that way. I earn my opportunities through my talent and merit, that's it. I don't put out for jobs ever and if that doesn't work for you, I'll find someone else to work for."

"Finley—"

"No. I'm serious, Gia. I love working here and you're a great boss, for the most part. And I don't give two shits if you sleep with everyone in here but it's not going to happen with me."

Gia holds her hands up, as if she's surrendering. "I get it, Finn, I do. And, I apologize for upsetting you. You're not like most guys around here... in a lot of ways, in fact, and I respect you for that. I'll lay off, I promise."

I relax my stance, nodding my acceptance of her words. "Thanks, Gia. I appreciate it."

She pulls a piece of paper out of her back pocket and hands it to me. "You can thank me after your meeting next week."

"What meeting?" I ask, looking down at the paper.

"Your meeting with Lola Carradine. She asked for you by name, so don't screw this up." Gia gives me a smile then walks off, leaving me completely dumbfounded and staring at the paper in my hand.

"Hey, Finn. Here's you a fresh beer."

I look up and see Suki, one of the waitresses here holding out a tall glass for me.

"Oh, thanks, Suki. I guess I forgot I ordered another one," I reply, taking the beer from her.

"Nah, it's on the house. I saw Gia was cornering you again, so I thought I'd interrupt and bring you a drink but then I got slammed and missed my chance. Better late than never, right?"

"Absolutely." I tip the beer toward her before taking a long drink.

"Have a great set," she calls out as she walks off to check on her tables.

Oh, shit, I still have another set. I've been completely distracted since Gia said the name *Lola Carradine* but I can't think about that right now.

One more set then, I can go home and freak the fuck out.

I CAN OFFICIALLY MARK *RIDE A STREETCAR* OFF MY NEW ORLEANS to-do list.

I wasn't sure what to expect once I paid my fare and sat down but it's actually not too bad. The wooden seats are more comfortable than you'd think and with the windows partially open, the breeze blowing through feels nice.

The best part, though, is the view and seeing a part of New Orleans I haven't had a chance to explore yet. The streetcar is taking me to a part of the city I haven't seen yet and I can't help but feel like a tourist again, staring out the windows as if I'm a kid on a train ride.

Jette will get such a kick out of this.

Speaking of Jette, I feel bad for turning down her offer to grab lunch today. She texted me last night and asked if I had plans, I said I did but didn't elaborate on what those plans were. I haven't told anyone I'm meeting Lola Carradine at her studio because I know they'll lose their shit, and believe me, I'm losing mine enough for everyone.

My stomach is twisted in knots, which is weird for me. I sometimes get a little anxious or excited before a gig but this is different. I'm meeting a fucking rock star... about a fucking job... so, yeah, you could say I'm nervous. I didn't eat breakfast or have any coffee before I left, which had CeCe practically chasing me through the shop, trying to see if I was running a fever, but there's no way I'm gonna risk puking all over Miss Carradine.

When I called the number Gia gave me the other night, someone named Casey set up the meeting and gave me the address I'm following now. I've been to a couple of the recording studios around town but never to one in the Garden District. All I've seen so far are homes with a few businesses sprinkled throughout. Definitely not the typical area for most musicians to hang.

Stepping off the streetcar, I check the GPS to make sure I'm in the right area. Once I have my bearings, I start walking, looking at the house numbers until I come to the correct one.

Casey told me she'd have the gate open and to go on up to a side door and ring the bell, which I do. While I wait for someone to open the door, I look around. It's a really nice neighborhood, nothing shady about it at all, but it's definitely not what I was expecting.

As luck would have it, as soon as I set my sax case on the ground, the door opens and Lola Carradine steps out.

Her smile is bright as she eyes me and then my sax. "Finley?" she asks.

"Uh, um, ye-yes, ma'am." Ma'am? Really, Finn. For fuck's sake. "Yeah, I'm Finley," I amend, offering my hand for a shake as I get my shit together.

"Finley Lawson. Someone by the name of Casey gave me this address... and the code to the gate."

I can picture what my tombstone will say: Here lies Finley Lawson. He died of embarrassment because he forgot how to speak like an adult.

Thankfully, Lola only smiles wide as she replies, "Casey is my sister. And I'm glad you didn't have any problem with the gate. It's a little tricky. No trouble finding the house?"

"No trouble at all." I wasn't expecting to walk up to her door. When Casey gave me the address, I assumed it was an actual studio. "Didn't expect it to be in a neighborhood. I take it you have a home studio?"

"Sure do. Makes life much easier. Why don't we go inside and play some music?" She opens and holds the door for me and as I walk past her, I say a silent prayer that I don't fuck this up.

Please, God, don't let me fuck this up.

Two hours later and I'm a crazy mixture of exhaustion and exhilaration. I've always loved playing with super talented people, and I feed off their creativity like a vampire to blood, but today was something otherworldly. I've been a fan of Lola's for years, but I had no idea how insanely gifted she is.

"Damn, Finn, that's the most fun I've had in the studio in ages," Lola says as she tosses me a bottle of water. "I don't know how much Gia told you, but I watched your set the other night."

I swear, it takes everything in me not to choke on the water I just poured into my mouth. Once I manage to remove the bottle from my lips, I cough out, "Oh, yeah?"

"Hell yeah. I love using local musicians as much as possible and was on the hunt. As soon as you stepped on that stage, I knew you had something special about you."

"Gia mentioned you asking for me by name, but I didn't really know what she meant. I was too surprised you wanted to meet with me at all to ask her about it."

"Well, after seeing you that night and what we just experienced here today, I have no doubt you'd make a great fit for my next album. If you're interested, that is."

Did Lola Carradine just ask me to join her band?

What the fuck?

Like I'd ever say no to that.

"You're serious?" I ask, waiting to be punked or something. "Of course, I'd love to. I'm honored you're even asking. Thank you so much." I walk to her with my hand stretched out for a shake, ready to seal the deal, but she blows it off and pulls me in for a hug instead.

"We hug a lot around here. I hope that doesn't scare you," she says, giving me a tight squeeze. "Welcome to the family, Finn."

Just then, a throat clears and it's a deep one, so I practically jump out of Lola's arms before turning and seeing a big, muscled dude eyeing me carefully.

"Babe!" Lola squeals, running into the guy's arms. "I have the best news. Come meet Finley."

Lola grabs his hand and pulls him farther into the studio until we're face to face. "Finn, this is my boyfriend, Bo. Bo, this is Finn, the saxophonist we saw perform at Good Times the other night. He's going to play on the album!"

Recognition must dawn on Bo because he quickly changes from cautious and protective to smiling and welcoming. "That's awesome, man. Great to meet you." He shakes my hand and just like Lola warned, pulls me in for a one-armed man hug. "You were amazing. I know you'll fit right in."

"Thanks, man. It's great to meet you, too."

The more I look at Bo, the more I feel like I've seen him somewhere before. I don't follow celebrity magazines or web sites, so I have no idea who Lola's boyfriend would be but I know his face from somewhere. As I start taking apart my sax and cleaning it before I pack it up, I can't help but watch how Lola and Bo interact with each other. They're obviously in love but I also see a deep and mutual admiration and respect between them. It's how I thought Jette and I would be if we would've stayed together.

They're just so normal together.

He asks her what's for dinner and she asks him how his day was.

Totally normal.

I mean, I guess. I really have nothing to go off of, seeing as how I grew up with drug addicts for parents and then went to live with Maggie. The only married people I witnessed on a regular basis was Shep's parents, but they were far from normal.

When Bo mentions batting practice, something in my brain finally clicks.

"Holy shit, I just realized who you are," I say, feeling stupid and somewhat embarrassed by my outburst. *But holy shit.* "You're Bo Bennett!"

Like, *the Bo Bennet*, third baseman for New Orleans MLB team, the Revelers. He's basically a household name. Every magazine in the grocery store has had his picture on the cover—Rookie of the Year, All-Star, you name it.

I don't follow celebrity gossip, but I can guess they had a field day with Bo Bennett and Lola Carradine, which makes their normalness even more exceptional.

Laughing, he turns to me and nods. "Yeah, are you a baseball fan?"

"Hell, yeah, I am," I say, still reeling from the fact I'm standing in Lola Carradine's kitchen talking to Bo Bennett about baseball. "I'm a huge fan, but I've never been to a game."

"Is there not a team where you're from?" Bo asks.

"I'm from Dallas so, yeah, there's a team but I've never been to a game."

Bo pulls Lola into his side, kissing the top of her head. "Well, as soon as the season starts, I'll get you some tickets so you can come check us out. Maybe Lola will even let you sit in her fancy pants box seats."

She smiles and swats at his chest, but he loves it. And so does she.

Free baseball tickets *and* a job playing with Lola Carradine?

Maybe I should go buy a lottery ticket, because I feel like this is my lucky day.

10

Georgette

"**Knock, knock!**"

I peek my head around the corner and look at the door, relief filling my body as I see Dani Landry walk into the gallery.

"Dani, hi! What brings you here?"

"I'm here to help, didn't Cami tell you?" She pushes her sunglasses up to sit on the top of her head, pulling her incredible auburn hair away from her face in the process.

"She did, but I wasn't sure when you'd be starting and I didn't want to be presumptuous but the phone has been ringing off the hook this morning and I could really use some help." I spit out the words quickly and on one breath, not caring if I sound like a crazy person because that's exactly how I feel. Crazy. On top of dealing with clients all morning, my realtor is breathing down my neck to get me to make a decision and Trevor is pissed at me because I'm even considering buying something, making this move more permanent, and I just cannot deal right now.

"Okay, okay. Let's sit down and talk all this out." Dani grabs me by the hand and leads me to the comfy couch near Cami's desk and I don't even care that she's talking to me as if I'm a child on the verge of a meltdown. "Can I get you some tea? Coffee? Bourbon? You name it and I'll get it."

A laugh escapes my mouth and I relax, allowing my body to sink fully into the couch. "No, I'm fine. I was just feeling a little in over my head. You showed up at the perfect time to talk me off the ledge, thank you."

"That's what I'm here for. Now, tell me how I can help. I am officially your beck and call girl, so use me!"

I look up at Dani and I'm suddenly overcome with gratitude. Not only because she's here—it's bigger than that. Of all the jobs, locations, bosses, and by default, friends, I landed the absolute best and I have no idea how or why. Rather than accept things for how they are and how fortunate I've been, my anxiety is causing me to question everything and believe I'm not good enough, that I'll fail spectacularly. Even so, I know Dani and everyone else in my new life here in New Orleans won't let that happen and for that, I'm so very thankful.

I don't want to burden Dani with all of that, though, so I give her the shortlist.

"Naturally, it's been the busiest day since I've started working here… you know, since Cami isn't here. It's like all her clients know she's on bedrest and are testing me." My eyes narrow at the thought, causing Dani to laugh.

"Well, I'm putting myself on phone duty for the rest of the day, so that should help some. What else can I do?"

Don't do it, Georgette. Don't you spill your guts to this nice woman. She's only here to help, not to be your therapist.

When I don't say anything, she continues. "If you don't tell me now, I'm only going to badger you until you do. I may be a Landry by marriage but I'm nosy as fuck, just like those related by blood. Besides, things are quiet right now; let's take advantage of it."

I wait a few seconds before blowing out a deep breath, ready to give in to Dani's demands. I don't really have anyone to talk to about things like this, besides Finley. He knows I'm struggling to make a decision about where I want to live but I don't feel right griping about Trevor to him. It feels… awkward. The last thing I want is to mess up what progress we've made.

"I've been looking at places to buy or rent so I can stop living out of my suitcase," I start.

"That's very stressful. Do you have someone to help?"

"I do. Maverick and Shep have given me advice, Finley has been going with me to see the properties, and I have a realtor, as well, but it's just overwhelming. I thought about renting a place but I'd really like to invest in something and have a place that's mine, you know? And I found a fabulous townhouse I'd love to buy, but my boyfriend loses his shit every time I bring it up. He was against me moving here and hasn't really changed his tune. Most days, I feel like he's not even trying to understand."

Letting out a heavy sigh, I think about spilling even more confessions, but stop there. That's the gist of it, but not everything. Trevor's lack of understanding is just the tip of the iceberg lately. The longer I'm here, the more distant he feels. I'd hoped it would be a case of distance making the heart grow fonder, but now, I'm not so sure.

"Ahh, so there's a boyfriend." When I nod my head, Dani presses her lips together, deep in thought. "I used to have one of those… a boyfriend in New York City. Pretentious and uptight? Thinks he knows what's best for you and doesn't listen when you disagree?"

Again, I nod my head.

"Yeah," she says, blowing out a breath. "I'm not going to tell you how to live your life but I will say, my life improved greatly when I kicked my ex to the curb."

"What happened?"

"I caught the bastard cheating."

"Oh, shit, Dani. I'm so sorry."

She laughs. "I'm not. Don't get me wrong, I was devastated when it happened but I had a friend who helped me through it and eventually, that friend became my husband."

I cover my mouth to try and hide the gasp that escaped. Color me fascinated. I want to know more about Dani's story but I don't want to pry too much. Plus, I can't help but think about how what she shared with me is similar to me and Finley. Except the cheating. Trevor isn't a cheater. I don't think he really cares about sex enough to cheat anyway, but everything else she said is really hitting home with me.

Dani's presence was just what I needed. She did as promised and manned the phones while I met with three potential buyers. One of them is interested in some of Cami's work, which is wonderful. I wish we had more to show at the gallery, but I let them take home her portfolio and we're planning to meet back up in a few days.

Hours later, I'm nestled in a small, corner table at Good Times, drinking from a bottle of champagne while I wait on Finn to finish his last set. For a day that started out to be the most stressful day I've had yet, it turned out not so bad.

When Finn sees me, the look of surprise on his face makes me smile.

Then, he starts cutting his eyes at me, smirking, and that makes me giggle.

And the giggle turns into full-on laughter.

Finley's always had that effect on me—childlike giddiness and the ability to forget my problems—although, it could also be the champagne.

When he finally is able to join me at my table, I'm well on the tipsy side.

Damn, he looks good.

Maybe I should lay off the champers.

"What's this all about? What are we celebrating?" Finley asks while sitting next to me.

"I did something big today and I wanted to share the news with you. But, first, you need a glass!" I hold the bottle up, ready to pour.

He laughs before declining my offer. "I'll stick to beer, but thank you. Now, tell me your news."

"I bought the townhouse!" It's pretty loud in the club tonight, so I make sure to lean close to Finley when I speak. You know, so he can hear me, *not* so I can smell him.

"Jette, that's awesome! Congratulations." He wraps his arm around me and pulls me to his side, kissing the top of my head. It feels so good to be this close to him, I want to snuggle closer and never leave. "You really did it, Jette. I'm proud of you." He gives me another squeeze before letting me go and setting me to rights. I feel the loss of him immediately but it's what I need to sober up.

You have a boyfriend, Georgette. And you're not a cheater.

The temptation of Finley has been getting stronger and stronger, but I keep telling myself it's nostalgia and pushing it down… down, down, down. Taking another sip of champagne, I regain the composure he stole and redirect my thoughts.

"Thanks, I'm really excited and I can't wait to start moving in and furnishing the place. Of course, I have to find some time to fly up to New York and pack up the rest of my things, but I have a little time."

There's a change in Finley's demeanor that almost slips by me. If I were completely sober, I'd be able to pinpoint the difference better but even so, I know something has changed.

"Have you told Trevor your big news?" he asks, focusing his attention on the label of the beer bottle in his hands.

"Not yet. He won't be happy, but I don't care. He can either support me or not." I wish I felt as brave as my words sound. I mean what I said but I can admit to myself I'm avoiding telling Trevor because I know it'll cause a fight… a fight we may not recover from.

"Hey, you wanna have some fun tomorrow?"

Finley's change of topic has me perking up immediately. "Sure, what do you have in mind?"

"Mardi Gras World!"

"What is that? I thought New Orleans *was* Mardi Gras World."

He smiles, meeting my eyes, as he shakes his head. "It's this place where some of the parade floats are created and stored. It's supposed to be pretty cool and they offer tours."

"If you were anyone else, I'd be worried they'd think this is a stupid idea, but I know you and I know how you get a kick out of oddities as much as I do. And what better way to immerse ourselves in this new city than with a tour of Mardi Gras World? I've heard the parades are insane, so this way, we can get an up-close and personal look at the floats without all the crazy people."

"That sounds so fun," I say, my face beaming with excitement. "I'd love to!"

"I'll meet you at the gallery around four, okay? We can get an Uber from there."

"I'll be ready," I say while trying to stifle a yawn.

"Alright, party animal. Let me take you home." Finley stands up and holds his hand out to me.

I take his hand and stand up; happy I only wobble a little. "Don't you have another set? I don't want to get you in trouble. I can stay here and wait for you." I know I'm lying and so does Finn. Once I start yawning, I'm down for the count.

"Let me tell Gia I'll be a little late for my next set and then we can go."

He's back a lot sooner than I expected and I'm relieved. It's been a long day and I really am tired. The champagne didn't help any, but I couldn't think of a better way to celebrate signing on the dotted line than to be here tonight, watching Finley play.

When we step outside, the cool breeze blowing by and the feel of Finley's hand grabbing mine work together to wake me up.

"You never could hold your liquor. Funny how some things never change."

I elbow him in his side, making him bark out a laugh. "Oh, hush. My reaction to alcohol may be the same but at least my choice of beverages has improved."

"Oh, so you've quit Boone's Farm for good?"

Now it's my turn to laugh. "That's right, no more Strawberry Hill for me. I'm all grown up."

I swear, it sounds like he murmurs "that's a fact" under his breath but I pretend I didn't hear. Instead, I privately enjoy the feel of my blood buzzing throughout my body at his words.

All too soon, we're standing in front of the hotel that's been my home for the past month.

"Thank you for walking me home, Finn. I really appreciate it."

"Any time, Jette. You know that." And I do know. I know how fortunate I am to have Finley back in my life. I make a silent vow to never take him for granted again or leave him.

If I can help it.

"I hope your boss isn't upset with you when you go back."

"Don't worry about that. Besides, your safety is more important than my job." He opens the door to the hotel for me and kisses my hand before letting it go and nudging me inside. "Night, Jette."

"Goodnight, Finn. I'll see you tomorrow."

I watch him walk down the street until he turns a corner before I head to my room.

Then, I take my time showering and getting ready for bed, daydreaming about what life will be like once I'm in my new place. It's not until I'm in bed that I turn my phone on and see a missed call from Trevor. He rarely initiates conversations these days, unless he needs something, so I can't help but worry about his reason for calling.

With New York being an hour ahead of New Orleans, it's probably way too late to call but I dial his number anyway. I should be able to call my boyfriend at any time, right? Besides, he called first. I'm being nice and returning it.

"Hello."

I can't tell by his voice if I woke him up or not, but he doesn't sound particularly happy to hear from me.

"Hey, Trevor. Is this a bad time? I just saw that you called."

"Where have you been? It's too late for you to be out by yourself."

"I wasn't out by myself; I was with Finley."

"Who's that?" he asks, sounding more alert now.

"My friend from high school, remember? I told you that we've reconnected."

"And what were you two out doing?"

Here goes nothing. "We were celebrating me being a homeowner."

Silence.

"I decided to buy the townhouse I looked at the other day," I continue.

"I gathered that, Georgette. I'm not stupid. How exactly are we supposed to make this work with us being in two different states permanently? Do you have any idea how hard this has been on me? How embarrassing it is to attend social gatherings by myself? I can't bring myself to explain to people where you are right now because it's so preposterous and now you're planning on living there?"

A rush of indignation flows through me and I sit up in bed, throwing the covers off.

"You know, Trevor," I start, squeezing my eyes shut and rubbing them furiously, trying to remain calm. "If the roles were reversed, I would support you and your career—"

"Career?" he barks out, cutting me off. "Is that what we're calling it now? Because last I checked, this resembles a childish stint of sowing your wild oats. I thought you got past that the last time you backpacked through Europe."

He scoffs, his heavy breath coming through loud and clear, along with his distaste, which makes my blood boil.

How dare he?

How fucking dare he?

Tears prick my eyes, but I inhale deeply and brush them away. "This is my career, my decision. And as I was saying before I was so rudely interrupted, if you were the one who had to move for your job, I would support you. I would try to make the best of things and I would use this time to try to figure out if this is what I really want."

My words end in a quiet whisper and we both sit quietly on opposite ends of the phone, feeling not just thousands of miles away, but millions... light-years.

"*What I really want*?" Trevor repeats. "Is this a fucking ultimatum... is that what this is? A... stunt to force me to... what? Ask you to marry me?"

I feel the stab of his words, right in my heart.

Unlike Trevor, I would never throw something in his face that means so much to him. I also wouldn't accuse him of something so low. How could he think I'm using this job opportunity as an ultimatum?

"I would never force you to ask me to marry you," I finally say, a feeling of resignation taking over. "I hope whoever I marry doesn't have to be forced to do anything when it comes to me. I want my future husband to choose me and make me a priority."

Trevor sighs, the same resignation ringing through. "I think we should both get some sleep. I have an early meeting tomorrow."

That's it?

He has an early meeting tomorrow?

Swallowing down my emotions, I clear my throat before replying, "Me too."

"Good night, Georgette."

"Good night."

11

Finley

As I walk to the gallery to meet Georgette for our
not-a-date date, I can't help but bask in the sunshine. It would've been a
perfect day to play in the Quarter and I'm sure there were tons of tourists
to entertain. Instead, it was my first official day in the studio with Lola,
which was pretty amazing in its own right, so no complaints from me.

Stepping onto Royal Street, I spot Jette immediately. She's standing
in front of her hotel, rather than the gallery, and I assume she's changed
her clothes because she looks way more casual than she normally does
when she works.

I like it. I like it a lot.

Wearing a thin sweater, jeans, and sneakers, she looks like she did
when we were in high school. Her blonde curls blowing wildly in the
breeze are the same, too, and I welcome the nostalgic feeling overcoming
me. I've always loved that, no matter how hard she tried to tame those
curls, they rebelled and did their own thing. It seems as though she's
finally embraced her hair and that makes me very happy.

I can't help but wish I could run my fingers through them to see if they're still as soft as they used to be, but that's where I must stop myself.

If I allow my imagination to go farther, I'll be dreaming about cradling her face in my hands and pulling her mouth to mine but none of that can happen. She's with Trevor, not me, and I have to respect that. I *do* respect that. As her friend, I want her to be happy, even if that means she's happy without me.

"Finley! I'm over here!"

I wave back at Jette to let her know I see her and pick up my pace until she's standing in front of me. Fuck, she smells good, like the warm sunshine I was just basking in, and the smile she's giving me in greeting is better and brighter than any stage light I've been under.

Reign in it, man. Just friends, remember?

"You haven't been waiting long, have you?" I ask.

"No, not at all. Dani agreed to close up the gallery so I left a little early and went to my room to change clothes. This is okay, isn't it?" she asks, pointing to her outfit. "I assumed this wasn't a dressy kind of excursion."

Chuckling, I reply, "You're perfect…" I start but catch myself. "I mean, what you're wearing is perfect. You look great, by the way. New Orleans suits you."

Jette seems to tense at my words, probably because of my slip of the tongue, but then relaxes into another smile. "Thank you, I agree. I had no idea I'd love being here as much as I do but I'm happy I'm adjusting so well." For a second, we just smile at each other, like we're two of the luckiest people on the planet because we're standing here in each other's company on a sidewalk in New Orleans.

Eventually, Jette nudges me with her elbow and nods toward the sidewalk. "I'm also happy I have you here to explore with, so let's get going!"

"Yes, ma'am." I give her a quick salute before pointing her in the direction we need to walk.

"I found out there's a shuttle a couple of blocks over that will take us to Mardi Gras World and it's scheduled to leave soon, so we need to hurry," I tell her, fighting the urge to grab her hand like I did last night, which I justified because she was tipsy.

Thankfully, there is only a small handful of people waiting for the shuttle and when we're all on board, there's room for us to have our own row of seats.

"So, how has the gallery been without Cami?" I ask as the shuttle starts moving.

"Not too bad. There are busy times and slow times, but it's been a lot of fun having Dani to hang out with. She keeps trying to get me hooked on her true crime tv shows. She's obsessed."

"Oh, yeah, Shep is hooked on those, too. He's tried to get me to watch some but I just can't. I don't want to know about the crazy shit that goes on outside my small world, you know? I'm perfectly fine watching reruns of *The Office* instead."

"Right?" she says, laughing. "If I want to be freaked out, I'll watch the news."

We continue to make small talk for the short ride. I've missed this, easy conversations about everything and nothing at all. Jette and I have always been able to fill the silence or enjoy it. Neither ever feels forced and it makes me feel good to know that hasn't changed.

When we arrive, I pay for our tickets and the tour starts shortly after. We're not the only ones here, but we get to take our time going through the floats and it's pretty damn cool.

"Whoa," Jette says, her eyes wide and child-like, taking in the monstrosities around us. When she turns and smiles that familiar smile, I'm a goner, and so fucking glad I invited her to come.

It's so wild seeing all the floats and props up close. The attention to detail and pure artistry of these things are incredible; I'm in awe as

Jette and I walk around, inspecting each piece. Some of them are pretty creepy, too, if I'm being perfectly honest. More than once, Jette has to stifle a scream after turning a corner and coming face to face with a large character made of Styrofoam.

I try not to laugh.

I fail.

"Shut up." She pushes on my shoulder when I can't hold back my laughter any longer. "That was scary and you know it!"

"Okay, I admit, that big-ass jester was pretty terrifying, but did you see the Louis Armstrong one? That was amazing."

"It was," she agrees, smiling up at me. "Was it your favorite?"

I ponder her question for a few seconds as we walk outside. "It was definitely in my top two." When we make it to the metal railing, we stop and lean against it, taking in the Mississippi River. With the sun starting to set behind a nearby bridge, the view is breathtaking. Almost as breathtaking as the woman beside me.

"What was your other favorite?" she asks.

"Oh, the Yoda, for sure. I mean, Louis Armstrong is a Nola legend, but Star Wars is the best."

"Wow, speaking of things never changing," she teases. Jette never has passed up an opportunity to poke fun at my obsession with Star Wars but I don't mind. I used to pick on her for her love of Broadway show tunes but, secretly, I loved that about her. I used to daydream about taking her to all her favorite shows, knowing I'd be watching her more than the actors on the stage.

Our laughter dies down and, if I were a betting man, I'd say we're both remembering how things were between us back in high school. Even though I was crushed when Jette left, I never regretted what happened between us but I've always wondered if she did.

It's on the tip of my tongue to ask, but I don't want to ruin this moment, so instead, I tell her my good news.

"So, I got a new job."

"What? Were you fired last night for walking me home?"

"No, I'm still at the club but I was given an opportunity that may eventually take me away from Good Times." I know I'm still in the early stages of working with Lola but I'm hoping this becomes something more permanent, more stable.

"Well, stop stalling and tell me!" She grabs onto my bicep and shakes it a little. Does she not feel the buzz of electricity when we touch? I can't be the only one.

"I'm a studio musician for Lola Carradine now." I try really hard not to sound like I'm bragging but, dammit, I'm proud. And I want Georgette to be proud of me, too.

"Lola Carradine. *The* Lola Carradine? Holy shit, Finn! When did this happen and why am I just now hearing about it?"

"Calm down," I say, even though I love her enthusiasm. "Yes, it's the Lola Carradine and I just started this week. Gia, my boss from Good Times, said Lola came by a while back and after watching me play, she asked Gia to give me her number. I went to her home studio last week and we hit it off, so she asked me to join her band. We started on her new album yesterday."

"Oh, my god! That's incredible news. I can't believe you didn't mention it last night."

"Last night we celebrated you. My news could wait."

"No, Finley, your news is way more important than my townhouse. I wish you would've told me sooner; we could've celebrated together."

"Jette, it's fine. Besides, we're celebrating tonight."

"Okay, but that means dinner is on me. Whatever you want." She's daring me to argue but she knows I'll give in. I always do. I'll never be able to deny her.

And, I know she means well but I want to be the one to spoil her, not the other way around.

Doing things for others makes Jette happy and I always want to make her happy, so I accept her offer and say, "Lagniappe, it is, then."

12

Georgette

"HELLO?" FINN SOUNDS A LITTLE OUT OF BREATH AND I'M afraid I caught him in the middle of a set or something.

"Are you busy?" I ask, in greeting. "I can call back—"

"Uh, no," he replies, sounding a bit distracted, but when he continues with, "I'm never too busy for you," my heart melts.

How does he do that with one sentence?

Why does he still have that effect on me?

Because he's Finley, that's why. It's the only explanation I can give. He's *my* Finley. But he's not actually mine, is he?

His heavy breaths increase and I pull the phone back briefly, my heart picking up speed, but not because of what he's saying but how he's breathing. There're only a few reasons people get that out of breath… walking stairs, moving heavy furniture, having sex…

Oh, God.

What if Finley was busy *with someone*?

"Uh, Finn?" I ask, feeling my cheeks heat up. "Did I interrupt you or—"

Deep breathing.

Lots of deep breathing.

"No, why?"

I swallow, feeling a surge of jealousy and then beating it down. I have no right to feel that. I just clarified that he's not mine. Finley can be with or do anyone he pleases.

"Jette?"

"Yeah."

"Did you need something?"

I can't help it, my stomach turns at the idea of Finley with someone, but I push through, getting to the point of my call. "I, uh... I was just calling to see if you'd like to drive to French Settlement with me tomorrow. I need to pick up a couple of pieces from Cami's studio. Deacon was going to drive them to the gallery, but he's had a few people call in sick, so I'm the only one who can do it." My words come out in a rush, so I take a second to breathe, brushing my hair out of my face. "We'd drive the van, so yeah... don't feel obligated."

Finley laughs and it's music to my ears. "I'm in, if for no other reason than to see you drive that big ass van."

"Hey, don't doubt my awesome driving skills."

"I'm sure you did a lot of driving while you were in New York," he says, sarcastically, "and we both know you didn't drive much in high school. I mean, y'all had a freaking driver." He pauses, and I'm worried he's thinking about the fact my family really did have a driver and all that entails. There have been a few times over the past month where our financial differences have come up in conversation and I hate Finley has carried that with him all these years. I wish there was a way I could prove to him that none of that matters to me and I had no choice in the family I was born into.

"You know what?" he continues. "On second thought, how about I drive the van?"

I huff, but the smile on my face is anything but annoyed. "Fine, but I pick the playlist."

"Fine."

We've always been good at compromising.

After hanging up with Finley, I make myself useful in an effort to occupy my mind so I won't start thinking about that feeling I had when I thought Finley might've been with someone else... like a woman. A woman who isn't me. Because he totally could and, honestly, I'm shocked he isn't.

And why is that? Why hasn't some lucky girl snatched Finley up?

As I'm going through invoices, I wonder how many people Finley's been with since we were together.

As I'm checking messages and scheduling appointments, I wonder if he's ever been serious with anyone.

As I'm dusting, I wonder how long ago it's been since he was with someone.

Who was she?

What did she look like?

Stop.

"Ugh," I groan out my frustration just as Dani walks through the front door with what I can only guess is takeout from Lagniappe. If Cami was trying to kill me with carbs, Dani is doing her best to fatten me up with Cajun cuisine.

She stops short when she looks at me. "What's wrong?"

"Nothing," I say, turning toward a canvas and continuing to dust.

"You're cleaning," she states. "So, you're either mad or stressed out."

I laugh, because, after a couple of weeks, she already knows me. "Neither."

"Then what?" she asks, walking over to the desk and setting down the bag. "You've sorted and filed all of the invoices, logged the messages, and made appointments. I was only gone for a couple of hours."

"Tell me I have no reason to be jealous or obsessing over Finley's girlfriends."

Dani's green eyes turn my way. "Wait, Finley has girlfriends... plural?"

Walking over to the couch, I ungracefully plop down, the duster dangling from my fingertips. "No, he doesn't have a girlfriend, at least not one he's told me about, which he would, right? Because we're friends and friends tell friends about girlfriends."

"Okay," Dani drawls, eyeing me suspiciously. "So, why are you obsessing?"

"I don't know," I whine, feeling completely childish. This is ridiculous. "I called him and he sounded out of breath and my wild imagination took over and the next thing you know he's Casanova."

When Dani laughs, I cover my face in embarrassment. "I know, it's stupid."

"Well," she starts, cocking her head. "It might be a little, but I get it. You have feelings for him."

That stops me in my tracks. "Of course, we're friends."

"And you have history together and unresolved feelings. It's natural. Sometimes, I wonder if anyone ever truly gets over their first love."

"Do you still have feelings for... what's his name? The New York cheater."

Dani snorts. "Absolutely not. But Cami's told me about her and Deacon. They were childhood sweethearts, too, you know."

"Yeah, she told me."

"She moved to New Orleans to go to college and pursue her passion for art. Deacon was off doing his own thing. But fate eventually brought them back together. Maybe it's doing the same for you and Finley."

The gallery is so quiet as we both sit there. I'm sure Dani is waiting on my response, but I don't know what to say. Is it something I've thought about while lying in bed at night? Yes. Do I sometimes wonder what it would be like to truly pick up where we left off? Yes. Every time we're together, I feel the pull and I have to fight it.

And it's getting harder and starting to take its toll. Maybe that's where this temporary insanity is coming from.

"Don't get caught up in the what-ifs and assumptions. If there's something you really need to know, just ask him. I'm sure Finley would tell you anything you want to know."

He would, and that scares me. I don't know if I want to know the answers to every question floating through my brain. And more than that, I don't know if I deserve an answer to them. I'm the one who left without a word. Finley and I had something special, we both knew it, which is why when I got that acceptance letter to New York, I packed up and left.

I left before my parents could talk me out of it.

I left before Finley could make me change my mind.

Do I regret it? No. But I do wish I would've done things differently. I wish I would've stayed in touch with Finley. Hindsight being twenty-twenty, I realize how selfish I was. I owed it to Finley to give him an explanation. And I owed our relationship the benefit of the doubt that it could've survived the long distance.

Unlike Trevor, I know Finley would've put in the work.

That's the other thing, though, I didn't want him to kill his dream to make mine happen. And I knew he didn't have the means to move to New York.

"Maybe we were just brought back into each other's lives to give each other some closure… and be friends," I tell her, my eyes turned to the tall, open ceiling. "Maybe that's all we were ever meant to be."

"Lies," Dani says, sounding an awful lot like her sister-in-law.

Popping up off the couch, I turn on her. "What?"

"You keep telling yourself that you and Finley Lawson were just meant to be friends," Dani continues. "And I'll keep praying for your soul, because that's a lie and anyone who's ever been in the same room as the two of you knows there's an unmistakable spark. It's so freaking obvious. You better hope that boyfriend of yours never visits, and if he does, make sure Finley doesn't come around."

With my mouth gaping, I stare at her, unbelieving.

"Close your mouth, Georgette. You're going to catch a fly."

"We're not like that."

"Like what? Touchy-feely?" She walks to stand in front of me, arms crossed. "No, you're not, but when there's something special, like what you and Finley share, you don't need to touch for everyone to see it."

But I do need to touch.

I need to touch Finley *so bad*.

"I'm going to New York," I blurt out. I was meaning to talk to her about it. Now seems like as good a time as any. "I'll just need a day. I'm going to pack up my things and have them shipped here."

"That's good," she says, her eyebrows raising knowingly. "I'll man the fort, so don't worry about that. And I'm going to give you the address of my favorite restaurant. It's a great place to say goodbye to New York."

Is that what I'm going to do? Say goodbye?

To New York, to Trevor…

"Good morning," Finley says as I open the door to the gallery, just before he gets the chance to knock.

"Good morning," I chirp back.

Finn smiles. "Someone's in a good mood."

I shrug. "Guilty as charged."

Maybe it's the anticipation of adventure causing my good mood. We're heading outside of the city and I have plans to take Finley to one of the Landry's other restaurants. Maybe it's the fact I get to spend the day with my most favorite person. Maybe it's a little of both.

"Ready to go?" I ask, noticing a bag in Finley's hand. Then I notice the other has a carrier with two coffee cups.

"Yes, and I brought provisions from CeCe." He holds the goods up higher for me to see. "She tried to pack us a lunch, but I assured her we'd be fine."

I laugh. "She's quite the motherly type, isn't she?" I ask, wishing I knew CeCe better, but knowing I love what I've seen so far. Her most becoming attribute is the way she cares for Finley. And anyone who is good to him, is good with me. The fact she was able to make a monogamous man out of Shepard Rhys-Jones—a man who was only committed to his business and growing his fortune, before convincing CeCe to marry him for his inheritance—is impressive in its own right. She's like a modern renaissance woman—business owner, married to a real estate mogul, entrepreneur, patron of the arts. She and Shep have been some of our biggest clients since the gallery opened. Not only does she have the coffee shop, but she and Shep are currently working on transforming the space beside Neutral Grounds into a roasting facility, where they'll roast and bag their own coffee beans.

"She definitely likes taking care of people," Finley says, walking through the door. I shut it behind him and lock it.

"The van's parked out back," I say, motioning to the exit.

As Finn suggested yesterday, he drives and I take over the coffee and breakfast CeCe packed up for us. And the playlist.

We start out the trip listening to music and devouring the croissants and coffee. Once we're out of the city, it's a gorgeous drive. The day is sunny and bright and there's not a lot of traffic.

"So, I bet this is way different than New York," Finley says, breaking the silence.

Looking out the window at the mix of green and water, I chuckle. "So different. But it's different than Dallas, too."

"It is," Finley replies. "I love it."

"Me too."

We go back to sitting in silence for a few moments until the questions plaguing me yesterday rear their ugly heads. "Hey, Finn," I start, rubbing my palms down the legs of my jeans.

"Yeah?" he asks, glancing out the side mirror as he changes lanes.

"Are you, uh, seeing anyone?" Inwardly, I facepalm myself. God, that sounded much more awkward out loud than it did in my head. *Real smooth, Jette.*

Finley laughs and my head snaps up to look at him.

"What?"

"No," Finn replies. "I'm not seeing anyone." He sighs, eyes straight ahead. "I'm also not sleeping with anyone or hooking up. Anything else you need to know?"

"No," I say, swallowing down the relief I feel at his confession. "Sorry if that was nosy or overstepping boundaries."

Finn reaches over and grabs my hand. "You know there are no boundaries where I'm concerned, at least not like that. We've always been open books with each other and that hasn't changed, at least not for me."

"Me either."

He squeezes and then let's go, but I wish he wouldn't. I wish we could drive down this Louisiana highway, holding hands, with nothing between us. But that's not the case, and I can't do anything about it right now, so I'll just take what I can get and enjoy the day.

Half an hour later, we're driving into French Settlement and my eyes are soaking it all in.

Quaint.

Small.

Peaceful.

"I love it," I murmur as we venture into their downtown. The address to Cami's studio is plugged into the GPS and my British guy has been guiding us here, much to Finn's amusement.

I didn't know you had a thing for British guys, he said about fifty miles up the road.

What I didn't say was if I could record him giving me all the directions, I would, but that's not an option. So, I'll settle for my British guy who I've named Edward.

"It's a nice little town," Finn agrees. "I can see why they'd all live here and commute."

I nod, trying to wonder what that would be like. Even though I love what I've seen so far of this small town, I think I'd miss New Orleans too much to live somewhere like French Settlement. I'm a city girl, through and through. I love my conveniences and hustle and bustle. But I can see myself getting away from it all and driving down here every once in a while.

When we pull up in front of the studio, Finn backs the van up to the curb, and I'm grateful he drove. He's right, I really have very little experience on the road and I sure as hell couldn't have backed this big van up like he just did.

And why is that so hot?

Focus, Georgette. Focus.

After using the spare key to the studio Cami left with me, we walk inside and I immediately feel my face light up.

"Wow," I say, turning in a wide circle. This place is amazing and filled to the brim with canvases of all different shapes and sizes, all adorned with Cami's signature style.

"My thoughts exactly," Finn says, whistling. "She's really talented."

"I know."

The three paintings we're supposed to pick up for the clients who came by last week are propped against the back wall, already wrapped up and ready to be loaded into the van. Courtesy of Deacon, no doubt.

Finley and I grab an end of the largest canvas and load it up into the back of the van.

I might've been able to do all this on my own, but I'm really glad he came along.

"Thanks for coming and helping me."

"Anytime," he says with a smirk as he runs his hand through his dark curls. His bicep is on full display when he does that. I wonder if he knows how gorgeous he is, surely he does. I can't be the only person who notices. As a matter of fact, I know I'm not.

I remember the stuck-up girls back in high school who would talk about him in the locker room.

If he wasn't so poor.

If he came from a better family.

He's the kind of guy you fuck, but never take home to meet the parents.

Those kinds of comments used to make my blood boil, but I also liked that they didn't see what I saw. I liked that the goodness of Finley Lawson was all mine. Because I knew he was more than his family and his background or socioeconomic status. He was more than his drug-addicted parents. And he was definitely good enough to take home to meet the parents, even if those parents forbid you to have a relationship with him, like mine.

Nothing they ever said about Finley made me change my mind about him or change how I felt.

And it wasn't about wanting something I couldn't have.

I just loved him, with a deep, unwavering love.

My stomach leaps at that thought and I press my hand there to keep it still.

Once we're finished loading the art, I take one last look around the studio, my eye landing on a gorgeous painting of a magnolia tree. I've been ogling a real one in Jackson Square, waiting for the day it finally blooms like the one in this painting. Walking over to it, I squat down and get eye level, taking in the brush strokes and Cami's choice of colors.

It's breathtaking.

Standing, I pick the painting up and hold it out at arm's length, picturing it in my mind's eye on display.

"Ready?" Finley asks.

"Yeah," I reply, my focus still on the painting. "I'm taking this one too."

"For the gallery?"

"No, for my house."

Finley helps me put it into the van and I shoot Cami a text letting her know I took it, just in case it was spoken for. If so, she'll just have to make me another one. I also tell her to take it out of my paycheck. One of the many benefits of being an art junkie working at a gallery.

Or maybe it's a pitfall.

Now that I have a house to furnish and decorate, I might be tapping into even more of my trust fund… because art.

"Where to next?" Finn asks as we climb into the van.

Cami's reply comes almost immediately.

Cami: The painting is yours, for free, just because you're awesome and the best employee I've ever had.

Me: I'm the only employee you've ever had.

Cami: Potato, potahto.

I laugh, shaking my head.

"What's so funny?"

"My boss."

"So, you confessed about your art thievery?"

I swat at him, but he dodges the blow. "Hey, I have every intention of paying for it. But she's probably going to be stubborn and refuse. Which just isn't going to work for me, since I have big plans of making my house a shrine to all things Cami Benoit-Landry."

"Sounds kind of stalkerish," he teases, but I see the approving smile on his face as we pull away from the curb.

"Let's go to Pockets," I say cheerfully, feeling practically giddy at the thought as I plug in the other address Cami gave me and let Edward guide us to the Landry's French Settlement establishment.

A few minutes later, we're pulling into the parking lot. Sitting just off the main road, it's full of customers already, even though it's just now time for lunch. The building is newly built because, according to Cami, the original restaurant was destroyed in a fire. Deacon was inside the building when it happened and from the sounds of things, it was a scary time for them.

I can only imagine.

My thoughts drift to Finley and what I would do if he was in a situation like that. It's not lost on me that my first thought wasn't Trevor, which only solidifies the decision I've made to end things with him. I can't see how we're ever going to make this work. During our argument on the phone the other night, when he accused me of using this job opportunity and move as a way to give him an ultimatum, I realized just how far removed we are from each other.

In all honesty, it's been happening for a while, but they were small cracks in our pavement. But since my move, those small cracks have turned into large divides.

"Welcome to Pockets," a girl with big blue eyes and a bouncing, blonde ponytail greets as we walk through the front door. "Just the two?"

"Yes," Finley answers. "Could we have a booth?" he asks, pointing at a line of them against one wall.

The restaurant is really nice, low-key, but nice. In a way, it has that same industrial feel Lagniappe has, but on a more rustic scale, fitting for the location and environment.

"Here are a couple of menus and I'll be back to get your drink orders in just a minute."

"Smells amazing," Finley groans as we both get comfortable in the booth. A stage takes up a good chunk of the corner and I see his eyes go straight to it. "Tucker told me he used to play gigs here, even when he was out touring with his band, he'd still stop in here and play."

"I didn't realize Tucker was in a band," I say, perusing the menu as Finley talks.

"Yeah, he was a pretty big name and one day, he just walked away. His tour bus dropped him off in French Settlement and he's pretty much been living the small-town life ever since."

I try to recall if Cami has ever said much about that part of her brother's life. We talk about a lot of things and she's told me plenty about her family, but most of the stories about Tucker are either from their childhood or about his little girl and fiancé.

"Well, isn't it funny how life just puts you in the right place at the right time," I tell Finn with a warm smile, happy things are falling into place for him, just like I always knew they would. The world just had to get ready for the greatness of Finley Lawson. He's always been an old soul and man before his time, even as a teenager. "I always knew you'd get your break one of these days."

I swear Finn's cheeks turn a light shade of pink. Another thing I've always loved about him is his humbleness. He's never flaunted his talents, just quietly let them speak for themselves.

I don't know where the next thing out of my mouth comes from, but it's there before I'm able to stop it. "Part of the reason I left was because I never wanted you to have to choose between me and your dreams."

Finn's gray eyes meet mine and a myriad of emotions pass through them.

"Did y'all decide?" the waitress asks, interrupting the moment. Part of me is thankful for the distraction, but part of me wants to ask her to leave, because now that it's out there, I know we really need to clear the air.

Lay all our cards on the table.

"I'll have whatever you have on draft and a crawfish pocket," Finley says, his eyes still on me as he hands his menu to the waitress.

"Uh," I start, breaking away from his intense stare and glancing back down to my menu. "I'll have a sweet tea and a gumbo pocket."

"And we'll share a basket of fries," Finley adds with a polite smile.

She takes my menu and returns Finn's smile. "Coming right up."

For a split second, I think he's going to ignore my statement, but then he looks back at me and says, "That should've been my choice."

Suddenly, there's a lump in my throat the size of Texas and I can barely swallow around it.

"We were just kids, Finn. You had your music and I knew you'd eventually get where you were going. But you didn't have the means to uproot and move to New York. I couldn't ask that of you, but I knew if I didn't get out, I'd be under my parents' thumbs forever. It was my chance and I took it."

The look on Finley's face breaks my spirit and my resolve. I want to cry at the pain I see there, knowing I caused it. If I could erase it and take it away, I would, but I can't.

"I went to New York," Finley says quietly, thumbing his lip as his eyes drift away, lost in memory. "After months of trying to reach you and failing, I saved up all the money from my gigs and bought a plane ticket."

"What?"

Finn laughs, but it's not in humor. "When I got there, I went straight to your campus, planning on surprising you. But instead, you surprised me. I saw you out in front of the student center and you were smiling... happy. There was a guy with you and a couple of girls. My biggest fear, what I had been losing sleep over those first few weeks, was that you were in this big, new city alone. I couldn't stand it. I had to go find you... but when I did, you were happy and I couldn't mess that up. So, I turned around and left. Spent the night in the airport and flew back to Dallas the next day."

"Finley." Pressing a hand to my mouth, I feel tears trying to spill over, but blink them away.

He shakes his head. "Don't... don't be sorry. It was the best thing you could've done for me, honestly. At that time, anyway. I needed to see you happy so I could go on with my life. I figured if you wanted to get in touch with me, you knew where to find me."

"I did," I insist, leaning forward in the booth. "I did want to see you and I tried to. The few times I went back to Dallas, even though I knew it would be harder to go back if I saw you, I still looked for you when I was out. You were never in our usual spots and it felt like you dropped off the face of the earth."

I could've tried harder, I think to myself. *I wish I had tried harder.* But it was hard enough being away from him and had I ran into him on those few times I was back, I'm not sure I would've been able to leave him again. So, maybe, subconsciously, I was avoiding him even when I was searching him out.

Finley sighs and then swallows, like he's reigning in his emotions. "Sometimes, it was like you were a figment of my imagination, until the night you walked into Lagniappe."

He came to New York.

Reaching across the table, I lace my fingers through his. "Maybe it just wasn't our time."

"And now it is?" Finley asks, cocking an eyebrow as his thumb strokes the top of my hand.

I shrug, unsure of what to say. I'd like to tell him I'm going back to New York and breaking up with Trevor, but I don't want to speak too soon. Finley's always been an actions speak louder than words kind of person.

"Well, I'm here and you're here… seems pretty serendipitous."

He bites down on his lower lip, fighting back a smile as he drops his head on a slow nod. "I'm really glad you're here," he says. "I'd give anything to go back, but I'm happy to have you in any capacity I'm allowed."

When he looks up at me, that intensity is back in Finley's eyes, but this time it's different. No longer are they full of resentment or unresolved emotions, they're full of tempered heat. I've seen it before, seen that heat unleashed, and I remember what it was like to be on the receiving end.

I'd heard stories about other girls' first times having sex.

I'd prepared myself for it to be a rite of passage and nothing more, but Finley blew every rumor and expectation out of the water. Sure, it wasn't super pleasant in the beginning, but he was slow and passionate, and he took his time, making sure I was taken care of in the process.

After all these years, it's still the single most intense moment of my life.

"One draft and an iced tea," the waitress says, bursting the bubble we've been in since she last walked away. "Your food will be out shortly."

Finley picks up his glass and holds it out. "To us and new beginnings."

"Cheers to that," I say, holding up my glass and clinking it with his.

"Someone once said," Finley begins, setting his glass back down and locking eyes with mine, "being deeply loved by someone gives you strength, while loving someone deeply gives you courage."

My heart begins to beat wildly in my chest, but I wait for whatever else he needs to say.

"I have no regrets, Jette. Sure, there was a time I resented you for leaving me. But we can't change the past and it shaped us into who we are today." He pauses, his eyes feeling like an extension of his hands as they roam. "I really like who you are today."

"I like who you are too," I admit, wanting to say more, but content with this for now.

"I could've let that resentment turn to hate, but I didn't, because loving you gave me courage. When times were tough, I'd always think of you and it kept me going. Even though I had no guarantee I'd see you again, I told myself that if I did, I wanted you to be proud of who I turned out to be."

God, my heart feels like it's breaking and rebuilding all at the same time.

"I'm so proud, Finley," I say, reining in my emotions. "So proud."

"One crawfish pocket, one gumbo pocket, and a basket of fries."

I glance up at the familiar voice, seeing none other than Sam Landry, Cami's father-in-law.

"Sam," I greet, standing to give him a hug. "I didn't know you worked here."

He raises his brows, shooting a look to Finley. "Yeah, it's a new development."

Finley chuckles, standing to shake his hand. "Good to see you, sir."

"Don't *sir* me; we're family, son." Forgoing Finley's outstretched hand, Sam pulls him into a hug. The look on Finley's face is comical, but I expect nothing less from the Landrys.

Now that I've been properly introduced to all of them, I can't think of a better family to be adopted into. Finley could use some of that fatherly love, so I don't even tempt to break up the man hug happening in front of me.

13

Finley

"THAT'S A WRAP!" LOLA YELLS INTO THE MIC FROM THE sound booth as I play the last chord of the song we've been working on. "Get your ass in here, Finley, and let's celebrate!"

What a fucking surreal moment.

As I place my sax back in its case, I'm literally vibrating with excitement—something I created is going to be included on Lola Carradine's album—and in the same breath, I'm sad because it's over. But fuck yeah, I'm here and I did this shit.

What is this life?

How did I get here?

I've only been recording with Lola and her band for about three weeks, but it's been such an amazing experience and one I'll never forget. As I step out of the recording booth, I feel my cheeks starting to ache from smiling so damn much.

"Finley Lawson," Lola says, standing from her chair and giving me a slow clap. I love that she's so involved in every aspect of the process. From laying down the vocals to mastering the songs, she's there with her hands in it all.

I feel my cheeks heat up with her praise and I wave her off, setting my case down at my feet. "Stop, I should be giving you a standing ovation. My part is so small and wouldn't be anything without your genius, God-given talent."

"Well, if we're going to talk about God-given talent," she starts, just as Bo walks in the door.

He waves at me and grabs Lola into his arms to kiss her. They're not always super touchy-feely, but he's been gone to Spring Training and is only home for a day or so. I felt bad that I was even here, but Lola insisted the show must go on.

I don't know how they make it look so easy—this busy life and long-distance thing—but they do.

"Finn," Bo greets, slapping my shoulder. "Did I interrupt an ego session?" he asks, cocking his head. "No, you're great... no you. You're the best."

Lola whacks him with a notepad from the desk, laughing. "Shut up! He is great and he needs to start embracing his greatness because I have some news for him." Her eyes dart to me and I look at her in confusion.

"What news?"

"I sent your tracks to some of my friends in the business," she says, cringing a little. "I hope you're not mad I did it without telling you, but it was a very spur-of-the-moment kind of thing and I didn't know what, if anything, would come from it."

"But something did?" I ask, feeling my blood start to pump faster through my body.

"Oh, yeah, something did," she says, shaking her head and smiling a very conspiratorial smile. "Practically every producer I sent your tracks to has an artist who can use you on a song, if not their entire album. If you're interested, I could keep you busy with studio work from now until kingdom come. *If* you're interested, but only—"

"Yes, I'm interested!" I say, cutting her off, unable to fight back the enormous smile and wide-eyed shock that has to be on my face. I never saw this coming, not in a million years.

For the first time in my life, I can see a light at the end of the tunnel, a way to make music and follow my passion and still make a decent living. Not that I'm starving now, but playing gigs all night and day will eventually wear on me, and it doesn't leave a huge amount of time for other things.

Like relationships.

But with studio work, I could cut back at the club and only play on the street when I wanted.

It's the best thing I never saw coming, except for Georgette. I never in a million years dreamed she'd show up here, in New Orleans, but she did and right now, she's the only person I want to tell my news to.

"Thank you," I tell Lola, pulling her into a hug. "I appreciate this opportunity so much."

She laughs, squeezing me tight. "You don't have to thank me. I just sent some files to some people, it's all on you."

After I say my goodbyes and head out, leaving Lola and Bo to their last few hours together, I practically run down the street to catch the streetcar. I consider bypassing it, but fuck, I'm kind of out of breath. After playing for hours, my lungs are tired. So, I hop on the next one that stops and try not to look like a tweaker as my knee bounces up and down.

Once the streetcar stops at Canal, I hop off and haul ass to Royal Street, straight to the gallery, hoping to catch Jette before she goes home. Now that she's not staying at the hotel, if she's not at the gallery, I'll have even more blocks to go before I can tell her my news, and I don't think I can contain it much longer.

Thankfully, the open sign is still on the door when I get there, so

I take a few deep breaths and then walk inside. The gallery is empty, except for one person.

The only person I want to see.

The only person I want to share my good news with.

The same person I want to see every morning and every night.

"Finn," Jette says, her smile growing as she walks toward me. "I thought you had your studio work today."

"I did. We finished," I tell her, still trying to catch my breath.

She frowns. "Is everything okay?"

"Better than okay." For a second, I just stare at her, wanting nothing more than to pull her to me, just like Bo did to Lola... just as easy and sure. I wish I could make Georgette Taylor mine in every sense of the word. My hands twitch as I fight the urge to reach out and touch her, so I distract myself by setting my case down at my feet and then running a hand through my hair.

Her eyes scan my face and I watch as they go from concerned to happy again. "Tell me."

"I finished up with Lola today, but she sent some tracks of me playing to some of her contacts and they want to use me. This is going to turn into a very permanent gig, one that pays a shit ton more than what I make at the club. It's... huge, for me, at least."

"It is huge," she says, her smile beaming. "I'm so happy for you!"

The next thing I know, Jette is launching herself at me and I have no choice but to catch her. And it's the best damn thing I've experienced in a long time. Better than working with Lola Carradine. Better than my news. Better than my next breath, but I take it anyway, inhaling her sweet scent and soaking her in while I can.

When she pulls away, her expression shifts and she rights herself, smoothing down her black skirt. Jette always looks amazing, but today, she's stunning. The red blouse she's wearing sets off her blonde curls and light complexion, putting her beauty on display.

She's like one of the paintings on the wall of the gallery, but better, because she's real.

So, so real.

"I, uh, have some news too," she starts, fidgeting like she does when she's nervous. "Not the exciting kind of news you had, but… well, I'm flying to New York tonight. I'll be back Monday. So, I'll just be gone a couple of days. Dani is going to cover the gallery for me while I'm gone. I wish I could celebrate with you tonight, but maybe when I get back?"

Her question is hesitant and I wonder what has her so unsure of herself—me or New York?

The thought of her going and seeing Trevor is like a bucket of cold water being poured over my head, but I try to hide it. "Of course. Yeah, no, that's great. You've been needing to do that so you can get your things."

"Yeah, I need to do it," she says on an exhale. The smile she throws up doesn't reach her eyes and I want to force her to talk to me… *and to stay.* But she walks behind the desk and rolls out a small suitcase.

"Wow, you really are leaving right now." Was she going to tell me before she left this time? I can't help to feel a little wounded that she would leave without telling me, but decide, instead, to let it go. "You'll call me when you get to the airport?" I ask. "And when you get to New York?"

She nods. "I will. I promise."

"Be safe," I say, wishing I could say so many more things—*Don't go. Stay. I still love you.* Instead, I wrap my arms around her shoulders and pull her in for one last hug, hoping it holds me over until she comes back.

And, she *will* come back. I have to believe that.

.

14

Georgette

Me: Hey. Made it to NYC.

It's late and I'm exhausted. After a busy day at the gallery, Dani stopped by, informing me she'd be on location with her photography quite a bit for the next couple of weeks and if I wanted to make the trip to New York, now might be my last chance for a while. So, I hopped online and booked a last-minute flight, ran to my townhouse and threw a few things in a suitcase, and made it back to the gallery to close up. And just in time to see Finley.

That last part wasn't planned, but like everything else in my life lately, felt serendipitous.

I was hoping to at least talk to him before I got on the plane, so I'm glad he stopped by, and more than that, I'm glad he had such great news to share. And that he wanted to share it with me.

My only regret is I had to leave him standing on that sidewalk and I didn't get a chance to celebrate with him. I know what he was thinking—about the last time I went to New York and left him. I get it. I was thinking about it too. But this is different.

This time, I'm saying goodbye to New York instead of running to it.

Pulling out my phone, I open up the Uber app and schedule a pickup. Trevor still hasn't returned my text from before I left New Orleans, but that doesn't surprise me. It's the way things have been between us pretty much the entire time I've been there. Since our fight over the townhouse, things have gotten worse. But he did promise me he'd be at the apartment when I get there so we can talk.

Just as I'm confirming my location on the app, a text from Finley comes through.

Finley: Glad to hear it. Can you text me when you're in for the night?

I smile, just seeing a few words from him somehow makes me feel better. This is just one example of the many differences between Finley and Trevor.

Trevor gets so preoccupied with his own life and business; he can completely forget about me.

Finn, on the other hand, can have a million things going, but he always takes the time to check on me and make sure I'm okay.

What they say, about it being the little things, is so true.

I don't need grand gestures; I just need someone who's going to make me a priority and *show* me they care. That's all.

As completely insane as it sounds, I wish he was here. Yeah, my first love/best friend/person I'm currently battling feelings for does not make a logical companion on a trip to call it off with my current boyfriend and pack up my things.

It's twisted, I know.

But I can't help what I'm feeling. And I'm here to hopefully make things right, free up my conscience and my life. Lately, I've felt like I need to have one of those voodoo people who sit out on Jackson Square come and sage my house, or my life. Between the gallery, setting up the townhouse, worrying about Trevor, and fighting my feelings for Finley, I'm spent.

Something has to give, which is my main reason for being here.

Me: Sure. How's the club tonight?

Walking out of the airport, I go to the curb and keep my eyes open for a black Prius. According to my app, Siobhan should be here in approximately three minutes. Thanks to my late arrival, it's not too busy.

Finley: A good distraction since I'm already missing you.

The slow smile that pulls at my lips is inevitable. God, I love him. I never stopped. With Finley and I, it's always been this multifaceted kind of love. I love him like a best friend. And I love and admire the person he is. I love his heart and his talents. And I love *him*—the boy who stole my heart and the man who still keeps it safe.

When the black car pulls up, a very tall woman gets out, reminding me of Brienne of Tarth from *Game of Thrones*.

"Welcome to New York," she greets as I slide into the back of the car, shoving my suitcase across the seat. "Where to?"

"89 Wall Street," I tell her, feeling the day weigh me down, pushing me further into the small back seat.

"Manhattan," she comments.

Glancing up, I make eye contact in the rearview mirror and nod with a smile. "Yeah."

"Coming home from somewhere or just visiting?"

You just never know what you're going to get with drivers. Some of them don't want to talk at all. Others don't speak fluent English. And a few are extreme conversationalists. I once got into a van with a few girls from Sotheby's and the guy was running some kind of social experiment. He grilled us all the way from Chinatown back to Manhattan.

"Just here for a couple of days." I decide to go with that, because I don't feel like this is a homecoming, but I also wouldn't consider it a visit. I'm just here to take care of business.

Blessedly, she pulls out onto the highway and conversation ceases. Pulling out my phone, I send Trevor another text.

Me: in a car headed to the apartment

Since he rarely texts me back, I don't feel obligated to give him complete sentences or punctuation.

Opening my messages from Finley, I read back over his last one and then stare at it. When that isn't enough, I close the text and open my photos, scrolling to the one we took outside of Pockets a week ago.

That was a good day. But then again, all days with Finley are good ones. He makes it so. The world could be falling apart, but as long as I'm with Finley, I know everything's going to be alright.

Switching back to the text messages, I shoot him a short one.

Me: I miss you too and my only distraction is Brienne of Tarth's look-alike.

Finley: She was my favorite character on GOT. Can you get an autograph?

Me: Your favorite, really? What about Jon Snow... Jaime? KHAL DROGO? I mean, I love Brienne too, but I'm not sure I'd say she's my favorite.

Finley: Of course you'd pick one of the hot guys as your favorite. *rolls eyes*

Me: *evil grins*

Instead of an evil grin, I sit in the back of the car as we make our way through New York with a stupid grin, courtesy of Finley Lawson. It's so crazy to think that a couple of months ago, I had no clue what was in store for me. I knew I was getting ready to embark on a new career in a new city, but I had no clue my past would come back and flip everything upside down... or maybe set it right.

Deep in thought, I don't even look for my usual landmarks. The same ones that took my breath away when I came to this city for the first time. All the lights and buildings are a blur and the next thing I know the car is stopping in front of a familiar building.

"Have a good night," Brienne of Tarth calls out as I open the door.

Pulling my suitcase across the seat, I smile over at her. "You too. Thanks for the ride."

Before I step inside the lobby of the building, I make sure to leave her a tip and a quick review, telling her how much I loved her in *Game of Thrones*.

Finn will get a kick out of that.

Stepping away from the curb, I take a deep breath as my eyes scan up the building. "Let's get this over with," I mutter to myself, watching my breath in the cold New York night.

I brace myself the entire ride up the elevator, wondering what Trevor's greeting will be like. Is he going to try to kiss me? Is he going to be pissed and give me the cold shoulder? Will this be a shouting match before I even get in the door?

God, I have no idea and the unknowing is killing me.

When the elevator stops, I take a fortifying breath and step out into the hallway. As I approach the door of the apartment, I hesitate for a second. With my hand curled into a fist, poised to knock, I check myself. Do I knock?

Even though I have a key and some of my things are still inside, I don't feel right barging in.

This isn't my home, not anymore.

Knocking lightly, I step back and wait. When the door doesn't open, I knock again, a little more forcefully this time.

Still no answer.

Leaning forward, I place my ear close to the door to see if I can hear

Trevor on a call. I can picture him in the pristine, white space, pacing the floor in his perfectly tailored suit and wingtip shoes. With one hand in his pocket and the other holding the phone to his ear, he always looked like someone powerful and important.

Swallowing down my nerves, I open my bag and dig out the key inside. As I slide it into the lock, I still expect the door to swing open and Trevor's hazel eyes to be staring back at me expectantly. But he doesn't. And as I open the door and pull my suitcase into the foyer, I notice the lights in the kitchen and living room are off.

As a matter-of-fact, the entire apartment is dark, except for a dim light coming from the lamp at the end of the hallway that's always left on when we're away.

We.

When was the last time Trevor and I actually felt like a we?

Months.

Probably the weekend we celebrated his birthday last fall. After that weekend was when I applied for the job in New Orleans. It's basically been downhill ever since.

Guilt floods my chest. Is this my fault? Am I to blame for our relationship falling apart?

"Trevor?" I call out, walking quietly down the hall toward the bedroom, just in case he came home from work and fell asleep.

Nothing.

"Trevor?"

Both bedrooms are empty, as well as the bathrooms. Walking back toward the kitchen, I flip on the light and it looks exactly the same way it did when I left. So does the living room. Everything looks too perfect and like it's being staged, not lived in.

As I make my way over to the large windows, I stare out at the city and the pang in my chest increases. This isn't right. Nothing about this place feels right and I suddenly feel like I'm suffocating.

Unwelcome tears sting my eyes and I roughly brush them away.

Part of me can't believe he's not here—no call, no text, no note. But the other part of me isn't surprised. And honestly, I'm relieved. Except, I can't go back to New Orleans until I talk to him, so he has to show up at some point. I refuse to leave without closure.

Pulling my phone out of my bag, I send Finley a quick text letting him know I made it safely to the apartment and promise to text him tomorrow. Then, I open the message to Trevor and send another.

Me: I'm here. Where are you?

While I wait, I decide to pour myself a glass of wine. I'm going to need it to get through the next thirty-six hours. That's how long I have until my flight leaves to go home.

Home.

Back to Finley.

After my first glass, I pick my phone back up and see a reply from him, telling me to sleep well. I almost texted him back, but I'd probably say too much and I want to save everything I have to say for when I see him in person.

Still nothing from Trevor.

So, I wait… and wait… and wait.

Around one in the morning, I walk back down the hallway with my suitcase in tow and I pause in front of the spare bedroom. Walking inside, I shut the door and flop on the bed. There's packing to do, but I can barely lift my arms right now, so it can wait for tomorrow, just like Trevor.

Just as I'm getting comfortable in the bed, my phone lights up from the nightstand. Reaching for it, my heart hopes it's Finley, needing to tell me something, anything to make me feel like he's here with me, but it's not.

Trevor: Sorry, something came up. Go to bed. I'll see you in the morning.

Growling out of frustration, I sit up in the bed and toss the blanket back. Out of spite, I think about getting up and doing just the opposite, but I don't. Instead, I fall back on the pillow and stare at the ceiling until my eyes refuse to stay open.

The smell of coffee wakes me after a fitful night's sleep. It's always been like an alarm clock to my body. I literally cannot stay in bed when I smell it. Which is why, during college, I had always had a coffee pot with a timer set for when I needed to wake up. Trevor and I continued that tradition when we moved in together.

Assuming that's what's happening, I roll out of bed and throw on my robe and walk down the hallway. The cool tile further wakes me as I make my way to the kitchen, but then I stop short.

Trevor is standing with his back to me, already dressed in a pressed shirt and slacks, or maybe he never changed? Maybe he just came home?

"Hey," I mumble and watch as his back stiffens a little at my greeting.

Yeah, not the reunion I imagined we'd have after months apart.

"Good morning," he replies and I hear coffee being poured into a cup. Turning, he offers it to me along with a forced smile that almost resembles a grimace. "Sorry I wasn't here last night when you came home."

Taking the proffered cup, I let my eyes fall to the hot liquid, avoiding looking Trevor in the eyes.

"I'm not even sure you owe me an apology at this point. I think we both know this is over." Sometime over the last few weeks, a sense of resolve has come over me and last night it settled deep in my soul.

This is over.

Trevor and I are over.

My time in New York is over.

"Excuse me?" Trevor's tone shifts and I'm forced to meet his stare. Those hazel eyes blazing. "What exactly are you saying, Georgette?"

Taking a deep breath, I lay it all out on the table. "Something I've learned since I left for New Orleans is that I will never be a priority for you—"

"Oh, come on. Are you kidding me with this shit? I thought we were adults, Georgette. You don't need to be coddled." Bracing his hands on the counter behind him, his eyes narrow in annoyance.

"Let me finish," I demand. "I'll never be a priority for you and that's not okay with me. I want to be with someone who puts my needs above his job and career. I get it, that's not you, and that's okay. We're not compatible. I'm not trying to change you or give you an ultimatum. I'm just done."

He just stands there, his face stoic. After a minute or so of silence, he clears his throat and shakes his head like he's trying to clear the cobwebs. "You're done?" he finally asks, confusion replacing his stoic expression. "As in with us? Is that really how you feel? Because six months ago, you wanted to get married. Six months ago, you were pushing me to make a commitment. What happened to that and what happens when you're finished roaming the country and are back in New York? Do you expect me to be here waiting for you?"

"I'm not coming back," I tell him. "I love my job and I love the city and I realize now that pushing you for a commitment was wrong." Pausing, I take a second to center myself and keep my composure. Nothing good will come from losing my cool or saying things out of anger, so I try to stick to the facts. "No one should ever pressure you to do anything you don't want. Whether that be moving forward in a relationship or staying in a job that doesn't make you happy."

I let that marinate for a second, before continuing. "We were friends before we were anything more, so I'm trying to end this on the same note we began. You'll always hold a special place in my heart and I'll think back on my time in New York, and with you, fondly. Because we've had some good times. But it's time for me to move on with my life and I can't do that here... I can't do that with you."

This time, when he looks at me, it's not spiteful or angry. He just looks sad and for a moment, I'm also sad. We did have happy times together, good times. And before I took this job in New Orleans and reunited with Finley, I thought what we had was enough for me, but it's not.

I want more.

I want someone who always puts me first.

I want the kind of love I thought I'd lost forever.

Maybe I'm being selfish, but I think that's okay sometimes. If we don't take what we want and make ourselves happy, no one else will do it for us.

"I can't believe you're standing here saying this," he confesses, taking a step toward me. Removing the coffee cup from my hand, he sets it on the counter beside me and pulls me into his chest, giving me the comfort I've been needing from him for so long.

But it's too late.

And the fact he didn't think anything was wrong with our relationship lets me know I'm doing the right thing. There's no way I could live the remainder of my life with that level of complacency. I want real happiness, not something that looks good on paper or to the outside world. I want happiness I feel from the top of my head to the tips of my toes. This isn't it.

Sighing, I push back to give myself some space. "It'll just take me a couple of hours to pack up my things and I'll find somewhere to stay for tonight."

"No," Trevor says, brows furrowed as he shakes his head. "You can stay here. The spare bedroom is yours. I have to go into the office for a few hours, so you'll have the place to yourself. Maybe we can get some takeout tonight, for old time's sake."

Inhaling deeply and blowing it out, I finally let my shoulders relax. "Okay, thanks."

Picking up his to-go cup of coffee, he grabs his keys off the table and walks out the door, not even offering me a backward glance.

15

Finley

THE RAINY SKIES OF NEW ORLEANS ARE THE PERFECT
representation of my mood. Normally, I love sleeping during a
thunderstorm, the sounds being oddly soothing to me, but not today.
Today, I'm up after only a few hours of sleep but not because of the
thunder and lightning currently raging through the French Quarter.

No, it's because Jette is gone again and I feel lost without her.

Honestly, I didn't think it would be so bad this time around. I've been
through this before and it's only for a couple of nights, for fuck's sake, but
I feel like shit.

The agony is in the unknown.

This can go one of two ways, I think.

One, she breaks up with Trevor and comes back to me. This is, of
course, what I want and I pray it's what Jette wants, as well. I'll never
stop believing we're meant for each other, even if she chooses the other
option: staying with Trevor.

Fuck, it'd kill me to let her go again, but I'd do it if I knew it was what
she truly wanted. I've only ever wanted her to be happy; I just hoped

with everything in me I was the one to make her that way.

I guess there's another possible outcome. She could pick Trevor over me *and* bring him down here to New Orleans. God, I want to puke just thinking about it. After living here these last five months, I absolutely believe everyone belongs here, and is welcome here. But not him. Fuck no, not him.

I would certainly have to move. It's one thing knowing Georgette is happy but it's a whole other ballgame having to see it in person day after day. I know myself. I couldn't do it. I would drive myself crazy. We're too connected, not only personally, but with our circle of friends and New Orleans isn't *that* big. Definitely not big enough to keep us apart, that's been proven already.

So, yeah, I'd move. I'd probably go to Los Angeles and take a chance on a music career there. I'm confident in my abilities to make it work, just like I've done here, but I'd still be broken.

Ruined forever by Georgette Taylor.

Sighing, I rub a hand over my face and through my hair. That's enough interpersonal drama for me. Shit, that's enough for an entire room full of people.

After showering and throwing on some clothes, I make my way downstairs, expecting to find CeCe opening up Neutral Grounds. What I didn't expect was to see Shep here as well.

"Well, good morning, sunshine," he calls out. "What has you up so early? You trying to sneak out a lady-friend or something?"

"Ha, ha, no. I can't sleep," I mumble, stumbling toward the counter to grab a scone. Another perk to living above the coffee shop is all the pastry and coffee I want. When I first moved in, I would never accept the food CeCe offered me, because she never let me pay. Until one day, she told me it hurt her feelings when I turned her down. So, I make a point to always accept her graciousness and thank her profusely. Also, I know she likes it when I make myself at home, and the truth is, I *feel* at home. So, grabbing my own scone and a cup of coffee has become second nature.

I owe Shep and CeCe so much and one of these days, I'll pay them back. Thanks to my new gigs, that'll be sooner rather than later.

"If you want to go back to sleep, I can fix you some soothing tea. Otherwise, the espresso machine is fired up and ready," CeCe offers.

"I'll just grab some coffee, thanks." Taking a mug off the shelf, I fill it with some dark roast before adding cream and stirring it in. Once I'm seated next to Shep and CeCe at a nearby table, I notice them both watching me closely.

"What?" I ask.

CeCe clears her throat. "Nothing, Finn. We're just concerned. You're not usually this... mopey."

"Does this have to do with Georgette?" Shep asks. "Because the way you're acting now is very reminiscent of when she left for college."

Shep's mention of Georgette leaving causes my back to straighten, feeding into my fears—unwarranted as they may be—and I don't appreciate it.

"What makes you think that? Did it not occur to you that it's storming outside and that's why I'm up this early?" I don't even try to hide the petulance in my voice and I know it's only adding more fuel to their assumptions.

"No, because most guys only get this pissy when a woman is involved. *You* only get this pissy when a certain blonde-hair spitfire is involved. So, you've either been cockblocked or heartbroken. Which is it?"

Instead of answering, I sip on my coffee, not looking at either of the two know-it-alls.

"Spill the deets," CeCe demands. "As soon as you get it out, the sooner we can see about fixing whatever problem you're having."

Fuck.

When I look back at them and see they're still eyeing me intently, I decide to give in. "Jette left yesterday. She flew to New York."

They both look at each other warily, but wait for me to give them more, and I do.

I tell them everything—my fears about Jette going back and realizing she misses New York, her and Trevor reconnecting, and how afraid I am to lose her.

Once I'm finished, Shep and CeCe stay quiet while finishing their drinks. I welcome the silence, watching the rain fall through the window next to me. Jackson Square is beautiful when the sun is shining but somehow the rain doesn't diminish its beauty in the least. If anything, it enhances it. This place really is magical.

Eventually, CeCe breaks the peace and quiet. "Finn, you need to tell her how you feel. Even if the worst happens and she stays with Trevor, it could just be temporary. She could be waiting on you to make the first move, have you thought of that?"

I shrug. "It's possible but she knows I'd never put her in a situation where she'd be cheating. And I'd never give her an ultimatum."

"Exactly," Shep pipes up. "She does know those things because she knows you better than anyone. You know her just as well, so don't count her out just yet. I'm sure this situation is weighing on her just as much as you and I know waiting sucks, but give her time to make the right decision. She's a smart girl."

"You're right, she is."

"I've never been one to believe in fate and all that romantic bullshit," Shep continues. "But even I can tell you two belong together. You always have."

"Aww, honey. Who knew marriage would turn you into such a softie?" CeCe teases, standing up to kiss the top of his head as she picks up our empty mugs.

"There's nothing *soft* about me and you know it. Do I need to remind you again before I go to work?" Shep tries to grab her ass but she scoots out of the way.

"God, no, please," I mutter, standing and taking my napkin with me. "Just let me leave first and then y'all can do whatever you want."

They laugh as I run up the stairs but before I make it to the top, I walk back down and stick my head around the corner, only interrupting an embrace. "Thanks, you two. For everything." Their answering smiles give me the courage to do what needs to be done.

I'm going to do it.

I'm going to tell Jette I'm in love with her and that I've never stopped. Even if she chooses Trevor over me, at least there won't be any doubt in her mind about how I feel. You can't make a sound decision without all the facts, right?

Feeling re-energized, I grab my sax case and raincoat before heading out for the day. Jette isn't supposed to be back until sometime tomorrow so I need to keep busy, otherwise, I'll drive myself and everyone around me insane. The rain will most likely keep the tourists inside, but I don't care. I need to create. I need to perform. I need to lose myself in the music and feel whole again. There are two outlets in my life that allow for this and since one is in New York right now, that leaves just me and my sax.

I decide to set up in my usual spot on Royal St, across from Cami's gallery. Thankfully, there's a nice, wide awning I can stand under and stay dry. Today's soundtrack doesn't call for original songs or anything flashy; it calls for truth, so I play from my heart.

Starting with "Unforgettable", I practically play through every Nat King Cole playlist in my head, ending with "What a Wonderful World". I play for Jette and I play for myself. I play for all the heartsick fools out there and wish them all well.

When I see Dani give me a wave before flipping the sign on the door to "closed", I know it's time to pack up. I'm not scheduled to work at Good Times tonight and I'm glad. Now that I've purged my feelings into the notes of every song, letting them float out into the damp air, I'm tapped out. Plus, I want to be well-rested and ready for when Jette comes back tomorrow, whatever may happen.

Taking the few bills that were tossed my way by the generous people who passed by throughout the day, I grab some takeout food before heading back to the apartment. I watch YouTube videos of *Drunk History* until midnight and then finally crawl into bed and fall asleep thinking of Jette and everything I want to say to her.

The next morning, when I wake, the sun is peeking through the window shades, a bright contrast to the skies from yesterday. Grabbing my phone from the nightstand, I see I already have a message waiting for me.

Jette: I'm on my way home.

16

Georgette

AFTER A DAY OF PACKING AND ARRANGING FOR MY BOXES
to be shipped to New Orleans, I logged onto the airline's website to see
if there was an earlier flight than what I originally booked. Sadly, there
wasn't, so I took Trevor up on his offer and stayed at the apartment.

Once he left for the office, he didn't return until later in the evening,
and like he suggested, we ate takeout and it wasn't horrible. He didn't
instigate an argument or question my motives or decision. We just ate,
mostly in silence, and the words we did exchange were amicable.

Trevor reminisced about when we first moved into the apartment
and how exciting it was to live in Manhattan. It was. I remember. There
are actually a lot of good memories I'm taking with me.

Trips around the world.

Nights of takeout and dreaming about the future.

Mornings that turned into a comfortable routine.

A feeling of contentment.

But soon, that contentment turned into complacency and I wanted
more.

So, I'm sitting on this airplane headed back to New Orleans with nothing but anticipation for the future. There are no regrets, no what-ifs, and absolutely nothing standing in my way of going after what I want, what my heart wants. What it's always wanted.

Four hours later, I'm in another Uber, this time leaving the airport outside of New Orleans and wishing I could make the driver go faster.

As we make our way down I-10, I start to relax.

When he takes the exit for downtown New Orleans, my heartbeats even out.

Just as the colorful houses of the outskirts of the French Quarter come into view, I take my first easy breath. The past day and a half felt like forty. None of it was easy or fun, but it's over and I'm back.

Craning my neck to see down the block, not only can I see my house, but I see something even better.

Finley is waiting on my front porch, elbows resting on his knees as he watches the road.

"Thank you," I tell the driver as he pulls up to the curb. I don't even give him a chance to get out and help me with my suitcase, I grab it and bail out of the backseat, shutting the door behind me and giving him a wave.

A wide smile greets me as Finley stands slowly, squinting his eyes against the bright New Orleans sun. "Aren't you a sight for sore eyes."

"I was planning on dumping this suitcase and coming to find you," I tell him, unsure of what to say. His greeting has me smiling and my feet moving. Before I can make the few steps onto the porch, Finn leaps off and meets me on the sidewalk, scooping me into a hug.

"Damn, I missed you."

Laughing, I squeeze him so hard he grunts. "I missed you too."

"That was the longest two days of my life," he says into my hair, still not letting me go.

"Me too," I tell him. "I was just thinking it felt like a freaking month." As I rest my head on his shoulder and sink into his chest, allowing his arms to hold me up, I don't stop my stream of consciousness from spilling over. "Funny how we were apart for five years, but it's these past two days that torture us. Not that I didn't miss you every time I thought about you in those five years, but I think it was the realization that you're here and I'm here and we really have a shot at this thing…"

"I missed you every day," Finn says, his voice gritty. "Every day, don't ever doubt it."

We stand there, his arms wrapped solidly around my waist and mine clinging to his neck, for God only knows how long. The mild breeze swirls around us and the sun kisses our skin, as the world passes by, and for a moment, it's just me and him… Jette and Finn.

"I broke up with Trevor," I whisper. "Officially. It's over."

Finley pulls back, his hands gripping my shoulders until he's sure I'm steady on my feet. With those deep, dark eyes, he really looks at me, down to my soul. "Are you okay?"

I nod, a lump stuck in my throat, but not over Trevor. I haven't cried a real tear over that relationship in a long time. It's because of how Finley cares for me, even in this moment, when he could jump at the chance to swoop in and take what I know he wants, he holds back, making sure I'm okay.

I love that about him.

Along with so many other things, but his care for me is something that digs down into the center of my heart and lives there. It makes me feel whole and good and loved. And like I can do anything and be anyone. Finley has always done that for me.

"I'm better than okay," I finally tell him. "I'm here, with you, in a city I love, standing in front of my new home with nothing from my past weighing me down. I honestly don't know how I could be any better."

Finley quirks an eyebrow.

Okay, I can think of a few ways I could be better.

But I can be patient.

"Let's go inside," Finley gestures, taking my suitcase as he grasps my hand and leads me up the steps. "Tell me all about New York. I want to hear it all."

"Don't you have to work?" I ask him. Finley works practically every day of the week—playing gigs at the club, on the street, or at the studio. "I can come find you."

After I unlock the front door and step inside, feeling instantly at home, I sigh, closing my eyes. When I open them, Finn is staring at me, his expression soft and his eyes… happy. It's the only way I can describe them. He looks so much like I feel—at peace, at home, and perfectly content.

"I took the day off." Unlike our more recent close encounters, when one of us will make a comment that could lead to something more intense or personal, we don't look away. We don't close down the emotions and feelings; we lean into them.

My breath hitches in my throat as Finley's hand comes up to brush a curl away from my face. Something that is literally a tale as old as time when it comes to the two of us, but it feels different.

There's a stream of light coming in from the window above the door and it's shining perfectly on Finn's full lips and richly-colored skin. We're such a contrast, two different people. On so many levels, everything about us is different, yet we're the same where it counts the most.

"I want to kiss you," I tell him, my hands lightly skimming his soft, worn t-shirt, wanting to pull him to me.

Finn's head leans down and our breaths fill the space. I watch as his jaw ticks, the muscles fluttering. "Then do it."

Blinking rapidly, I lick my lips and will my heart to remain in my chest as it threatens to break through my rib cage. "I don't want to mess anything up between us," I whisper, needing to get a few things out in the open.

"I just need you to know this isn't a rebound or me trying to get someone out of my head. I've been needing to kiss you for a long time. Going to New York was two-fold for me. I needed to close out that chapter in my life, and along with that, I needed to break things off with Trevor because I'm not a cheater. It dawned on me that I probably did so without even realizing it."

Taking a deep breath, I inch back to put a little distance between us so I can think clearly and say what I need to say without getting sidetracked by Finley's nearness.

Just like always, he waits and listens.

"Emotionally, I've been leaning on you more than I should. You weren't the one in a relationship when we reconnected. I was. So, it should've been me to put up boundaries, and I tried to do that. But I'm sure I failed on some levels. And I just want you to know that I'm not that girl. I don't sleep around or jump from one relationship to another. Trevor was my only boyfriend while I was in New York. If the truth be told, *he* was my rebound. I needed him to fill some of the gaps in my heart that were caused by leaving you. *I* did that. Me. And I'm not putting the blame on anyone but myself. I'm sorry, for everything."

When I'm finished, I take a shuddering breath, not realizing how much I needed to get that off my chest.

Finn reaches forward and pulls me to him. "This is uncharted territory for both of us. And sometimes," he says, stroking my hair. "Sometimes life just happens and it's not perfect or easy… it just swoops in and says here I am. We can only walk through it the best we know how. You're not wrong or bad, Georgette Taylor. You never could be, because your heart is good and true. I'll always forgive you and I'll always be on your side, no matter what."

In that moment, I want to sink into him, like liquid mercury, our bodies melding into one.

"About that kiss," Finn mutters, reaching under my chin to tilt my head back, our eyes meeting.

Standing on my tiptoes, I use his body for leverage and press my lips to his. For a few seconds, it's just brushes of skin and shared breaths as my heart climbs up my throat.

But then, Finley's hand cups my jaw and his other tightens on my waist, pulling me impossibly close, and our mouths open to each other, releasing the floodgates of emotions.

As time stands still, Finley and I kiss with everything we have in us, connecting our past and present. It's everything I expected and so many things I didn't even know existed. For every ounce of heat, there is an equal amount of sweetness. And for every nip of his teeth on my lips, there's an answering caress.

It feels like coming home and also like I'm soaring on a new adventure, because as much as Finley hasn't changed, there are parts of him that have. Unlike our kisses from the past, this isn't tentative or exploring, it's claiming and demanding.

Finley, the man, knows exactly what he wants and he's currently taking it.

My toes curl as he dominates the kiss and my body, pushing me up against the wall.

I don't know how much time passes. While I'm wrapped in Finley's arms, lost to the world around me, I don't even know what time is. I barely know my name.

Panting, we eventually slow the kiss, each taking a much-needed breath of air.

"I've been waiting so long for that," Finley mutters, his lips brushing my cheek and then my nose. "God, I've missed you."

A tear slips down my cheek out of nowhere. "I've missed you too."

These *I miss yous* aren't about the two days I was in New York. These are for five years of missed kisses and everything in between.

After a few softer, slower kisses, we finally venture out of the foyer and into the living room. I still don't have furniture in the majority of my house, but yet it still feels warm and inviting.

Cami's painting is adorning one wall and it's always the first thing I see when I walk inside.

I love it.

"Want something to eat?" I ask Finn. "I don't have much, but I did pick up a few things at the market before I left. I can definitely make a grilled cheese or a PB&J." Glancing back, I see Finley standing in the wide opening between the living room and dining room. His strong arms are crossed over his chest and he's just staring at me. "What?"

Biting down on his bottom lip, he shakes his head and looks down at his worn boots. "Just you… here, I'm still trying to wrap my head around all of it."

"Well, get used to it, because I'm not going anywhere," I tell him, feeling my chest warm with the confession. "I mean, I bought a freaking house, for goodness sake."

Finn chuckles, swiping his thumb over his bottom lip. "You did, huh."

"Sure did," I retort, quirking an eyebrow as if I'm asking him to challenge me on this… on us. I know what he's thinking, because I know him better than he knows himself on some days, or at least I see him clearer. Finley always thought good things didn't happen to someone like him. Although, if you didn't really know him, you'd never guess that, because he's always so positive. He's probably one of the happiest, most cheerful people I've ever met.

But I know the Finley no one else sees. I know his fears and doubts.

And I refuse to let them ruin this moment or us.

"Here's what's going to happen," I tell him, walking into the kitchen and opening the refrigerator. "I'm making us sandwiches and then we're going to have an inside picnic."

"Like old times?" Finley asks, his eyes still searching, still trying to convince himself this is real.

I shrug. "Like old times, like new times… whatever you want to call it."

"This is really happening?" he questions.

Turning toward him, I pause with one hand on the open refrigerator door. A moment passes between us where I'm silently telling him to take his own advice and just let life happen and he's silently telling me okay.

"Yes, Finley, this is really happening."

A rueful chuckle escapes his lips as he runs a hand through those dark curls, drawing my attention to his biceps and then down to the couple of inches of skin showing at his waist.

God, he's beautiful.

"Grilled cheese or PB&J?" I mutter, my eyes still glued to that patch of skin as my mouth goes dry.

"Do you have Doritos?"

"Yes."

"PB&J."

After making our gourmet meal and pouring glasses of wine, instead of the milk cartons we used to drink—because we're adults—we settle in the dining room on a few blankets and pillows I grabbed from upstairs.

For hours, Finley and I talk about everything. I tell him about New York and the conversation with Trevor. I tell him about some of the travels I've been on and show him pictures from one of the photo albums I packed into my suitcase. Finley gets the most enjoyment out of my backpacking in Europe because that's something the two of us used to daydream about.

He was going to take his saxophone and play in the streets at night and we were going to tour every museum during the day. Our daydreams were so specific, we even knew what hostels we wanted to stay in and where we wanted to eat.

"I stayed at the Circus Hotel, you know," I say, leaning on one elbow as I look over Finley's shoulder.

He pauses, turning his head to the side. "Really?"

"Of course," I say with a snort. "How could I pass up a hostel with its very own David Hasselhoff museum?"

Finley gracefully turns over until he's lying on his side facing me. "Was it as cool as we thought it would be?"

I'm trying to gauge if me telling him all this is cutting deeper, because I did the things we dreamed about together without him or if it's the opposite and he's happy I did the things.

"If I'm being honest," I start, taking a sip of wine to help wash down the memory, "it was one of the best and worst days of my trip. I was about a week and a half in when I made it to Berlin, so I was kind of starting to feel homesick, but not in the typical sense. I wasn't crying in my pillow at night because I missed New York… or Trevor," I add, my eyes drifting down to the mostly-empty glass. "I missed you. Everything we had read about it was true and as happy as it made me to be there, doing the things, I missed you so bad that first day it literally hurt. I sat at the rooftop bar and just tried to imagine where you were and what you were doing."

The confession hangs in the air between us, heavy, like a wet blanket.

After a minute, maybe more, Finley takes the wineglass from my hand and pulls me to him, nestling me into his chest, as we lie on the blankets. "Is it wrong for me to say I'm glad you missed me?"

"No, if it had been you who went, I would want to know you missed me like I missed you."

Kissing the top of my head, Finley breathes deeply. "Let's go there one day, together."

"I could show you all of it, everything, you'd love it."

We lay in silence for what feels like forever, the sun already setting in the evening sky, beyond what can be seen from the large windows. Finley holds me and we soak up each other's presence.

"I'm glad you went," he finally says. "I love that about you, your fearlessness to go after what you want. It's one of the things I love the most."

"What else?" I ask quietly.

He doesn't say anything for a few moments and I wonder if he's fallen asleep, but then he starts listing things like they're being read from an old piece of paper that has folds and creases from being read so many times.

"I love the way you see people beyond the obvious. I love your heart. I love how you love others the way you want to be loved. I love that you're caring and nurturing even though you weren't raised with that kind of love in your life. I love your wild, untamed curls and the fact you don't try to hide them. I love the shade of blue in your eyes. It's not royal or navy or pale... it's your own color. I love your lips. If I could spend every moment of the rest of my life kissing them, it would be a life well-lived..."

He continues naming things from serious to silly and I drift off to the cadence of his voice.

17

Finley

AFTER HELPING JETTE UPSTAIRS TO HER BED, ONE OF THE few pieces of furniture she has right now, I tuck her in and kiss her one last time before leaving and locking the door behind me.

I could stay.

It would take nothing to convince me to slip under the covers behind her and pull her to me, but I know she's tired and we've covered a lot of ground in the small amount of time she's been back.

There's plenty of time to take things slow. It's always been how Jette and I work best. We've always been willing to let things unfold naturally between us. I see no reason to change that now. As badly as I want her and want to make her mine in every sense of the word, I don't want to rush things and mess it up.

We've come so far and waited so long, what's a little while longer?

Making my way down the steps of her townhouse, I see a Jeep pull up alongside the curb across the street. Shaw O'Sullivan steps out and looks my way.

"Finley?" he asks, unable to see me clearly in the dimness of the streetlights.

"Yeah," I reply, walking toward him. "Hey, Shaw. How's it going?"

"Good, everything okay at Georgette's?" he asks, motioning over my shoulder to where I just left.

I glance back, wishing I was still there and missing her already. "Yeah, fine. Jette just got back from New York and we were…" I drift off, unsure what to say, but realizing there's no need to skirt the truth or make excuses. "Catching up."

Shaw's coy smile tells me he's probably reading more into things than necessary, but he's always a man of few words, so in true Shaw O'Sullivan fashion, he merely gives me a nod, no questions asked. "Need a ride home?"

"No, no," I tell him, shoving my hands into my pockets. "I'm good. Just going to enjoy the cool New Orleans night while I still can."

"Better believe it," he says, walking around the Jeep and grabbing what looks like to-go bags, probably from the cooking school he runs that's next door to his bar. "Hungry?" he asks, holding up a bag.

"No, thank you, though."

Shaw smiles, nudging the door shut with his shoulder. "Probably a good thing you turned me down. Avery would kick my ass if I gave away this crawfish etouffee. She's usually up with Shae when I get home from the bar. We have late night rendezvouses in the kitchen once she puts him back to sleep." He waggles his eyebrows and I have to laugh.

"Enjoy your night," I call out with a wave as the two of us go our own way.

"Be careful," Shaw calls back.

A look further down the street and I see Shep and CeCe's lights are out. But something about knowing they're all close and everyone kind of leans on each other makes me feel something I've never felt before in my life.

It's like community… a sense of belonging.

I want it all, things I never dreamed of, especially since Georgette walked out of my life. Every person since her has never lived up to the extremely high bar she sat. And I've never been the type to be with someone I don't see a future with, which means, I haven't really been with that many people in the last five years.

Sure, there have been a few hookups and I've dated a few girls, but nothing of substance and nothing that's lasted beyond a few dates.

Standing in Jette's kitchen earlier, watching her and realizing we actually have a shot for a second chance at… us… well, it was more than I could wrap my head around. I've hoped for it, dreamed about it, longed for it… but never really allowed myself to think about the true possibility.

Every time I looked at her tonight, it felt like I was dreaming. But she's not a dream, instead, she's the most real person I've ever met. So, along with taking our time to keep from making any rash mistakes, I'm also hoping this new reality will settle in and I'll start to believe it.

Georgette Taylor is back and she's mine.

Georgette

WAKING TO MY ALARM CLOCK, I STRETCH AND TRY TO GET my bearings. The smell of coffee drifting up the stairs brings me upright.

In my bed.

In my house.

But no Finley.

Finley.

Touching my lips, my mind drifts back to yesterday and images play like an old movie—Finley waiting on my porch, kissing in the foyer and later on the blankets in the dining room, a vague memory of him helping me upstairs and a soft kiss in the dark. By the time I'm finished remembering each kiss and touch and need and want, my cheeks ache from smiling so hard.

I think I'd forgotten what it was like to be kissed by Finley Lawson.

I'm not sure how, but maybe my mind had blocked it out as a method of saving me the heartache of missing out on something so wonderful.

But now that I had experienced it again, and I remember, I want more.

There's probably some sort of unspoken rule about how long you should wait to reconnect with your lost love after breaking up with your ex-boyfriend, but I'm not sure rules apply to me and Finley. We've always gone against the grain, pressed boundaries, and done things on our own terms and timeframe.

I don't see that changing now.

Climbing out of bed, I slip on my robe and walk downstairs, inhaling deeply as the coffee aroma grows stronger. Just as I'm walking into the kitchen to pour myself a cup, my phone rings from the counter where I plugged it in last night.

My first thought is Finley, but upon further inspection, I see it's my mother. Sighing, I swipe to answer the call. It's useless to send her to voicemail. When she finally decides she's ready to talk to me or has something pressing to tell me, she's relentless. We might go weeks without speaking, but when she's ready to talk, the whole world better stand still.

"Hello," I speak into the phone, answering on the fifth ring.

"Georgette," my mother greets, in her typical no-nonsense tone.

Glancing at the clock on the stove, I see I only have about an hour before I need to be at the gallery to open it for the day. I also have two scheduled appointments before lunch and Dani won't be there much for the rest of the week. So, I decide to get this over as quickly as possible.

"How are you?" I ask, going about making my coffee.

She huffs something between a laugh and a sound of disapproval. "I guess I should be asking you that."

Trevor. That's the only answer I need. Since he's closer to my parents than I am, I'm assuming he's already called to tell them about my quick trip to New York and the result of that trip.

"Well, I'm great. Thanks for asking," I say as cheerfully as possible, just to piss her off even more. When she starts respecting me and my decisions, I'll try to lay off the sarcasm. Until then, this is the best I can do.

"What has gotten into you?" she asks and I can picture her trying to rein it in and not completely lose her cool. She'd love nothing more than to go off on me right now. I can feel it through the phone. "First you take this job in New Orleans, of all places, leaving poor Trevor to fend for himself. Then, you decide to make it permanent and buy a house. Lovely of you to ask us our advice on that, by the way. I'm sure your grandfather would be so proud to know how you finally decided to spend your inheritance. And now I find out you've packed up the remainder of your belongings and broken things off with Trevor."

Her tone increases in volume and ire as she goes along. By the end, she's practically screeching in my ear and I'm forced to hold the phone at a distance to save my hearing. Although her accounts are accurate, so I merely reply, "Yes, mother, that about sums it up."

"Well, you've made a huge mistake," she continues. "Your father and I have let you sow all the wild oats we can stand at this point. Running off to New York, chasing this silly dream and career path, backpacking across God knows where." When she breaks for a breath, her huff almost sounds like she's on the verge of tears, but even if she were, it's not because of love for me. No, the only thing that would upset her to the point of tears would be me embarrassing the family name. That's it. "You're going to fix this, Georgette. Call Trevor and make amends, and as soon as possible, let this job and all the frivolity go and get back to your life. Salvage what you can before it's too late."

Staring at the cabinet in front of me, my mug of steaming coffee in midair, I inhale a deep breath and center myself before replying, "I'm not going to do any of that."

My voice is quiet and calm and I wait for the storm brewing on the other end of the phone.

"You will," she retorts.

I hear the "or else" in her tone, but she doesn't say it. However, I know what she wants to hold over my head. The trust fund I recently dipped into for the purchase of my townhouse is the inheritance I received from my grandparents, not what I'll eventually get from my parents. And she still thinks, after all these years, I care about that.

"I won't, and there's nothing you can do to change my mind."

I hope she hears the finality in *my* tone and *my* words.

"Don't do this, Georgette," she pleads, something resembling desperation in her voice. "You're our only daughter… we… well, we care about your life and only want what's best for you. Trevor is what's best for you. He can provide the kind of life you deserve and he will help you make the choices to further yourself. Walking away from him is a mistake."

She just can't bring herself to say it.

We love you.

That actually would've gone a hell of a lot further than *we care about your life.*

Bullshit.

"The only person who knows what's best for me is me." At this point, my voice is trembling from anger and frustration and hurt. In my twenty-three years, she's never shown an ounce of motherly love. Not once. Sometimes, I wonder if it would kill her to say something kind. Maybe it's not in her DNA. Maybe it's because she was raised by a shrew and doesn't know any different. Whatever it is, I refuse to let her pass that on to me.

"I have to get ready for work," I continue. "Goodbye, Mother."

Hanging up, I don't give her another chance for a rebuttal. She'll call back, I'm sure of it, but it won't matter. There's nothing she can say that will change my mind.

After a few seconds of breathing to clear my mind and regain my composure, I take a sip of coffee before placing it on the counter. If I hurry and get dressed, I can make it to Neutral Grounds before Finley heads out for the day.

I need to see him. He'll be able to erase the bad juju my mother's phone call brought. He's always been able to do that. It's like his superpower.

Running upstairs, I quickly shower and pick out a simple, yet put-together ensemble for the day and slide into comfortable flats for the walk to the gallery, but put my power heels in my bag. Letting my curls run wild, I add a little product to tame the ends and swipe some mascara and lip gloss on and call it good.

There are some things about me that are a bit high-maintenance, my love of expensive art and well-made clothes and shoes, but I think I balance it out in other areas.

As I'm locking my front door, I hear a familiar voice call out from across the street. Turning, I see Avery walking out with a baby strapped to her chest. "Hey, neighbor!"

"Good morning," I call back.

We both make our way to the sidewalk and then I check the street before running across.

"Headed to the gallery?" she asks, nodding toward the Quarter.

Taking a peek at a sleeping Shae O'Sullivan, my heart warms and expands. Gently, I swipe a finger down his perfect little cheek. "Yeah," I whisper. "I'm headed to work, but stopping at Neutral Grounds first for a coffee."

"Just a coffee?" she asks, quirking an eyebrow. "Shaw told me he saw Finley leaving your place late last night."

Word does travel fast around here.

Chuckling, I bite back a smile. "Yeah, we…uh—"

"No need to explain," Avery says with a gigantic smile. "Really, totally judgment-free zone here."

"I would say it's complicated, but that couldn't be further from the truth," I tell her. "It's a long time coming and we're taking things slow."

Her smile softens and she reaches out to give my hand a squeeze. "I'm glad to hear it. And I haven't had a chance to tell you, but I'm really glad you decided to settle in here. It's so great to have more familiar faces on the street. Let me buy you a coffee this morning," she says, looping her arm through mine as we begin to walk down the street toward Neutral Grounds.

19

Finley

WALKING DOWN THE STAIRS, MY PHONE IN HAND, I'M JUST getting ready to send Jette a text to tell her good morning, when I hear her voice floating through the shop.

"Good morning," she calls out to CeCe, who's making her way around the counter to steal the baby sleeping on Avery's chest. Like a ninja, she has Shae out of the wrapped fabric and in her arms with Shae none the wiser.

CeCe starts cooing to the baby and speaking to the adults in the room in a soothing tone that resembles a character from a Disney film. "Y'all know where the coffee is," she sing-songs. "Help yourselves. Aunt CeCe is on baby duty."

Avery shakes her head as Jette laughs, the both of them making their way to the counter, until Jette sees me and her face lights up even brighter.

"Ladies," I greet, pulling an apron from the hooks on the wall near the stairs, tossing it over my head and wrapping the tie around my waist. "What can I get for you?"

Jette visibly swallows and then averts her gaze, clearing her throat and I can only wonder if she's thinking what I'm thinking—she wants more than what's on the menu at Neutral Grounds. Because that's all I've thought about since our kiss in the foyer of her townhouse yesterday.

My need for her has always been all-consuming, but knowing she can actually be mine and that I can have her—in all the ways I want her—that need has exploded. But I play it cool and smirk at her, winking as she looks back up to me and then to the menu.

It's a ruse. She knows what she wants. Georgette Taylor always knows what she wants and she's not afraid to go after it. "I'll have an americano and a chocolate croissant."

"A decaf latte," Avery adds. "But I can make it myself, if you need me to."

Shaking my head, I give her a smile. "Coming right up," I tell her, looking back to Jette. "Have a seat, I'll bring it to you."

Avery pulls Jette's arm and directs her to a table, whispering, "God, he's a keeper."

I can't help the smile on my face as I literally whistle while I work, drawing shots of espresso, adding steaming milk, and pouring up the drinks, just like CeCe taught me. When I'm finished with those, I grab two chocolate croissants and plate them, carrying it all to the table where CeCe, Avery, and Jette are talking quietly. Jette's cheeks flush when she sees me and I'd love nothing more than to know what they've been saying behind my back.

"Anything else, ladies?" I ask, my eyes glued to Jette's.

Swallowing once again, Jette shakes her head slightly. "No, this is great."

With a dip of my head, I walk back to the counter to clean up my mess. A few more customers walk in, most of them wanting their usual drip coffee and the occasional breakfast item, so I take care of them, giving CeCe a break to visit before the insanity that is the week before

Mardi Gras descends on her shop.

Just as I'm getting ready to tackle another order, Paige walks in with a smile on her face and immediately gets to work. "Hey," she greets, bumping me with her hip. "Thanks for pitching in. It's good to see CeCe taking a break every once in a while."

I look back at the table of women. "Yeah, it's the baby."

Paige nods. "She'd close this place down if Shae needed her," she agrees. "However, she could be on her deathbed and still try to work."

"Babies, man."

She sighs. "Yeah, they get you right in the feels."

Honestly, I haven't thought much about babies before now, but seeing them gush over the little guy is definitely making my chest do funny things. Jette is now holding him and the way she lets the entire world fall by the wayside and focus solely on him makes me wonder what she'd be like with her own child.

So good.

I already know that. She'll make an incredible mother one of these days. And I know it's something she's always wanted. Even when we were in high school, she'd talk about what she wanted to name her kids. One time, she asked if her talking about her theoretical children freaked me out, to which I replied, no. Not that I wanted a baby at that moment, but even then, I could imagine having one with Jette one day.

"You headed to the studio today?" Paige asks, pulling me out of my thoughts.

Folding the towel I've been using to wipe down the counters, I sigh, thinking about my busy schedule. "Yeah, studio this morning and then gigs at the club this evening and tonight. With Mardi Gras kicking into high gear, it's insane."

"I bet," Paige says, stocking the cups and lids while the shop isn't busy. There's always something to be done around here and when the roastery gets going next door, it will be even busier. "We've been slammed every day this past week."

"Hey."

Turning, I see Jette leaning over the counter expectantly, and feel the need to do the same and claim her perfect lips.

"Hey," I reply, glancing over to Paige. "Jette, this is Paige," I say, pointing to my side. "Paige, this is Georgette Taylor."

"I've heard a lot about you," Paige says, reaching across the counter to shake Jette's hand.

"All good I hope," Jette replies, shaking her hand.

Paige smiles. "All good. Can I get you a refill?" she asks, pointing to the empty cup on the counter.

"No, thank you," Jette says, glancing back at the door. "I have to get to the gallery...but I was—"

Without hesitation, I pull off the apron and walk toward the end of the bar. "You okay on your own?" I ask Paige.

"Yeah, get out of here," she says with a knowing smile. "Have a good day, Georgette! Don't let the madness of Mardi Gras get to you."

Jette chuckles. "Thanks, I feel like I'm going to need it."

"See y'all later," I call out to CeCe and Avery. Jette stops back by the table, grabbing her bag and leaning in for hugs from the two women.

When we're out on the sidewalk, I wrap my arm around her waist and pull her to me. She sighs, sinking into me. "Well, that was a nice surprise," I tell her, kissing the top of her head and inhaling her sweet scent.

"You left me last night," Jette says and I stiffen a little, but continue to hold onto her.

"I thought you could use some good rest and if I stayed..."

Jette stops walking, turning into my chest. "It's okay. I just missed you when I woke up this morning and I needed to see you."

"Everything okay?" I ask, sensing something more in her tone.

She just stands there looking at me for a long moment. "Everything is great, especially when I'm here, with you. But I had a phone call from my mother this morning."

Should've known that was coming. "About Trevor?"

"Yep," she says on a deep sigh.

Wrapping my arms around her shoulders, I pull her in for a much-needed hug. "Don't let her get to you," I tell her, pressing my lips to the top of her head and then down to her temple. "She doesn't get to run your life anymore."

That's a fanfuckingtastic difference from five years ago.

Back then, her parents still had pull over her and could make her life miserable if she didn't do what they wanted her to do, which included keeping her distance from me.

Now, Jette's an adult and they no longer get to dictate who is or isn't in her life.

"I know," she says, leaning forward and placing her lips on my collarbone, light as a feather, yet wreaking havoc inside my chest. When the kiss travels to my throat, I have to focus on my breaths so I don't completely lose myself on this increasingly busy sidewalk in the middle of the French Quarter.

"You've always been able to make everything better," Jette whispers. "Thank you for that."

Tightening my grip on her, I bury my head in the cocoon of us. "No need to thank me, you do that just by being here."

Being mine, I want to add, but refrain for fear of moving too fast. In my mind, reaching this point has taken years and it feels like we've crawled here at a snail's pace. But in reality, it's been less than two months since Georgette walked back into my life, and only a short time since she left her past behind her.

I'm willing to wait, anything for her. And anything to make sure this time is for good.

When Jette tilts her head up, our eyes locking, I press my lips to hers and drink her in, giving in just enough to take the edge off.

After a few seconds, we both pull away, knowing we can't fully satiate the need, not here.

"Walk me to work?" Jette asks.

Once I kiss Jette again, at the front door of 303 Royal Street, like I've dreamed of doing every day for the past month, I make my way down to Canal Street to catch the streetcar to Lola's. I have some studio work to do this morning, which will keep me busy until I have to run back to the apartment and grab my sax and a quick change of clothes before going to the club tonight.

As I'm sitting on the streetcar, just a mere fifteen minutes after leaving Jette, I'm already missing her. The thought of not seeing her for the rest of the day is unacceptable, so I pull out my phone and send her a text.

Me: Come watch me play tonight?

Less than a second later, Jette's reply pops up on my screen, her quirk shining through and making me chuckle.

Jette: Does a woodchuck chuck wood??

Jette: You didn't even have to ask, I was planning on it anyway.

With a smile that belongs solely to the girl who stole my heart years ago and never gave it back, I enjoy the remainder of my ride to Lola's, soaking in the sights of the Garden District.

PEEKING MY HEAD OUT THE BACKSTAGE DOOR, I SCAN THE CROWD looking for Georgette. She sent me a text half an hour ago that she was closing up the gallery after her last appointment, but I still haven't seen her.

I did reserve her a small table near the stage, so at least she won't have to fight for a table.

It's a madhouse in here tonight. The roar of the crowd is almost enough to drown out the sound of the band. But the energy in the club is electric. Thankfully, most of the patrons are casually drinking and the party hasn't kicked up too high. Frenchmen has just enough of the Mardi Gras vibe without the overcrowding of the clubs and bars on Bourbon.

But if it's like this with six days left to go, I can't imagine what it will be like on Fat Tuesday.

"Let's go," Gia calls out. "We've got bills to pay and hearts to break!"

Someone passes me the bottle of whiskey, but I wave it off. "Finley," Gia says, saddling up beside me. "I haven't had a chance to ask you how things are going with Lola."

"Good," I tell her, my eyes still fixed on the crowd. "Great, actually. Thank you again for making the connection. I really appreciate the opportunity."

She waves me off. "Don't thank me. She would've tracked you down on her own if I didn't pass along the message. I'm glad it's all working out."

I assume she's moving along, doing what Gia does best and rallying the troops, but then she speaks again, making me jump. "Who is she?"

"Who?" I ask, playing dumb because I hate that I'm being that obvious.

Gia rolls her eyes, shaking her head with a laugh. "You can't fool me, honey. I haven't just been around the block; I've been around the whole damn city. Who is she?"

"Georgette Taylor," I tell her.

It's always been Georgette Taylor.

"Well," she drawls. "She must be something special to catch the attention of Finley Lawson. Lord knows me and every other warm-blooded female around here have been trying since the day you walked in the door."

I'm sure Gia has seen Jette in here before, but she sees a lot of people, so it's not a surprise she hasn't put two and two together.

About that time, Jette's blonde curls appear in the front door and I watch her as she stands on her own in the throngs of people, pushing her way to the front.

"The blonde," Gia says, still standing beside me in the doorway. "I should've known. I've seen the way you look at her."

"Yeah," I say, smiling at Jette when she makes eye contact. "She's the one."

Motioning to the small table by the stage, I meet her there. "Thought I was going to have to come find you," I say, pulling her chair out for her.

"It's insane out there," she says breathlessly. "Just as I thought I was getting used to the crowds, the mob descended. Have you been out there?"

Squatting down beside her, I can't help but smile at her wild eyes that match her even wilder hair.

"You're beautiful," I tell her and she stops what she's doing, her jacket half-way off, as her cheeks turn a lovely shade of pink.

"Thank you."

Helping her the rest of the way out of her jacket, I place it on the chair beside her and motion for Suki to take her drink order. "I wish I could sit by your side, but alas, I cannot."

"Instead, I'm going to sit here and ogle you while you play," she quips. "So, get on up there and give me something to look at."

Standing, I run a hand through my hair and chuckle. "Is that all I am to you? An object to ogle?"

"Yeah," she says, her perfect lips turning down. "I'm sorry you had to find out this way. I've only ever wanted you for your body."

Even though we're joking around, like we've always done, and we're surrounded by a club full of strangers, for a split second, it's just me and Jette and the spark that's always sizzled between us. In a silent promise of things to come, I lean down and kiss her like I mean it.

When I pull back, Jette's eyes are still closed and there's a soft smile on her lips where mine just were. Hovering over her, I lower my voice just for her. "There's so much more where that came from."

"I'm counting on it," she replies as her eyes flutter open.

Suki walks up about that time and it's my cue to get my ass on stage. The rest of the band is already tuning up and I have to hustle to catch up.

Once we start playing, I try to stay focused, but it's nearly impossible with Jette so close and so much unresolved tension coursing between us.

Between sets, I head straight to the table. "I'm only playing one more set," I tell her, accepting a bottle of water from Suki and wiping the sweat off my brow with the collar of my shirt.

Jette's eyes grow hooded and I pause with the water bottle halfway to my mouth. "What?"

"You," she says, her words lazy and low. "This, watching you play... knowing I'm leaving with you and not just as friends..." She drifts off, shaking her head slightly as she fights back a smile. "It's a heady feeling."

"You're killing me," I mutter, leaning forward and inhaling her sweetness before capturing her lips with mine. After a few moments, I pull away. "Sorry, I know I'm sweaty, but I can't help myself."

"Don't apologize." Her lips brush mine and I swear a drop of my sweat lands on her lip. "Nothing about this moment is a turnoff." She laughs lightly, putting a few more inches between us. "Quite the opposite actually," she says under her breath, shifting in her chair.

Standing, I down half the bottle of water and set it on the table. "One more set."

"I'm not going anywhere."

Jette's always been my biggest fan. Unlike other people I've been with over the years, I know it's genuine interest where she's concerned. Even though we both have better things we'd like to be doing right now, she'd stay and listen to me play as long as the club is open.

The next set feels like it's in slow motion, but once it's done, I'm off the stage and headed to the back. I clean my sax in record time and store it in its case. Going into the bathroom, I tear off my shirt and splash water on my face, freshening up as much as I can before putting on a clean shirt. I know Jette said she doesn't mind it, but I do.

She smells so good.

It wouldn't be right for me to taint that.

But I would like to dirty her up.

Fuck.

Okay, that's good enough.

Shoving everything into my bag, I toss it over my shoulder and grab my sax. When I walk back out into the club, I stop short. Jette isn't sitting at the table. There's a large man with a mullet and a busty redhead now sitting there. The club is even fuller than it was earlier and I start to worry about where she might've gone.

I know she's tough and she lived in New York for five years, but she's, well, *her*, and I'd never want anything bad to happen to her. I've always felt protective over her, even when it wasn't necessary. I can't help it.

I'm seconds away from calling her name when I catch a glimpse of her standing by the bar, a couple of guys blocking my full view of her.

"Jette," I call out, getting her attention. She slips the bartender a tip into his jar and then quickly makes her way over. "I thought I lost you," I tell her, pulling her to me and keeping her close as we make our way out of the club.

A few people offer me a head nod or high five as I'm walking out. "Nice set," one of the bouncers says as we pass by.

"Thanks, man."

Once we're finally out in the cool night air, I take a breath. "Damn, I don't think I've ever seen it that packed."

"You had them eating out of the palm of your hand," Jette says, leaning closer. "I'm not sure if you're aware, but you've got quite the following. Possibly even a fan club."

I laugh, kissing the top of her head. "I seriously doubt that. Most people who go in there are barely even paying attention to the band on a night like tonight."

"Not true. I saw it with my own eyes."

"With your own eyes, huh?" I tease. "What else did you see with your own eyes?"

She shrugs. "There was this really hot sax player. I mean, I wouldn't kick him out of my bed."

"Oh, really?"

After we pass another large group of people and make the turn around the corner, Jette stops, pulling me against the side of a building. "Your place or mine?"

"Um, well." When she's looking at me like this, eyes full of fire and determination, I forget what to say, what to think. "I was thinking maybe we should—"

"If you're going to say anything besides my place or yours, it's the wrong answer, Finley." Leaning forward, she kisses me softly, pulling me closer by the front of my shirt. "I know you," she says between kisses. "I know you're probably trying to do the right thing, take things slow, but that doesn't work for me."

"It doesn't?" I ask, my heart starting to pound in my chest. "Why not?"

Biting down on her lip, she grabs my shirt tighter. "See, I've kind of been waiting five years to be with you again. So, I feel like I've paid my dues. And unlike the first time we were together, which by the way, was one of the best nights of my life, maybe *the* best night, I'm older and wiser and I know what I want. This isn't a rash decision or a mistake. *We could never be a mistake.*" Standing on her tiptoes, she nips at my jaw and then grazes her way to my earlobe, driving me insane as her teeth scrape against the sensitive skin. "I want you and I know you want me, so let's not waste any more time."

"Your place," I reply, using my free hand to cup her jaw and kiss her stupid. If I could fly us there or use some sort of teleportation device, I would. Instead, I pull away from her and take her hand, walking as fast as possible.

When we make it to her front porch, we're both a little breathless, partly from the brisk walk and partly from the kisses we've been stealing along the way. Jette fumbles with the key a few times, but finally manages to unlock the door. Once she opens it, I drop my shit in the foyer and take Jette's bag from her, adding it to the pile.

Next is her jacket and then we both kick off our shoes.

Without another word, Jette offers me her hand and starts up the stairs. I've been up to her room several times since she moved in here, helping the furniture people with her bed, tucking her in, but this feels like uncharted territory.

At the top of the steps, Jette turns and pushes me against the wall next to her bedroom door, devouring my mouth with hers. "I forgot how good it was to kiss you," she whispers. "I think my mind shut it out in an effort to save me from years of disappointment because no one has ever measured up to you or this, the way I feel when we're together."

Running my hands around her waist and down her ass, I lift her into my arms and carry her into her bedroom. "You ruined me for everyone else five fucking years ago," I growl. "No one has ever come close, Jette… not even a little bit."

Once I'm standing at the edge of her bed, I lean forward, laying her down as I hover over her.

"Remind me," she whispers, her hands gripping the edge of my shirt and pulling it up. I help her out and yank it over my head, discarding it on the floor. When I look back down, she has her own shirt up and over her head and she's working on the zipper of her skirt.

I want to tell her to slow down or to let me, but there will be time for slow and patient later. Tonight, Jette and I both need something from each other. It might not be the most perfect moment or the best sex, but it will be what we need.

Once she's lying there in only her bra and panties, I take a second to just look at her.

She's still the same girl I fell in love with so long ago, but there're also parts of her I've yet to get acquainted with. Her full hips and breasts, her waist that curves in at just the right place… that's all part of the woman she's become. Trailing a finger across her collarbone and between her breasts, I commit these new traits to memory. "You're so beautiful," I tell her, leaning down to taste the skin I was just touching. "So much more beautiful than I remember and I don't even know how that's possible."

"Finn," she moans, her hands raking through my hair, holding me to her.

"Let me taste you, Jette." Nudging the waist of her panties with my nose, I kneel before her and kiss a path down her center, inhaling her through the thin, silky fabric. Her fingers wrap around strands of my hair and when she pulls slightly, it only spurs me on, making my cock strain against the fabric of my jeans.

Yeah, we'll get there, but first, I'm going to make Jette remember.

20

Georgette

OH. MY. GOD.

The feel of Finley's mouth is so much better than I remembered. Granted, the one and only time he went down on me was a first for both of us, and although it felt amazing, we both knew it would only get better with time and practice. I don't want to focus on why his skills have improved—it's obvious he hasn't been a monk while I was in New York—but I'm woman enough to appreciate the difference five years have brought him.

One thing that won't be very different from our first time together is how quickly he makes me come. I've been a quaking, horny mess all night thanks to him. Watching Finn perform is foreplay for me and it's not only because of how his mouth and fingers work his sax or how his hips and ass instinctually groove to the beat, but it's also the passion he emanates. He plays like he makes love and I'm more than ready to reap the benefits.

A few more flicks of Finn's tongue coupled with the pressure of his finger on my g-spot has me screaming his name in no time.

"Pants off. Now," I gasp out, still reeling from my orgasm.

He chuckles while rising to his feet, already undoing his jeans. "Your wish, my command."

The moment his cock springs out from its confines, my mouth begins to water. I've never really stopped to appreciate a penis before but I can't help myself as I stare at Finley's. It's so hard, it's throbbing and when Finn wipes my moisture from his mouth then rubs it on the head, I can't help but whimper.

I've never been this turned on. Or needy. But, that's what I am. I need him. I need him inside me, and I need it now.

Sitting up, I try to grab for him but he pulls back, a worried look covering his face.

"What's wrong?"

"I wasn't expecting tonight to happen," he says, running a hand down his face and then back up into his hair. That damn forearm on display in the dim light of my bedroom. "I don't have a condom. Do you?"

Condom.

I feel a smile stretch across my lips. Leave it to Finn to always be the responsible, thoughtful one. But I don't want that, I don't want anything between us. So I tell him.

"I don't have any, but it doesn't matter because I don't want to use one. I want to feel all of you. You know I've been on the pill for years and I promise I haven't been with Trevor in months, even way before I moved here. And no one before him… except you."

There's a shift on Finley's face, a growing intensity.

His throat bobs when he swallows as he processes my words.

"Months?" he asks.

I only nod, swallowing down the tightness in my throat as my eyes rove his body, taking inventory of every new muscle, the broadness of his shoulders in contrast to the narrowness of his hips… grown-up Finley is perfection. And knowing him, he's now contemplating the idea that it's been so long since I've been with Trevor and equal parts happy and pissed. Happy it's been months, but pissed my needs haven't been taken care of in so long.

"Finley." My voice brings him out of his thoughts and he looks at me. "I want you. Please, make love to me."

As my words register, he slowly crawls back over me, kissing me until my toes curl into the bed. Settling between my thighs, his tongue enters my mouth. When he reaches between us, his fingers sliding along my sensitive flesh with ease, he groans so deeply I feel the vibrations against my chest. "You're so fucking wet. I'm afraid I won't last long."

"I'm not worried about that," I tell him, my words coming out in pants. "We have a lifetime of this ahead of us." Not to count my chickens before they hatch or anything, but this is it. Finley is it for me and all I'll ever want. What I don't tell him is that I'm so turned on right now, I'll probably orgasm as soon as he enters me.

When he pulls back to look at me, his smile is glorious and it tells me we're on the same page, as usual. With our eyes locked, I feel his tip push inside and I hold my breath, trying to remain patient.

Gripping onto the blanket at my sides, I'm so close to telling him to fuck me. Not slow, not patient, just take what he wants and give me what I want. I appreciate him wanting to take his time, though, especially now that I'm registering the size of him.

Holy hell.

He's bigger than I remembered.

My body stretches around him, welcoming his intrusion, and when our hips are flush together, I sigh in relief. I'm full and complete and even without moving, it feels perfect.

And, then he moves.

Every push and pull is exquisite and my body is on fire, lit from within, and so close to detonating. I run my hands down his back, relishing the feel of his muscles tensing and relaxing in response to his thrusts. When I reach his ass, I grab onto it, encouraging Finley to push harder as I bring my knees closer to my chest, giving him room to thrust deeper.

Harder.

Oh, God.

"Fuck, Jette," Finley breathes out, his voice broken. "God, you... you feel amazing. I can't... I'm so close."

For the second time tonight, a bead of Finley's sweat drips onto my skin. He's so primal and raw in this moment—just like when he performs—but this time, his passion is only for me.

"Yes, Finn... yes... please don't hold back."

He buries his head in the crook of my neck and pounds into me. It's relentless and perfect and too soon, my orgasm explodes throughout my body, causing me to cry out as I spasm around him. Finley soon follows, his body going rigid as he spills inside of me, my name a whisper on his lips.

I can tell he's trying not to crush me with his whole weight but I want it. I'm desperate to be this close to him, even more so after what we just shared.

"Don't you dare move yet," I tell him, causing him to snicker.

"Woman, I don't think I could move if I wanted to."

He looks at me with eyes so tender and I want to cry at how beautiful he is, how special this moment is. I can feel the unexpected tears building and I don't try to stop them when they spill over, running down my cheeks and into my hair.

"Baby," Finley whispers. "Why are you crying? Are you hurt?"

"No." Shaking my head slightly only causes more tears to slide down my skin. "I'm perfect and you're perfect and we're finally together again. It's overwhelming in the best kind of way."

He kisses me before rolling onto his back and pulling me into his chest.

"This is just the beginning," he says, kissing the top of my head. "Promise."

UNLIKE YESTERDAY, WHEN I WAKE UP THIS MORNING, IT'S NOT THE coffee that wakes me up, it's the warm, heavy arms of Finley.

Also, I realize I passed out and didn't set up the timer on my coffee pot or set an alarm.

I'm blaming that on the fantastic orgasms Finley gave me. Not only did we have a round two, but at some point, in the wee hours of the morning, Finley woke me up with soft caresses, sliding into me from behind.

It was slow and sensual and perfect.

In another world, where I'm not the sole person responsible for opening and running a gallery, I would call in sick today, not from a physical illness, but pure exhaustion.

The best kind of exhaustion.

And so long overdue, in so many ways.

Rolling over in Finn's embrace, I gently brush my thumb over his cheek, soaking him up in the early morning light. As I glance over his shoulder at the alarm clock, I see it's only six-thirty and I'm relieved I have plenty of time to get up and around.

When I slip out of bed, Finn stirs, blinking slowly as he wakes. "Good morning."

His voice is like honey poured over coarse salt—sweet and gritty.

"Good morning," I reply with a slow smile. "How did you sleep?"

"Best sleep ever," Finn says, raising up on his elbow and looking behind him at the clock. "But not nearly enough."

"Thanks for that, by the way," I tease, turning and walking into the bathroom. I hear the rustle of the sheets and then Finley's behind me, wrapping his arms around my middle and pulling me into his chest.

He's naked.

So am I.

And this, feeling his skin against mine, just became my newest obsession.

"Are you trying to say all those orgasms were my fault?" he asks, his voice husky in my ear and his breath warm against my neck.

Swallowing down the rush of lust, I press into Finley's growing length. "You're really good at what you do."

Finn's growl is his only response before he walks me forward toward the shower. Leaning around me, he turns the water on, waiting for it to heat as he nips at my neck, stirring up every hormone in my body. When the water is warm, he nudges me into the shower.

First, we get dirty... again.

Then, Finn takes his time washing my hair and every inch of my body. When he's done, I take the soap and return the favor, savoring each moment with him as we reconnect on every level, even ones we've never been to before.

After we get out and dry off, Finley slips on his jeans from last night and grabs a fresh t-shirt from his bag. I give him an extra toothbrush and we go about getting ready, like it's the most normal thing in the world.

It feels like it.

This morning had the potential to feel awkward and uncharted, but it just feels natural and right.

Good.

So, so good.

"Here's your coffee," I tell Finn as he walks into the kitchen with his bag. "I thought we could stop by Neutral Grounds and grab some breakfast before I have to open the gallery."

Finn chuckles. "CeCe is going to love this."

"What?"

"You, me... walking in together."

I shrug. After my impromptu girls' chat with CeCe and Avery yesterday morning, this won't come as a surprise. They were trying to get me to ditch the gallery and drag Finley up to his apartment and *make this thing official.*

Talk about some horny floozies.

My cheeks still heat up at the memory of what they were suggesting. And God, do I love them even more than I already did.

"What's that blush for?" Finn asks as we make our way to the front door and he stops to grab his sax.

"Nothing," I tell him, checking to make sure I have everything I need for the day loaded in my bag. "They're just a bunch of pervs. They were probably taking bets on how long it would take us to do the deed."

Finn chokes on a sip of coffee and rolls his eyes as he holds the door open for me and I slip under his arm. "Is that what y'all were talking about yesterday?"

"Mmm-hmm," I hum, locking the door and then looping my arm through his as we walk down the steps and onto the sidewalk. Glancing over at Avery and Shaw's and then to CeCe and Shep's. Both houses have lights on, but no one is out and about this morning.

"And women always say guys are bad," Finn mutters. "What exactly were you talking about?"

"Oh," I begin, keeping my tone casual. "You know, just seducing you and taking you upstairs and *blowing...* your mind."

I hear him choke again, but smirk and keep walking. It takes him a couple of blocks to recover.

"I don't think I can face them," he admits, and now it's my turn to chuckle.

"Well, if you need some ammo, I have plenty of dirt on the two of them." We pause at a corner and check the street before crossing. "I had to listen to more sexcapades than I care to admit."

Finn sighs. "I'm good, thanks."

Pausing, I pull him to a stop. "We're good," I tell him. "And that's all that matters."

"You're right," he says, brushing a strand of hair behind my ear and cupping my cheek. "Fuck the rest of the world, right?"

"Yeah, fuck 'em," I agree, my eyes trained on Finley's full lips.

He groans. "You can't say that in public." His voice is low and gravelly, a warning that shoots straight to my core. "That sweet, perfect mouth uttering a dirty word is liable to be my undoing."

Closing my eyes, I inhale, trying to center myself.

How is it possible that we've spent the better part of the last ten hours screwing each other's brains out and I'm still burning with desire for this man?

Finn's mouth melds into mine and I lean into the kiss, hoping the fire never dies.

21

Finley

"THANKS, MAN," I TELL THE GUY WHO JUST TOSSED SOME dollar bills into my sax case.

Honestly, I wasn't expecting to make any money today. I assumed people would be too hungover to be out and about just yet but I was wrong. There are people all over the Quarter and they're extremely generous, for which I'm very thankful.

Gotta love Mardi Gras.

I was too antsy to stay at home. My studio work has slowed down this week and I'm not due to be at the club until much later, so I decided to come play Royal Street for a few hours. Really, though, I needed something to keep my mind off Jette. Since we've been together—*really* together—I've been insatiable. I feel like I'm going to lose my mind if I don't see her, touch her, or have some kind of contact with her. It's weird to feel this way because I've never been a clingy guy and I'd never want to get on her nerves but that's how I feel.

Thankfully, Jette feels the same. She texts or calls me almost every time I think of doing the same to her. I love that we haven't lost our ability to be so in sync.

I suppose it's also good we have to be responsible adults and do our jobs throughout the day. Otherwise, we'd be fucking like bunnies. I have to remind myself that being apart during the day makes the nighttime even better.

"You take requests?"

Turning, I find Shep walking toward me with two coffees in his hand. When he's close enough, I eagerly reach for one before giving him our usual one-arm man-hug.

"So, about that request…" he starts.

"Dude, if you ask me to play Led Zeppelin, I'm walking away."

"What's wrong with Zeppelin?" Shep tries to look offended but I know better. He's more of a Stones guy anyway.

"Nothing is wrong with them, but do you know how many times a day I have people ask me to play 'Stairway to Heaven'? On a freaking sax, no less?"

Laughing, Shep concedes. "Yeah, I imagine that would get old pretty quick. Looks like you've had a good morning, though."

"Yeah, it's been great. What brings you out here today?"

"I was scoping out a property nearby and hoped you'd be playing, so I took a chance and grabbed some coffees for us."

I take a tentative sip to make sure the coffee is cooled off enough to drink before taking a hefty gulp. There's a different kind of burn with this coffee and it causes me to cough a little.

"What is this spiked with? And why?" I ask, wiping my eyes.

"Oh, I'm not exactly sure what CeCe puts in her special coffees. It could be Irish cream liquor or vodka… or both. It's sure to keep you warm, that's for sure."

"Damn, she has a heavy hand, but tell her I appreciate it. I just hope I'm able to walk across the street to the gallery after this," I say, chuckling.

"No worries, man. Everyone stumbles down here, thanks to the open container law. Just don't knock any of those paintings off the walls and make Georgette kick your ass. Speaking of, how are things between you two now that she's back from New York? I haven't seen you much, so I assume things are going really well…"

I expect my cheeks to get hot at what he's insinuating but they don't because I'm not embarrassed. Not even a little bit. I won't kiss and tell but I sure as hell won't deny what's been going on between me and Jette either.

"Things are perfect. I had no idea it could be so good, to be honest."

Shep's smile is genuine as he claps a hand on my shoulder. "That's great, Finn. I'm thrilled for you both. I always knew you two would find your way back to each other."

"Oh, really? Since when? Because if I recall correctly, and I believe I do, your advice to me after Jette left was to *go out and 'get some' while I'm still young.*"

He scoffs, waving me off. "That was the old me. The new and improved me knew you and Georgette were made for each other." His expression is completely serious but I can't help but call him out.

"Does this new you have anything to do with you being married now?"

"Well, I can't deny being with CeCe has shown me the error of my ways, but I'd like to think I would've matured on my own eventually."

"Yeah, doubtful," I say, laughing, earning a light punch to my shoulder. Looking past him, I notice people clearing paths along the streets. "What are those barricades up for over there?"

Shep turns and looks over his shoulder. "Road closures, man. They are the bane of the locals' existence during Mardi Gras, or so CeCe says. This is my first time to be in the city during the carnival season, but I do know parades are everywhere and at random times, so watch out if you have to be somewhere you can't walk to."

"So, that means a parade will be making its way to Royal Street?" I ask, still scoping everything out as people pass by. "I haven't seen one yet. I wonder if Jette would want to watch."

"Most businesses close early between now and Fat Tuesday because of the parades, but she might not know that. Why don't you go relay the message," he says, raising his eyebrows suggestively. "You've barely taken your eyes off the gallery since I've been standing here. I'm guessing you're about to jump out of your skin if you don't see her soon, am I right?"

"Shut up," I mutter, refusing to make eye contact with him because he's damn right. "But, thanks for the heads up."

Giving my shoulder one last strong clap, he starts walking down the sidewalk toward Neutral Grounds. "Don't be such a stranger, jackass," he calls out. "And bring your girl over for dinner soon."

"Yes, sir!" I yell back before packing up my things and heading across the street.

When I step inside the gallery and see Jette speaking with a client, I can't help the smile that covers my face. It still feels a bit surreal that she's really here and she's really doing what she loves—what she was meant to do.

And she's all mine.

And I'm so damn proud of her.

I try to sneak by and hide my case in the office in the back but she sees me anyway, giving me a quick wave before turning back to the woman she's been speaking to. While she works, I decide to walk around and look at the new art she's brought in this past week.

The gallery is actually a lot bigger inside than it looks from the street. I love how these spaces are deeper than they are wide. With the columns and rooms off to the sides that open into each other, it's easy to get lost in the art and forget where you are.

Thankfully, it doesn't take long for Jette to find me and when she does, she greets me with a smile and a kiss that's not nearly long enough.

Fucking jobs and workplace protocol.

"You cut your set short?" she asks.

"Yeah, they're setting up for a parade that looks like it's about to start, so I thought I'd see if you want to go watch it with me?"

Her face lights up. "I'd love to. Dani mentioned something about closing early if I wanted to this week, but I didn't realize we'd be this close to a parade. This is so exciting!"

An hour later, we're locking up the front door when we hear music coming from down the street. Taking Jette's hand, I take off down the sidewalk, finding a space in the crowd just big enough for the two of us to squeeze in.

I don't even know what kind of parade to expect but everyone around us seems really excited. There are a lot of kids running around, as well, so I assume it's a family-friendly one. But you just never know in New Orleans.

"Look! I see something coming!" Jette shouts, standing on her tip-toes and pointing down the street.

When the procession gets closer, I'm able to read the large banner being carried by a few people leading the way. It says "Krewe of Barkus" but that doesn't mean anything to me. There are so many krewes, I can't keep them all straight. A few weeks ago, I didn't even know what a *krewe* was.

But, from first glance, it's easy to tell this isn't a typical parade.

For one, instead of large floats coming down the street, I see a bunch of people walking. Also, instead of tossing beads and cups into the crowd, these people have leashes in their hands and those leashes are attached to, you guessed it, dogs.

Ah, Krewe of *Bark*us. Very clever.

But the look on Jette's face is what really is entertaining me. The excitement on her face when she realizes what we're watching is contagious. Like every time I'm around her, I can't help but be happy.

Jette is happiness incarnate.

"It's a dog parade!" she squeals, grabbing onto my arm and jumping up and down.

I spend the majority of the parade watching her clap and laugh and wave at every dog that passes us. Don't get me wrong, the pups are great. They have breeds ranging from Frenchies to Great Danes and everything in between and they're all so fun to watch. Some are even in costume, which is freaking hysterical.

But nothing compares to my girl.

And, when she turns to me with sparkles in her eyes and says, "Let's adopt a dog," there's no way I can turn her down and kill this pure, unadulterated joy.

Which is how we end up at a local animal shelter a few blocks away not even an hour after the parade ends.

"Hey, y'all. Looking to adopt a pet today?" the woman at the front desk greets as we walk in.

"We are," Jette gushes. "We just watched the doggie parade and thought it'd be a great time to get one of our own. I'm not sure what kind we want, though. Do you have any recommendations?"

The lady smiles warmly, glancing from Jette up to me. "The Krewe of Barkus brings us lots of visitors. It's a good thing you got here as quickly as you did. Right now, you have the pick of the litter, so to speak." Walking around the counter, she opens a door that leads down a long, wide walkway. "We have all kinds of dogs right now, some pure breeds, some mutts. I suggest you just browse and see which one grabs your heart the most. Nine times out of ten, it's the dog who picks its owner."

Jette and I thank the woman and walk past her, the barking getting louder as we approach the kennels where the dogs are kept. She wasn't lying when she said they had a little of everything.

Big ones. Small ones. Puppies to old dogs.

"What kind do you think we should get?" Jette asks, her voice a mixture of amazement and overwhelmed. She stops at each kennel, giving each dog a minute of her time as she brings her hand to the gate and lets them sniff her palm.

"I don't really have a lot of experience with dogs," I say, shrugging and kneeling down beside her. "One that's hopefully easy-going, since we've never done this before, and maybe one that can be left outside during the day, since you have to be at the gallery."

"I agree," she says thoughtfully, rising to her feet.

As I stand to follow her, Jette grabs my hand and squeezes. For a second, I assume she's found a dog she can't live without. But when I try to look at her, she turns the other way. That's when I hear the sniffles. Pulling her to me, I cup her jaw and bring her face to mine.

"Hey, what's wrong?"

Jette bites her bottom lip to keep it from trembling, fighting back tears. "It's just so sad, Finn. I want them all but I know we can only get one."

Wrapping her in my arms, I let her cry. "I know. I don't like it either, but you heard the lady out front. Thanks to the parade, they'll get lots of people looking to adopt. We have to leave some for them, okay?"

She nods her head and wipes her eyes. "Okay. You're right. Sorry for getting so emotional."

"You never have to apologize for that. Your big heart is one of the things I love most about you."

Georgette looks up at me with a small mischievous smile fighting to the surface. "Are we saying our first 'I love yous' in a dog shelter?"

"Nah, we'll save it for a more romantic time, if you want. Like, tonight, in bed." I grab her ass and kiss the top of her head. When she laughs, the tension in my chest eases. I've never liked seeing people cry, but Jette's tears have the ability to kill my soul. I hate it.

As we begin to walk again, a dog in a kennel a few feet away catches my attention. "Hey, Jette, look over there."

Inside, there's a dog with blonde and white fur and kind eyes, and it seems to be patiently waiting for us to make our way to it. Walking up to the gate, we read the card attached.

King is a Border Collie/Labrador Retriever mix. He's four-years-old and was found abandoned on Royal Street. He enjoys cuddling and long walks around the French Quarter.

"Finn," Jette whispers, looking at the card and then back at me. "He was found on Royal Street. *We* work on Royal Street. It's like we were meant to find him."

I smile, looking down at the dog and back up to Jette. "Also, *King*... like Nat King Cole," I muse, mostly to myself as I continue to make eye contact with the dog, feeling an immediate connection.

"He's perfect!" she declares, her smile widening as she squats down to the dog's level. Once she's there, he paws the cage, trying his hardest to lick Jette through the small openings.

"I think you've been chosen, babe," I say, kneeling down beside her and sticking my hand out for him to sniff me. Giving me his approval, he starts trying to lick at me too.

The three of us sit there for a minute, bonding, before Jette leans into me. "Look at that, Finley Lawson. I think we just became parents."

22

Georgette

THIS WEEK HAS BEEN HARD AND IT'S ONLY TUESDAY...FAT Tuesday.

First, Mardi Gras. I feel like that's a blanket excuse for everything these days. The streets are too crowded? Mardi Gras. The restaurants are packed? Mardi Gras. Too many drunk people wandering the French Quarter? Mardi Gras.

Second, Finley. He's all I think about. I'm sure it's the newness of being back together and I'm sure it will eventually fade, but for now, he consumes my thoughts and makes it impossible to work without being distracted.

Then, throw in our new baby and it's the perfect storm. King is the biggest cuddle bug on the face of the planet, more so than Finley, and I wish I could take him with me everywhere I go. Finn stops by the townhouse and checks on him when he can and I've been home for lunch a couple of times since we got him. He's a good boy and I know he's fine, but I still worry about him adjusting to his new life.

Add into all of that the pure exhaustion from working the gallery by myself and I'm struggling. Thanks to CeCe, she's kept me in a constant supply of coffee and food, knowing I'm here alone. Either she, Finn, or Shep drop by something a couple of times a day.

I'm grateful, for so many things, but at the top of my mental list is this new family I've acquired by moving here.

When I accepted the job, I knew it would be an adventure and a challenge. I already felt incredibly thankful for the opportunity. Not many people would hire someone like me, with so little experience under their belt, to hand over their gallery to. But Cami saw my potential and took a chance. What she didn't realize was bringing me here would put together pieces of my heart that have been missing, helping me in more ways than just professionally.

For that, I'm not sure I could ever repay her.

Glancing down at the appointment book in front of me, I take a sip of the coffee Finn dropped off on his way to the studio. His schedule has been a bit off lately too. We're all just trying to keep our heads above water.

Thankfully, I've already met with my one appointment for the day and the schedule is pretty open until Thursday. Most people in the city have other plans with today being Fat Tuesday.

Walking over to the window, I watch for a while as throngs of people pass by.

Some are dressed in the traditional purple, green, and gold. Some have elaborate costumes with glitter and bare body parts mixed in for good measure. And I can also hear more music filtering through the closed door of the gallery than usual.

Occasionally, on a slow day, I can hear Finley when he plays, and it's so surreal.

He's here.

I'm here.

We're us again.

I had no clue I could be this happy.

Checking my watch, I see it's after one o'clock. When I spoke to Cami yesterday, she told me I should close up the gallery for the entire day and just enjoy Mardi Gras, but I didn't want to reschedule the appointment from earlier.

Now that I'm standing here and have been the only person inside these walls for over two hours, I'm considering taking her up on it. But first, I'm going to rearrange the back wall and make room for a few new pieces one of our artists is bringing by later this week.

An hour or so later, I'm standing back, looking over the wall I've been working on, when my phone rings. I assume it's Cami asking me why I'm still at the gallery—she watches the video feeds and alarm system like a hawk—or Finley, so when I see Deacon's name on the screen, my heart jumps in my chest.

"Hello?"

For a second, there's no response and I wonder if he butt-dialed me or something.

"Deacon?"

When he finally speaks, he sounds out-of-breath and my heart kicks it into high gear again. "Georgette? Can you hear me?"

"Yes, I'm here. Is Cami okay?"

"Uh, yeah… she's, well… her water broke and I brought her to the hospital. We're going to have a baby today, but the doctor said the cord is wrapped so he's taking her by c-section."

Her.

It's a girl.

They've been keeping that a secret.

But now, I'm worried. "Should I come? Can I come… to the hospital?"

"Of course," Deacon says, sounding distracted and a little unnerved, which makes me feel unnerved because he's always so laid back and calm. "Cami wanted you to know, she'd want you here."

That settles it. "I'll be there as soon as I can," I tell him, walking over to grab my bag as I run down the mental checklist of closing up the gallery: back door, lights, alarm. "And Deacon?" I ask, making sure he's still on the line.

"Yeah?"

"She's going to be fine... better than fine. I just know it."

Please, God, let it be so.

After locking up, I pull out my phone and dial Finley. I'm not sure if I should try to get to him or have him come to me, or if he'll even be able to come with me, but I want him to know what's happening. Logically, the van seems like the best mode of transportation, but then I remember... Mardi Gras.

When Finn's voicemail picks up, I step back from the door and look down at my phone. It's not like him to not answer, but he might still be in the studio with Lola, in which case, his phone is on silent.

He had to go in to fix a track for an artist.

Apparently, even Mardi Gras doesn't come between big names and deadlines.

Feeling stuck, I walk to the edge of the building and look around to see if I would even be able to get the van out onto the street. The immediate vicinity is open, but that doesn't mean I'd be able to make it all the way to Canal or Decatur, which are my two best bets of getting to I-10. New Orleans is a tough city to navigate on a good day.

Looking down at my phone again, I think about texting Finn, but that wouldn't really do any good. I need to talk to him and get him to help me figure this out.

I could walk to Canal and take the streetcar down to the Garden District and then call him again. At least I'd be closer to him and then maybe he'd have an idea on getting out of the city.

Standing here in this back alley is making me feel antsy.

Going back into the gallery isn't an option. There's no way I can go back to work and the place was already making me feel stir crazy even before I found out Cami's water broke.

And the baby.

God, I need to get to her or at least do something that feels productive.

Walking down the sidewalk, I squeeze my way through and around groups of people, feeling more claustrophobic than I ever did on the streets of New York City. By the time I make it to the corner where Finley typically plays, another idea comes to me.

Pulling my phone back out, I dial Dani.

No answer.

Shit.

Shit, shit, shit.

My next phone call is to CeCe, who thankfully picks up on the fourth ring.

"Neutral Grounds?" she answers, sounding uncharacteristically frazzled. What the hell is happening with all of my even-tempered friends today? "Oh, shit. Sorry… I forgot this was my cell," she mutters to me or herself, I'm not sure. "Hello?"

"CeCe?" Looking around me I realize it will take me a good while to get just about anywhere. The street I normally cross over to get to Canal is blocked again by a barricade.

"Georgette?" The sounds of the espresso machine are drowned out by voices. I'm guessing Neutral Grounds looks a lot like the sidewalk I'm standing on—packed to the gills. "Where are you?"

"Uh, Royal Street, trying to figure out how to get out of this madness!" My voice rises as a smidge of panic sets in. "Cami went into labor and I'm worried about her so I closed up the gallery to drive to the hospital but now I don't know how I'd even get out of the Quarter, let alone the city…" I pause, feeling the weight of the moment crash down on me. "I just wanted to go to the hospital and be there."

"Deep breaths," she says, regaining some of her usual calm, cool demeanor. "What about Cami? I missed a call from Deacon earlier but when I called him back it went to voicemail."

"I don't know much… he couldn't talk long," I tell her as a guy pushes me into the side of the building I'm standing next to. Not on purpose, but due to the lack of space as people pass by.

When I let out a grunt, CeCe asks, "Are you okay?"

"Fine," I say, wincing as I rub the sting away on my shoulder. "Should've worn some football pads today. Anyway," I continue, "Deacon just said Cami's water broke and the cord is wrapped around the baby and they want to do a c-section. I know they don't need me there, but the thought of staying put had me feeling anxious, so I thought about driving to Baton Rouge, but now…"

"Not a good idea, babe," CeCe says, the phone rustling as she calls out an order. "And I'm sure the baby and Cami are going to be fine. She's a pro and Deacon would never let anything happen to her."

She's right.

I know she's right.

"We'll all go tomorrow when the dust settles," she urges. "Now, either get back in the gallery or get here. You don't need to be out on the streets by yourself. Where's Finn?"

"Studio," I tell her, glancing around and trying to decide my next move. "I guess I'm coming to Neutral Grounds. It's better than sitting at the gallery, worrying by myself."

"Okay," she says with a sigh. "Be safe and I'll see you soon."

23

Finley

WALKING INTO NEUTRAL GROUNDS, I FEEL LIKE I'VE RUN A
marathon and walked through a maze to get here. I knew today would
be crazy, but I had no clue on what level.

When CeCe sees me, she motions for me to come behind the counter,
which is a feat in itself considering every inch of the shop is occupied
with a body. I've never seen anything like it. It's like Black Friday at Wal-
Mart, which I've never experienced first-hand, but I've seen the news
when someone gets trampled as they open the doors.

That could totally happen today.

"Hey," I say, looking around to see if I can be of assistance. "Need me
to throw on an apron?"

She blows a strand of hair out of her face and glances over her
shoulder. "I think we've got it and Shep's on his way over to give us a
hand, but if you're going to be around for a while, maybe you could give
Paige a break?"

"Sure," I tell her, reaching over to grab an apron.

"Is Georgette with you?" she asks, standing on her tiptoes so see out over the people.

I shake my head as I fiddle with the strings of the apron. "No, I figure she'll call when she's finished at the gallery. I don't have to be at the club until six, so I wanted to stop by here and freshen up before heading back out."

CeCe's concerned expression has me pausing.

"What?"

She cuts her eyes to the door and then back at me. "Well, she called a while ago and said Deacon called her and Cami's water broke, but there're some complications and they want to do a c-section."

"What?" I ask, trepidation starting to flood my veins. Not only for Cami and the baby, but Georgette too. I know how she feels about Cami and she'll be worried.

CeCe huffs and then bites down on her lip, thinking. "Maybe you should go look for her. When she called, she'd already locked up the gallery and was on Royal trying to make her way here."

"How long ago?" I ask, taking the apron back off and tossing it to the side.

"Half an hour… maybe a little more." She looks over at the clock and then back out at the line of customers. "I'm not sure. I've kind of lost track of time and space today."

"Royal Street was a nightmare. I had to wind my way around and it took me forever. No telling where she's at and there are several parades going on…" That ember of worry is now blazing as I make my way toward the back hallway. "I'll be back. If she shows up, tell her to wait here."

Fuck.

I'm sure she's fine, but I hate the idea of her being out there alone. The urge to go all caveman and murder someone if even a single blonde curl is out of place is strong, but I try to tamper it down.

It's fine.

She's fine.

Everything is fine.

Cutting across the narrow back alley, I make my way out to Royal, keeping my eyes peeled for Jette and trying to guess where she'd go. As I make it to the first corner, it's just like the other end of the street and the road is blocked. Turning right and then left, I decide to head toward Decatur.

Maybe Jette tried to stay on the main thoroughfares.

Pulling my phone out, I see a missed call and kick myself for not checking sooner. Lola and I got straight to work when I got to the studio and we didn't stop until we were finished re-recording the track we've been working on. She didn't want to be in the studio today, which I don't blame her for. The excitement of the streets is distracting, if nothing else. And the fanfare is incredible. I've never seen anything like it.

However, I'd be able to enjoy it a lot better if I could find Jette and know she's safe.

Then, *laissez les bon temps rouler.*

Until then, I want to magically shut this place down until I find her.

Dialing her number, I close my eyes, praying she answers. Hearing her voice would do wonders for the panic that's building in my chest. "Pick up," I mutter, stepping into an alcove to avoid a group of people having their own parade down the sidewalk—whistles and horns and the whole nine yards.

"Hello?" Jette answers, sounding as out of breath as I feel.

"Jette?"

"Finn," she replies, relief flooding her voice. "God, this is insanity."

"Where are you?"

There's a long pause and I'm afraid the call has dropped, but then she answers, "Decatur and… shit, I don't know, I've lost track of how many times I've cut over and backtracked trying to get around these parade routes."

I want to yell at her, ask her what she was thinking leaving the gallery. We should've made a better plan for the day. But here we are, traversing this new city together, as long as she's okay, everything is going to be fine.

"What do you see?" I ask. "Just give me a landmark or two and I'll come to you."

She tells me the names of a couple of businesses by her and I use my GPS to locate her. Fifteen minutes later, I turn a corner and see her gorgeous blonde hair as she huddles next to a storefront that's closed down. "Finn!"

Running the rest of the way, dodging people as I go, I literally pick her up off her feet when I reach her, hugging her to me. "I swear, I'll always find you, but I wish you'd stop running away from me."

She laughs breathlessly, squeezing my neck. "I swear, I've never intentionally tried to leave you."

There's something about this exchange that's bigger than the moment. But I meant what I said, I'll always find her… always. Because she's mine and I'm hers and nothing or no one will keep us apart, not even a crazy-ass Fat Tuesday.

"Let's go," I tell her, placing her back on her feet. "CeCe will be putting out an APB on your ass if we don't. She'll need to see you with her own eyes to know you're safe."

Hand in hand, we make our way back to Neutral Grounds, taking the route I used to find her.

When we walk into the shop, the crowd has thinned some and Shep is behind the counter making drinks while CeCe and Paige stock the bar.

"God," CeCe exclaims, setting down a stack of cups and walking over to us. "You scared the shit out of me!" She pulls Jette into a hug and gives me a look over her shoulder.

She was genuinely worried.

Yeah, me too.

"I was about to call in some favors," Shep says when he sees us. "You good?"

The question is directed at Jette and she nods, taking a deep breath. "Yeah, I'm good."

"Let me get you something," CeCe says, always needing to feed somebody. "What sounds good? Sandwich? Coffee?"

"Maybe just a coffee… and a couch," Jette says with a laugh. "I feel like I've been walking for miles."

Once CeCe makes us both a drink, I turn to Jette. "Want to take these upstairs?"

She nods, silently agreeing, and follows me to the staircase.

While I'm in the shower, Jette makes herself at home on the couch, just like she said. After I'm dressed, I walk back into the living room to find her staring at her phone.

"Still no call?"

Sighing, she falls back on the couch. "No, and I know these things take time, but it's been almost three hours since Deacon called. Surely, there's a baby by now… right?"

I see the worry on her face and I wish I could take it all away. "How about you try Dani again? I'm sure she's made it there by now and even if she hasn't, she'll know something."

Jette blows out a deep breath and starts to dial, but before she can, there's a knock at the door.

"It's a girl," CeCe yells through the door before I can open it. "It's a girl!"

Jette is off the couch and flinging the door open before I can get to it. She and CeCe hug each other like one of them just had the baby. I can't help the stupid smile on my face and the immense relief I feel.

"Oh, my God," Jette gushes, wiping away a few tears. "What's her name?"

CeCe braces her hand on the door frame and catches her breath. "June Sunny Landry. Six pounds, seven ounces, and twenty inches long. Annie called the shop because she didn't have anyone's personal numbers, which she wasn't happy about, by the way. But she said she's perfect and Cami is doing great."

They hug again and then CeCe heads back downstairs.

"What a freaking day," Jette groans, walking toward me and falling into my chest. "How lame would it be for me to spend my first Mardi Gras in New Orleans at home with our dog?"

Kissing the top of her head, I hold her, wishing I could stay home with her and our dog too. And if that makes me lame, I really don't give a shit. But alas, I am a musician in New Orleans on its biggest night of the year.

"Come on, I'll walk you home."

24

Georgette

Lazily, Finn runs a finger up my spine causing chills to follow in its wake.

"Cold?" he asks, his voice just as lazy as his actions. It's Saturday, and for most people, that means a day off, but not for me and Finn. I have to be at the gallery in a couple of hours and Finley has another studio session with Lola today.

But tonight, he's taking me to Lagniappe for a date.

A smile stretches across my face. "Quite the opposite," I finally answer, loving the feel of his skin against mine. "I'm feeling very... very... warm."

I feel Finn lean closer and then his breath blows across my skin. Closing my eyes, I swallow the moan that tries to escape, biting down on my lip. Then, his lips replace his breath and I'm not strong enough to hold back my appreciation of his attention.

"You taste so sweet," Finn mutters against my skin. "The best thing I've ever put in my mouth... I knew it years ago, but it's even better now... somehow."

Straddling my body, he kneels behind me, hands caressing my hips.

I feel his hair brush my back as he bends over to kiss down my spine. When he works his way to my core, I'm a writhing mess, quietly panting and begging him for more.

And he delivers.

Finley always delivers.

An hour later, after separate showers, because we now know we can't get ready in a timely manner if we take one together, we're both dressing, King laying on the bed watching us like a Pong game.

"Maybe you can come with us one of these days, buddy," I tell him. "I've been thinking about asking Cami if King can come to the gallery with me sometime. He's such a good boy. I don't think she'd mind."

Finn smiles, shaking his head. "I knew that was coming."

"What?" I ask, slipping on my flats. "I hate that he's here by himself so much."

"You do remember he's a dog, right?"

Leaning over the bed to nuzzle his nose, I coo. "He's the best dog ever. Aren't you, King?" Standing up, I level Finn with my gaze through the mirror on the dresser. "Don't act like I'm the only one who babies him."

Finn tries to act like he's innocent, but he's so not. I've caught him several times feeding him straight from his plate, even though we agreed we wouldn't give him people food. *And* he lets him on the bed, even though we agreed he'd sleep on his own bed in the corner.

It seriously has a better mattress than the one we sleep on.

"Let's go," Finn says, patting his leg for King to follow, and I feel my heart fill even more as the two of them patter down the stairs, Finley murmuring to King as they leave.

I SWEAR, THIS HAS BEEN THE LONGEST WEEK IN THE HISTORY OF

weeks.

Fat Tuesday seems like a month ago instead of four days.

CeCe, Shep, Finley, and I finally got to go see the baby and Cami yesterday. After hearing everything was fine and Cami and the baby were healthy, we all decided to give Cami and Deacon some space and wait for her to be discharged from the hospital before visiting.

And I turned it into a multi-purpose trip, picking up a few of Cami's pieces while I was in town.

Little Junie is perfect, of course. She looks like Cami with her blonde hair and petite features. I have no clue how Cami is going to leave her to come back to work, but she swears she'll be back when the doctor releases her. However, that will now be closer to two months, instead of the four weeks she'd planned on, but we'll manage. I assured her of that.

The gallery is getting easier to handle on my own. With Mardi Gras behind us, the city is back to its usual buzz of activity, instead of the building roar of carnival.

Finley, King, and I have fallen into a comfortable routine that I could live with forever.

On most nights, Finley sleeps at my house, with extra-curricular activities added in. We sit on my small back porch and watch King run around the backyard. We snuggle on the couch. Some nights I go with Finn to Good Times and listen to him play.

All I want is to finish out this day and meet Finley at Lagniappe for our date.

And then stay in bed with him all day tomorrow.

The saying *living my best life* runs through my mind just as the gallery phone rings.

Hurrying over to the desk, I pick it up. "303 Royal Street. How can I help you?"

The person on the other end of the line, Mrs. Fitzpatrick, is interested in buying a small collection of pieces for her house in the Garden District. A friend of hers recently purchased a painting from us and she's looking for something by the same artist.

"I'd love to set up an appointment with you and show you what we have available. If none of our current collection fits what you're looking for, we could discuss a commission," I tell her, walking around to look at the schedule. "With our artists being local, it gives us the luxury of meeting our clients' needs in a variety of ways."

After I pencil her in for an appointment next Tuesday, she asks if I might know someone who would be willing to do a portrait of her dog. To which I tell her, I'd be delighted to find an artist and gather a portfolio for her to look over when she's here next week.

Sometimes, my job is straightforward and to the point.

Other times, it's unconventional and spontaneous.

No matter what, each client is different and I love that aspect.

Being a Saturday, the foot traffic on Royal is steady, but not many people have walked in today. However, as I'm looking over the schedule for next week, I hear the chime of the front door.

"Welcome to 303 Royal," I greet before looking up, my heart stopping in my chest.

25

Finley

Hopping off the streetcar at Canal, I have a little
extra pep in my step and loads of good news to share with Jette tonight
over dinner. I've never been one to care about a paycheck or how much
money I've made or have.

For my entire life, it's always been about following my passion—be it
the saxophone or Jette.

But I won't lie and say the check in my pocket doesn't mean something
to me, as does the new contract I just signed with Lola's production
company.

It means stability.

It means providing for Jette.

It means living my life in comfort while still doing what I love.

It means I've officially got everything I've ever dreamed of, with the
exception of a few things.

One of those being making Georgette Taylor my wife.

And the second, giving her the desires of her heart—a family, a home.

When I reach the corner of Royal and Canal, there's a woman standing with a bucket of flowers. Spontaneously, I walk up to her and pull out a twenty from my pocket. "How much?" I ask, pointing to the bouquet of wildflowers—untamed and free, just like my beautiful girl.

"Ten," she replies, pulling one of the fullest bunches from the bucket. "For you."

I smile, accepting them from her as I hand her the twenty. "Keep the change."

"May you be blessed with warmth in your home, love in your heart, peace in your soul, and joy in your life," she says, her smile in return as bright as the New Orleans sky.

Nodding my head in gratitude, I turn and continue toward the gallery. Mardi Gras was a rush and I made more tips this past week than I've ever made in my life, but I'm glad it's over. The streets are still busy, but comfortably so, and every person I've passed has a smile to offer.

There really is no place like this city and the people in it.

When I get to the gallery, I do what I always do and peek inside the front window, hoping for a glimpse of Jette in her element. Admiring her when she's not looking is one of my favorite pastimes.

But what I see stops me in my tracks.

My feet moving on autopilot, I walk to the door and open it, stepping inside the gallery.

Jette's mom is the first to notice me and the look on her face tells me I'm unwelcome and the last person she thought she'd be seeing today.

"What is he doing here?" she sneers, causing Jette to turn her attention from the man kneeling in front of her to me.

"Finley," Jette gushes, her eyes going wide, looking just as shocked as I feel.

Trevor stands, turning to face me and then looks back at Jette. "Wait? This is Finley?" His expression is confused as he looks back and forth between the two of us. "I thought…"

"Finley Lawson," Jette says, her confidence seeping back into her body as our eyes lock. "This is Trevor Armstrong. Trevor *this* is Finley."

Her mother huffs as her father steps forward, taking over the conversation and puffing out his chest. "What are you doing here? Georgette, what's going on here?" he demands.

Jette clears her throat, swallowing. "Finley lives here, in New Orleans." I watch as she squares her shoulders and faces her father. "And we're together."

"Oh, God, Georgette, not this again. I thought you got over this ridiculous crush when you moved to New York, which is one of the reasons your father and I didn't demand you return home. And then you met Trevor and we felt like it all happened for a reason. We couldn't have orchestrated it better." She pauses, glaring at me. "Please, don't throw your life away for *this*."

Throwing her arm out, she points at me, looking at Jette.

"Trevor came all this way to tell you he wants to marry you. Isn't that what you wanted? The reason you came to New Orleans in the first place? To prove your point?" Her mother's voice raises with each question, her sophisticated demeanor slipping. "Point proven, Georgette. Your little stunt can be over now and you can accept Trevor's proposal and get on with your life."

I watch as Jette's head falls to her chest and I see her breathing deeply, trying to get a grip on what's happening. Unable to watch her suffer in any way, I decide now is the best chance I'm ever going to get to say my piece, leaving my heart on the line… all for her.

"When I was sixteen," I begin, glancing at Jette, whose head snaps up to look at me. "You kicked me out of your house and told Georgette she couldn't see me anymore. I didn't really know any better... I didn't know to stand up for myself or that I could. I was a kid and I'd been beaten down my entire life before I went to live with Maggie. Unfortunately, for a time, I believed the hate you spewed. I believed you when you said I wasn't good enough for Georgette."

Pausing, I give Jette a sad smile, remembering back to the days when we had to sneak around to see each other and how much worth she gave my life every time she took a chance on me.

"Thank goodness, she didn't listen to you," I continue. "Thank goodness, she saw the good in me. Because now I know none of what you said is true."

Looking back at them, locking eyes with her father and hoping he hears every word I'm about to say. "I am good enough for Georgette and I know I can make her happy. I know what she wants and I want to give it to her. She would never have to doubt or question my love for her because I would show her every single day."

"Every single day," I repeat, my eyes finding hers, a promise I hope she feels down to her soul. "She would never have to doubt where she stands in my life because I would always put her first, above everything else."

Jette's mother is standing there, mouth agape, while her father clears his throat and adjusts his tie, trying to seem unfazed by my words. Honestly, I don't care. All I care is that Jette hears them, loud and clear, and knows they're true.

"You should want her to be happy," I tell them. "She's your only child and I've never even heard you tell her you love her."

I hear Jette, rather than see her—quiet sniffles filling the gallery—and I can't bring myself to make eye contact.

"And you don't deserve her," I tell Trevor, my hand gripping the door handle behind me, needing to get some air and clear my head. And more than anything, I want to give Jette a chance to make her own choices, hoping she takes this opportunity to stand up to her parents, once and for all. "You had your chance to make her happy and you blew it."

Before I walk out, I call back to Jette, telling her to call me. The ball is in her court, she deserves this chance to make her own choices and call her own shots. I won't force her hand. More than anything else in the entire world, I want Jette to be happy.

Before the door closes behind me, I hear her call my name but I don't turn around. I can't. If I see her upset, I won't be able to walk away.

When I make it down the block, just before crossing the street, I stop and brace my hands on my knees. Breathing deeply, I close my eyes and tilt my head to the sky.

"Please, God."

The prayer is barely out of my mouth when my phone rings. Not even looking at the screen, I answer, bracing myself for whatever she has to say. But it's not Jette.

"Finley?" a familiar voice asks, breaking through the haze. "Are you there?"

"Aunt Stella?"

When I hear her begin to cry, my body goes rigid. "Aunt Stella? Are you okay? Where's Maggie?"

26

Georgette

"**GEORGETTE?**"

My name coming from Trevor is somewhere between a question and a plea, pulling me from under the flood of emotions left in Finley's wake. Brushing away the moisture under my eyes, I inhale a cleansing breath, never more sure of what I want to say.

"Please leave," I say in a quiet, even tone.

"Georgette?" Trevor asks again, this time his voice shifting to anger. "I asked you to marry me. For months, that's what you've wanted. You can't tell me whatever happened between then and now changes your feelings about me."

"You already know how I feel about you," I tell him, crossing my arms over my chest. "That hasn't changed."

"Were you screwing him?" Trevor spits. "Is that why you're standing here giving me whiplash with this bullshit?"

His accusation feels like a slap in the face and I flinch at his words. "No," I grit, trying to keep my emotions under control. "My decision to end things between us had nothing to do with Finley and everything to do with me. We haven't been in a good place in a long time—"

"Because you're always giving me grief," he snaps, cutting me off. "For fuck's sake, Georgette. You went from wanting to marry me to accepting this ridiculous job, I couldn't keep up. You couldn't even give me a damn minute to figure out what I want."

Huffing a laugh, I shake my head. "And now you know what you want?"

"Yes," he says, softer this time, his eyes pleading. "I... I want what you want."

Feeling my parents' presence, pressuring me as always, I close my eyes and try to push it all away, remembering Finn's words and drawing strength from them. Specifically remembering when he told me my love gives him courage.

Same, Finn... same.

"And what is that, Trevor?" I ask, just wanting this to all be over so I can go find Finley. "What do I want?"

He gives me a confused expression, hands on his hips. "Marriage?" he asks, like he's choosing a multiple-choice answer. But this isn't a multiple-choice question. "You know what? Why don't you just tell me what you want and I'll make it happen. What's your price, Georgette?"

A coolness settles over me and I take a step back. "I'm not for sale."

"Georgette," my father warns. When I turn to look at him, I see the same warning in my mother's eyes, her unspoken threat from earlier this week coming back.

"I love Finley," I tell him...her, Trevor, and anyone who will listen. "He's all I've ever truly wanted. If you can't accept that, then you can't accept me, so please leave."

My mother's face is blazing with anger as she passes me without a backward glance. My father follows her and they both vacate the gallery. Then, it's just me and Trevor.

"So, this is it?" Trevor asks, resignation written all over his face.

"Yeah, Trevor, this is it," I sigh, feeling exhausted from it all. "Finley is it for me. It's always been him, I just lost him for a while, but now he's back and he's reclaimed what was always his. You don't want me, Trevor... it never would've worked out between us anyway. We're two different people who want different things in life. Consider this a second chance to go find what makes you happy, because I have."

Exhaling, he nods slightly before turning toward the door and walking out—out of the gallery and out of my life.

Packing up my things, I shut off the lights, turn on the alarm and place a note in the window that says the gallery will reopen on Monday morning. After locking the door, I look both ways, wondering if he's waiting for me somewhere close by. If I know Finn, he didn't go far, probably just out of view so he wouldn't have to deal with my parents or Trevor as they left the gallery. I'm close to calling out for him, expecting him to materialize from the side of the building, but he doesn't.

Where are you, Finn?

I begin to feel antsy as thoughts of where he might've gone start flooding my mind. I know he was upset, so maybe he went to talk to Shep or maybe he went back to his apartment to wait for me there. I know he said to call, but I just need to see him.

At this point, his embrace is the only thing that's going to settle my nerves and emotions. Finley is the soothing balm my soul needs. Plus, I know walking in on Trevor proposing was the last thing he expected to see today and I want to assure him Trevor has no place in my life.

It's only him.

It's always been Finley.

As I begin to jog down the sidewalk, a group of people block my path and I find myself throwing a few elbows to get past them. Normally, I'm not that aggressive, but the urgency I feel inside is taking over.

"Sorry," I call out, taking off in more of a sprint the closer I get to Neutral Grounds. By the time I open the front door, I'm out of breath and probably looking as frazzled as I feel.

"Welcome to—" Paige's words are cut off when she sees it's me and takes in my demeanor. "Georgette? Is everything okay?"

"Finley...is he here? Have you seen him?" Swallowing down air, I try to calm my breathing. All that King Cake Cami forced me to eat when I first moved here, paired with CeCe's chocolate croissants, and my lack of gym time have officially caught up with me.

She shakes her head wearily. "No, I haven't seen him."

Feeling close to tears again, I bite down on my lip. Surely he wouldn't have gone anywhere... he has to know I would never accept Trevor's proposal and that I would come looking for him.

"But I did just get here about twenty minutes ago, so you might call CeCe and see if he was here before I showed up. Is everything okay?"

I take a deep breath, assuring myself everything is fine before telling Paige the same thing and bolting out the door in search of Finley.

My next stop is Good Times. Music has always soothed his soul, maybe he needed to go there and clear his head or just escape for a while. On my walk there, I call CeCe, but she doesn't answer.

When I make it to the club, I open the door and expect to see him on stage or at the bar, but both are vacant. As I look around the space, I don't see any familiar faces, except the bartender, so I walk up and wait as he mixes a drink.

"What can I get for ya?" he asks before realizing who I am. "Oh, didn't expect to see you here without Finn." Cocking his head, he looks around. "Everything okay?"

Why does everyone keep asking me that?

"Fine," I tell him. "Just looking for Finn, but I'm guessing you haven't seen him?"

His face falls a bit and his brows furrow. "Haven't seen him today. You sure you're okay?"

"Yeah," I tell him, pushing away from the bar. "I'm fine." I start to walk away, but stop short of the door and turn back to him. "If you see him, would you please tell him I'm looking for him?"

"Will do," he says. "Take care."

Giving him the best smile I can muster, I turn for the door and walk back out onto the sidewalk feeling a bit lost and defeated.

"Where are you, Finley?" I whisper, willing him, once again, to appear out of thin air. When that doesn't happen, I start walking toward my house, hoping that's where he decided to go. Maybe he's sitting on my front steps waiting for me while I've been running around the French Quarter.

But the only person waiting for me, well dog waiting for me, is King.

Pulling my phone out, I dial Finn's number, expecting him to answer, just as out of breath and worried as I am, but he doesn't.

"Finn," I say, speaking to his voicemail. "It's me. You said to call you but I needed to see you so I went to Neutral Grounds and then to Good Times. You're weren't there...obviously." I feel my cheeks heat at the absurdity of my message. Of course, he wasn't there, and of course, he knows that. "Call me, please."

Once I let King into the house, I give myself a moment to cry into his fur, soaking up his affection as I let out the stress and frustration of the last couple of hours. When I'm done, he licks my cheeks and then we share a spoonful of peanut butter while we watch reruns of *Friends* on the couch.

Every once in a while, he looks toward the door, like he is anticipating Finley's presence even more than I am. "I know, buddy," I say, rubbing his ears. "He'll be back. Don't worry."

Those words are more for me than him, but we both take comfort in them while we wait.

27

Finley

FUCK, I HATE FLYING.

After nearly missing my flight from New Orleans to Houston and a layover that barely lasted long enough to get from one gate to the next, I'm finally on the last leg of my trip to Odessa.

Maggie, my grandmother and closest relative, had a heart attack today and I wasn't there.

In fact, I'm having a hard time right now remembering the last time we talked. When I first moved, she made me call her at least once a week so she could keep tabs on me but those calls fell by the wayside once Jette came back into my life.

I keep replaying the conversation we had when she decided to move in with her sister after Shep's parents fired her last year. Knowing I didn't want to move with her but still unsure of where I should go, she simply told me to follow my heart.

"You'll not only survive, you'll thrive wherever you plant your feet, Finley Lawson. You've fought your entire life and you deserve to be happy, so go where your heart leads you."

I doubt she had any idea how prophetic her words were at the time but they were exactly what I needed to hear at that moment and they led me to the French Quarter and back to Jette.

Jette.

God, I sigh and run a hand down my face as my gut twists at the mere thought of her name.

She has no idea where I am right now and I feel like complete shit for leaving her the way I did. Initially, I only planned to step out of the gallery to give her the opportunity to speak for herself without any added pressure my presence was bringing. The last thing I wanted was for her parents to have any doubt that whatever decision Jette made wasn't one hundred percent her choice.

She deserves that.

Then, I got the call about Maggie from her sister and just started running.

Thankfully, Shep was at Neutral Grounds when I got there. After I told him what had happened, he jumped into action and bought my plane ticket while I threw some clothes and toiletries in a bag and CeCe scheduled an Uber.

Now, here I sit, trying not to let my fidgeting upset the man sitting next to me while I deal with my guilt over so many things.

When I left the gallery and told Jette to call me, I didn't think she'd wait so long. The whole fifteen-minute ride to the airport, I kept checking my phone.

During my layover, I powered it back on, expecting a missed call, but nothing.

So, now my mind is running rampant, thinking the worst. I still can't believe what I walked in on today—Jette's parents and Trevor down on one knee.

Fucking proposing. To my girl.

The thought makes me want to punch something, but I can't. I'm on a flight and I don't need my ass getting kicked off between here and Odessa. Also, I don't have the brain space to think about that right now. All I can do is pray Jette is okay and that she made whatever decision is going to make her happy. The rest, I'll just have to live with.

Right now, I have to focus on getting to Maggie.

When Aunt Stella called to tell me Maggie had a heart attack, it was way too soon for any kind of prognosis, so I have no idea what to expect when I get there.

Please, God, let her be okay. I swear I'll call her more often and visit when I can. Just don't take her away from me.

I never even told her I'd found Jette again, but it'll be the first thing I tell her once I know she's okay.

She's gonna be so happy, I just know it. She used to always tell me how sorry she was that Shep and Jette, both, had such awful parents. I tried blaming their wealth on their lousy personalities but she disagreed.

"Some people are rotten, Finley, and money, whether you have it or you don't, can exaggerate a person's attributes. If you're hateful and poor, money won't make you nice all of a sudden and vice versa. That's why it's more important to focus on what's inside their hearts rather than their bank accounts."

She was so wise… *is* wise. I refuse to think of her in the past tense.

I owe everything to her. She took me in when I had no one else. She provided for me and helped me when I struggled with my studies at my fancy new school before I met Jette. She's always encouraged and supported me and even though I'm dying to be with Jette, and it's literally killing me to think about her being alone, Maggie needs me more.

Somehow, I manage to doze off mid-flight and wake just as the plane touches down. It wasn't much of a nap, but I do feel a little more alert. It could just be all the adrenaline and fear of the unknown.

Shouldering my bag, I deboard the plane as quickly as possible and power up my phone to schedule an Uber to take me straight to the hospital.

Thankfully, there's a missed call from Jette. Just seeing her name pop up on my screen puts my body at ease a little. Shep also called while I was mid-flight, because even though he knew I wouldn't be able to answer, it's killing him to stay in New Orleans and not be here in Odessa with me. Right now, I'm his connection to Maggie and he needs her to be okay just as much as I do.

First, I schedule the Uber and then just as I'm getting ready to call Jette, my screen goes black.

Fucking perfect.

Of course, my phone would die.

For a day that felt like it was going so right only a short time ago, it's sure gone to shit fast.

At least I remember the make and model of the Uber driver's car that's supposed to be picking me up, so I run to the rideshare exit to wait, convincing myself Jette will forgive me once I'm finally able to explain.

I'll grovel forever if I have to.

Once I'm at the hospital, I head straight to the emergency room admissions desk and give my name to the lady there. Aunt Stella said she'd give the nursing staff my name so they'd know to expect me since it's late and past normal visiting hours. The nurse informs me Maggie has been moved to a room in the cardiac care unit, which is a positive sign, and tells me her room number.

My stomach twists as I make my way down the corridor.

I think I hate hospitals more than flying.

When I get to the correct floor, a new nurse points me in the direction of Maggie's room. I don't hesitate, practically running down the hall before gently knocking on the door.

Aunt Stella opens it, peeking out. Relief washes over her face when she sees me. "Oh, Finley. I'm so glad you're finally here," she whispers, giving me a quick hug before leading me into the room.

"How is she?" I ask tentatively.

Like Stella, I'm relieved to be here, but I'm also nervous about what I'm walking in on.

"She's still in surgery," she informs me and it's then I notice the spot where her bed should be is empty. "Maggie has always been in perfect health; I'm just shocked over this whole ordeal."

Stella wipes at her eyes with a tissue. "The doctor said she needed a bypass. Can you believe that?"

I can tell she's scared for her sister and I can only imagine how traumatizing the day has been for her, so I pull her into a hug and try to be strong for her, but I'm scared, too. I can't even begin to think of a life where Maggie isn't here and I don't want to try.

Aunt Stella and I are only in the room for a short while before the door is suddenly pushed open, making way for a team of nurses to wheel in the gurney that's carrying my grandmother.

When one of them notices us, she politely asks us to wait in the hall while they get Maggie situated and promises the doctor will be by soon to give us an update.

"Of course," Aunt Stella says, taking my hand. "Come on, Finley, let's get a cup of coffee."

I follow her lead, my eyes scanning Maggie's face on my way out. She looks so pale, and in her unconscious state she doesn't look like herself, which causes more worry and dread to fill my stomach.

When we reach the alcove where the coffee is, Aunt Stella pours two cups with shaking hands, giving one of them to me. I welcome the familiar burn, even though my taste buds aren't registering the flavor, which is probably a good thing.

"How was your trip?" Aunt Stella asks, her eyes bloodshot from the tears, but her face still so comforting. She and Maggie look so much alike, it's uncanny.

"Fast, but yet slow at the same time," I tell her with a chuckle, running a hand through my hair. "This whole day has felt like an episode of the *Twilight Zone*."

"I'm sorry—" she starts to say, but doesn't get a chance to finish before a nurse steps out of Maggie's room to finds us.

Both Aunt Stella and I abandon our coffees and go to her. She informs us a doctor will be around soon to give us details about the surgery and Maggie's condition, but since it's after visiting hours, only one of us can stay.

I immediately volunteer.

There's no way I'm leaving her alone. Plus, Aunt Stella needs to go home and rest. This day has already been so hard on her.

"Are you sure?" Aunt Stella asks.

I nod. "I'm positive. But if you want to go inside and see her before you leave, I'll wait out here."

She gives me a soft smile, patting my cheek.

A few minutes later, she returns, tears in her eyes and her purse under her arm.

Dabbing her eyes with a hankie, she sniffles. "If you change your mind, we have an extra bedroom you're more than welcome to use. She won't even know you left, I'm sure."

Shaking my head, I look past her into Maggie's room, seeing her still form. "No, I'm staying," I assure her. "I don't want her to be alone."

"Such a good boy," she says, her hand squeezing my arm. "I'll be back bright and early in the morning, but please call me if anything changes." She looks back, hesitating for a moment, but then turns to me with a reassuring smile. "She's going to be fine."

I nod, leaning in for one more hug, and then she leaves.

Walking quietly into the room, I try to believe Aunt Stella's words, but it's hard to see someone who has always been a pillar of strength lying in a bed, looking so weak.

There are wires everywhere, connecting her to machines that beep and hiss, doing God knows what.

And I've never felt so helpless in all my life.

"Maggie." The sound of my voice is foreign to me, a broken whisper full of emotion I can't hold back. Standing beside the bed, I gently take her hand in mine, careful not to disrupt anything.

Reaching behind me, I pull a chair over and sit, not wanting to let go of her hand. I can't rub my thumb over her wrinkled skin because of the IV that's attached, so I hold onto her fingers, needing the contact.

The hardest part is seeing the tube sticking out of her mouth, breathing for her. It makes the reality of the situation hit me square in the gut.

Please, God... please.

Leaning my head on the railing of her bed, I pray more than I've ever prayed in my entire life.

At some point, I must fall asleep, because when the door opens behind me, I jump.

Turning, I see an older man in a white coat walk into the room. He introduces himself and sticks his hand out, forcing me to let go of Maggie's to shake it.

"How long will she be out of it?" I don't want small talk; I only want answers.

"She should sleep for the remainder of the night. We want her body to rest so it can start healing as quickly as possible." Walking around to the foot of her bed, he pulls out a chart, looking over it as he continues to speak. "As a warning, when she does wake up, she's going to be very disoriented and confused, especially once she realizes the tube in her mouth is keeping her from speaking. If a staff member isn't in here, please buzz the nurse as soon as possible."

I nod my head in understanding. "And then what? What will her recovery be like? I'm assuming the surgery worked?"

"Yes, the procedure was very successful but she still has a long road ahead of her. She'll be in pain for at least a few days. We, of course, will provide her with pain meds to help as much as possible. If all goes well, she should be able to go home in a few days but she'll need lots of rest. It's imperative that she not exert herself in any way."

My mind is racing at all the what-ifs and uncertainty I'm feeling. "How long will she be in recovery? Will she need any special services once we take her home?"

He replaces the chart, putting his hands into the pockets of his coat. "It could take up to six weeks, if all goes well, and as long as she's not overdoing it and her incision heals well, she won't need special services outside of cardiac rehab. But we'll worry about all of those details in a few days."

Pausing, he smiles. "I can tell you love your grandmother very much and she's lucky to have you and her sister to care for her."

I nod. "I do, and yes, we'll take good care of her. Thank you, doctor."

"Have a good night, Mr. Lawson. I'll be back in the morning."

A few minutes later, a nurse comes in with some blankets and pillows and shows me how to open the couch by the window into a bed. It's smaller than any normal-sized bed I've ever used and my feet dangle off the edge, but I'm still thankful for it. I'd sleep sitting straight up if I had to, whatever it takes to stay here with Maggie.

Before laying down, I plug my phone into the wall and wait for it to get a small amount of charge, enough to make a phone call. When it gets to about ten percent, I walk down the hall and find a waiting area, hoping it's a safe place to make a quick phone call to Jette. I know it's late but I can't stand it any longer. If I don't at least try, I'll never be able to sleep and if I know Jette, she's not sleeping well without me.

Tapping Jette's name, I wait.

And wait.

When the call goes to voicemail, I hang up and glance at the time. It's after midnight. Looking back at the phone and the list of missed calls, I growl in frustration. Part of me wants to call back, but I doubt she'll answer and it just doesn't feel right leaving a message, so I'll have to wait until tomorrow to talk to her.

When I'm back in bed and as comfortable as I'm going to get, I take advantage of the quiet and pray some more.

I pray for Maggie's recovery.

And I pray Jette is still mine.

28

Georgette

Sloppy, wet kisses wake me up and as I roll over, I realize I fell asleep on the couch and King is lying next to me, licking my face.

For a moment, I can't recall what day it is or where I'm supposed to be, but then I remember.

Oh, shit.

My phone.

Frantic, I search the couch until I find it nestled between the cushions. With my heart beating wildly, I unlock it, seeing a missed call from Finley.

He called.

After midnight last night.

Shit.

When I check my voicemails and there's none from Finley, my stomach drops. Why wouldn't he leave a message?

What the hell is going on and where the hell are you?

At least he called though, right?

That has to be a good sign. I have to stay positive or I'll lose my mind going through all the possibilities of where he is and why he's not here with me. After being apart for five years and finding each other again, I refuse to believe this little bump in the road is enough to derail us. Actually, the thought of it doesn't even register.

Finley and I are forever.

Hitting redial on the missed call, I wait, but only get voicemail.

Last night, I didn't want to have a conversation via text, but right now, it seems like my only hope, so I open up our thread of texts and quickly type out a message.

Me: Hey. Where are you? I'm worried about you and I miss you. I hope you know I didn't accept Trevor's proposal. I'd never do that to you. To us. Please call or message me back as soon as you can. I'm going crazy over here.

Me: BTW, King misses you too.

Snapping a picture of our dog, sprawled out on his back with all four paws in the air, I send it to Finley, with a prayer he'll reply, sooner rather than later. Hoping it's like a bat signal for him to come home.

For a few minutes, I sit and stare at the screen, willing those three magical dots to appear, letting me know he's there and he's replying, but they never come.

Thankfully, it's Sunday and I don't have to work but I'm at a loss at how I'm going to distract myself until I hear back from Finley. There's no way I'll be able to concentrate on anything constructive, like reading or binge watching a show. I have too much nervous energy for that.

Maybe I'll do some cleaning.

And I still have some boxes to unpack, so I guess I'll start there.

But first, I go into the kitchen and start a pot of coffee, dishing out some breakfast for King and I, and feeling Finley's absence immensely. "I know, buddy," I tell King, running a hand through his fur. "Let's go make ourselves useful and unpack some boxes."

A few hours later, I'm a hot, sweaty mess and in desperate need of a shower. I'm surprised my arm isn't sore, not from cleaning or unpacking, but from checking my phone a million times. Blowing out a breath of air and surveying my progress, I decide that's enough manual labor for a Sunday and I need to shower and then take King for a walk.

On my way up the stairs, the doorbell rings, and I run back down them at warp speed, hoping with all of my heart that Finley is on the other side of the door.

Without even looking, I throw the door open and find a visibly startled Shep in front of me.

"Oh, hey," I say, sounding every bit as disappointed as I feel.

Shep's face morphs into a half-smile. "I know I'm not the man you were hoping to see standing here, but I come with news."

"Sorry," I say, remembering I'm a sweaty mess. "I'm sure I look crazy right now because that's exactly how I feel. Come on in."

Shep follows me inside, stopping to love on King because the dog practically demands it. At least he's cute about it, though.

"Please excuse the mess," I say, pointing around the room and at myself. "I've been unpacking to keep myself distracted and it's only marginally working. Can I get you something to drink?"

"No, thanks, I'm fine. Why don't we sit down so I can put you out of your misery?"

I look at him and my heart sinks, but he gives me a small, reassuring smile, so I try not to jump to conclusions. "Yes, please," I reply, not even trying to hide the relief and desperation in my voice.

Settling into my couch, I pull an oversized pillow into my lap because I feel like I need to hold onto something. Shep sits in a chair close by, facing me with his elbows propped up on his knees.

"First of all, Finley wanted me to apologize for not getting in touch with you and he says he will most certainly call you tonight."

I let out a deep breath and sink back into cushions. "Okay, so he's not mad at me?"

Shep gives me a kind smile. "No, Georgette. He's most definitely not mad at you." Taking a deep breath, he exhales and then begins. "Finley received a phone call yesterday, just after he left the gallery, about Maggie. She had a heart attack."

"Oh, my, God," I gush, jumping off the couch. "Is she okay? I mean, is she…" With my hand over my mouth, I feel tears start to burn my eyes and I can't even bring myself to say what's in my mind.

Dead.

Is Maggie dead?

"She's okay," Shep says, standing with his hands in the air in an effort to calm me. "At least, she will be. She was rushed to the hospital and they did surgery last night. Finley's Aunt Stella called to let him know and he ran to the coffee shop in a panic and asked me to help him get on a flight out to Odessa. Once he got there, Maggie was still in surgery. But she's expected to make a full recovery. She'll be in ICU for a couple of days. He said when he got off the plane his phone died. That's why he's been radio silent."

Oh, God.

Poor Maggie.

And poor Finley.

"I can't imagine what he's…" I shake my head, feeling a tear slip out. I know how much Finley loves his grandmother. I love her too. Everybody who meets her loves her.

"Are you okay?" I ask Shep, knowing how close the two of them have always been. Just like Finley is more of a brother to Shep, Maggie is like his grandmother.

Shep exhales, nodding, and it's only now I see the dark circles under his eyes. "As long as Maggie is okay. That's all that matters."

I nod in agreement. That is all that matters.

"I just feel so awful. All this time I thought Finley left because of what happened at the gallery yesterday. I don't know if he told you, but he walked in on Trevor proposing to me."

Shep's eyes go wide and I know Finley didn't tell him. Why would he? I'm sure the only thing he could think about was getting to Maggie. My issues with Trevor and my parents seem so trivial now.

"He didn't tell me," Shep says, confirming my thought. "But knowing that was on his mind, in addition to the call about Maggie, explains why he was in such a panic."

My heart breaks for Finley even more now. "And, now knowing what's been going on with Maggie... Gah, it's all so terrible. Are you sure she'll be okay?"

"That's what Finn told me late last night… or well, early this morning," Shep says with a sigh.

"Wait, he called you?" I ask, feeling the hurt seep in.

Shep's hands go up again in surrender. "No, I called the hospital and they put me through to Maggie's room," he clarifies. "I couldn't sleep and I hadn't heard from him. With the little bit of information I had before he left, I knew Maggie should've been out of surgery, so I called. He told me his phone went dead while he was in the airport and then when he finally got a chance to charge it, he'd tried to reach you but you didn't answer. He just didn't want to leave a voice message about something like this."

I sigh, wishing I had heard my phone ring and needing to hear Finley's voice now more than ever. "That sounds like Finley," I whisper, wiping at the moisture under my eyes.

"It was probably after three o'clock this morning when he finally got to sleep," Shep says, sounding weary. "I told him I would come over first thing this morning and tell you everything. He'll call, I promise."

Falling back down on the couch, I pull my knees to my chest. "Okay."

"Don't ever doubt how crazy that kid is about you," he says, placing a hand on my shoulder. "You're his whole world."

I try to give him my best smile, but my heart is too sad for that.

"I really appreciate you coming over here and letting me know about Maggie… and Finn."

"No problem," he says, walking toward the door. "Try not to worry, okay?"

Easier said than done.

"I'm not sure how long he'll be gone," Shep continues. "But if you need anything, don't hesitate to call me or CeCe."

"Thanks, Shep."

Once he's gone, I finally allow the relief I feel to flow throughout my body. I hate hearing about Maggie, but feel better knowing where Finn is and that he's not upset with me. As soon as he calls me and I can hear his voice, all will be right again.

Until then, I'll wait.

29

Finley

AROUND EIGHT THIS MORNING, MAGGIE REGAINED consciousness. I hadn't really been to sleep, but her voice jolted me, making me jump from the bed. When I got to her side, she was trying to speak around the ventilator, but I stopped her, assuring her she was fine. The second our eyes met, and she realized it was me in the room with her, tears started forming. But I smiled, fighting back my emotions and telling her she was fine, everything was going to be fine.

I've never seen Maggie cry and the mere idea made my heart crack a little in my chest.

When I buzzed for the nurses, they came right away and gave her something to help her continue to rest. Once she was comfortable again, I tried to sleep, having not had any except for my nap on the plane, but it was impossible.

Aunt Stella came in around nine and insisted I lay down and rest. I guess it was a combination of someone else being in the room and total exhaustion, because I finally passed out on the makeshift bed and apparently slept like the dead.

Rubbing my eyes, I try to stretch, but can't due to the size of the couch. My neck is locked up and I can't tell from the amount of light in the room what time it is… or what day. Glancing across the room, I see that Maggie is sleeping. The beeps and hisses of the machines are the same, which I'm taking is a good sign.

The nurses assured me if something went wrong, everyone would know it.

Sitting across the room, in the chair beside Maggie's bed, Aunt Stella runs a needle and thread through a piece of fabric. When she hears me rustling around, her eyes find me. "Good morning," she says with a soft smile. "I left you a sandwich and coffee on the window ledge. The coffee might be cold, but there's a microwave in the waiting area down the hall."

Pulling myself up to a sitting position, I rub my face, trying to wake myself up.

"How is she?" I ask, standing to walk over to Maggie's bedside. "Has the doctor been back?"

She places what she's working on down in an open bag on the floor and stands, walking over and taking Maggie's hand in hers. "He did, just for a few minutes, but he didn't have any more news than what he gave you last night. Rest is most important right now, so they're keeping her comfortable and trying to let her body mend."

"What time is it?" I ask, my voice raspy from sleep and emotion.

Aunt Stella clears her throat and glances down at the dainty gold band on her wrist. "A little after five. If you weren't awake in an hour, I was going to wake you. You need to eat, Finley. I know you traveled for hours yesterday and haven't had anything since you've been at the hospital."

I try to give her a smile, appreciating her concern, but my heart is so heavy for the woman lying on the bed between us. Taking inventory of Maggie, I notice her color is a little better than last night, but all the wires and tubes are still in place.

"Did they say how long she'll need the ventilator?" I ask, taking Maggie's hand in mine.

"The nurse said they'll try to take it out first thing in the morning. They wanted to wait a full twenty-four hours after surgery, but that won't be until tonight. She said it'd be best to wait."

Waiting… I'm chalking that up there with flying and hospitals. I feel like I've been in limbo ever since…

Jette.

Letting go of Maggie's hand, I turn to find my phone still plugged in where I left it.

"Aunt Stella, I have to go make a call," I tell her, my heart pumping. I hope Shep kept his word and at least went and told Jette what happened, but I haven't spoken to her since walking out of the gallery nearly twenty-four hours ago and it's killing me.

"Take your time," she says, sitting back down in her chair. "Maggie and I will just be here cross-stitching, don't worry about us."

Clutching my phone tightly, like it's a lifeline to Jette, I make my way down the hall and into the waiting area I was in last night. But unlike last night, it's full of visitors. Seeing a stairway beside the bank of elevators, I decide to take it, hoping for some privacy.

As I walk down to the first landing, my hands are practically vibrating while I'm dialing Jette's number and waiting for her to answer. It's only been a little over a day since I last spoke to her, but everything was such a mess… and I left her.

And then there's Maggie.

And I'm not sure my heart can take much more if she doesn't…

"Hello?" she says, finally answering the phone and sounding out of breath. "Finley?"

"Jette," I reply, closing my eyes as I slump against the cold, concrete wall. My breaths echo off the vacuous space. "God, I…"

"I'm so sorry," Jette says, filling the void of my thoughts. "I'm so sorry about Maggie. How is she?" Her intake of breath tells me she's feeling as emotional as I am right now and all I want to do is reach through the phone and pull her into me, bring her here.

I need her.

"She's a fighter," I tell her, swiping under my eye then wiping the moisture on my jeans. Running a hand through my hair, I begin to pace the small landing. "She had surgery last night, it was late… I'm so sorry I didn't call earlier. So sorry, you have no idea… When I got the call about Maggie, I had literally just walked out of the gallery and had every intention of waiting for you outside. My intent was to give you some space and I needed some air."

Pausing, I chuckle, not out of humor really, just the absurdity of this whole ordeal.

"I get it," she says, her voice between a plea and prayer. "Please, don't worry about me. And don't even think about what you walked in on yesterday… it's over. It was over, long before then, you know that. But I also want to say thank you."

"For what?" I ask, turning back to the wall and letting it hold me up.

"For being wonderful and selfless. For standing up for me yesterday and pouring your heart out. Those words, what you said, they were everything, Finley."

Her voice cracks and I press a fist to my forehead, wishing I could split myself in two, part of me staying here with Maggie and the other part running as fast as I can back to my girl. "Don't cry," I beg her. "Please, don't cry. I can't take it, especially knowing I can't be there to do anything about it."

"Sorry," she says, sniffling and I can just picture her expression as she puts on a brave face, squaring her shoulders. Jette might be small, but she's mighty, and I know we're going to be okay. "Just do me one favor."

"Anything," I tell her.

"Come back to me."

"Wild horses couldn't keep me away," I tell her, pressing the phone closer to my ear, wishing it was her. "As soon as I know Maggie is going to be okay, I'll be back."

We both just listen to the other breathe for a few moments. Eventually, someone walks up the stairs, barely acknowledging me, but it's enough to bring me out of my Jette-induced haze.

"I need to get back to Maggie's room," I tell her. "But I'll call you." It's a promise.

"Hey, Finn," Jette says softly. "I love you."

Those words cause pieces of my heart to fall back into place. I'd rather say them to her face and follow it up with actions, showing her just how much, but I'll take what I can get for now.

"I love you too… always."

There was never a time I didn't love Georgette. I think even before we met, my heart knew she was out there somewhere and it was always searching, until a fateful day when she walked over to a fountain and sat down beside me, changing the trajectory of my life.

30

Georgette

"LET'S GO, KING. TIME TO EARN OUR BACON."

At the word bacon, his adorable ears perk up. "I know, buddy. Me too. Let's go see what CeCe has for us this morning."

On our way down the steps and out to the sidewalk, Shaw peeks out his front door and grabs the newspaper, waving. Shirtless.

I've never once questioned why Avery is with that man.

Yes, I'm taken… so freaking taken, but I can still appreciate a fine specimen like Shaw O'Sullivan. Actually, Shepard Rhys-Jones falls into that category too. When I was younger, I had a bit of a crush on Shep, but that was before I met Finley.

It's kind of strange to think about knowing Shep longer than Finley, but our connection to each other was distant, through our parents. I didn't really get to know Shep until Finley. At first, I thought he was like everyone else I grew up with—money-hungry and self-absorbed—but quickly realized he wasn't.

That also goes for his best friend, Maverick, who I haven't seen a lot of since moving to New Orleans. According to the few conversations I've had with Carys, he stays busy with the hotel and the properties he and Shep buy and sell. They've created a lucrative business for themselves, but the thing I love most is it's not all about the money.

They truly care about the community and seem to take on beautification projects more than anything, finding ways to make old buildings useful.

I honestly can't thank Shep enough for giving me the contact information for the townhouse.

"Wait," I tell King as we come to the corner. "Always look both ways."

My morning walks to work were lonely for the first few days Finn was gone, so I bit the bullet and called in a favor to my boss, asking if I could bring King to work. I promised Cami he'd be on his best behavior, but she didn't seem too concerned about it, telling me she thought it was a great idea and that clients would love him.

They do.

And so far, we haven't had any mishaps.

Except for his dirty paws. The first day I brought him, I found myself spot cleaning our gleaming white floor several times. One stop on Amazon for dog shoes, and problem solved.

It took an entire evening of us walking around the neighborhood with them before he stopped looking like a Clydesdale, taking big, wide steps. But he got used to them and I feel better about him traipsing around the Quarter with them on.

It protects his little paws and my white floors at the gallery.

Win, win.

Walking in front of the cathedral, I look up and then back over at Jackson Square. It's really breath-taking this time of morning. Without Finley here to give me a reason to stay in bed, King and I are usually out the door a couple of hours earlier than I normally would be. But that's okay. It gives us plenty of time to walk to Neutral Grounds, chat with

CeCe, and sometimes Shep is there and has an update on Maggie.

"Good morning," CeCe calls as we walk in the door. My eyes drift to the stairs leading to Finn's apartment, just like they do every morning. I've come close to asking CeCe if I can just go up there and sit and feel close to him, but I don't. It's fine. He'll be home eventually.

Until then, I have King… and two of Finn's t-shirts I found in a duffel bag from the club. They were probably sweaty when he took them off and I should probably wash them, but not until he's home. Call me crazy, but they smell like him and sometimes at night, it's all I need to feel close to him before falling asleep.

That and his late-night phone calls.

However, those sometimes amp me up instead of sedate me. Sometimes, Finn goes to the stairwell to call me and with no one around, our conversations turn from PG to rated R pretty quickly.

"Hey," CeCe says, setting a few drinks on the counter. I'm assuming they're to-go orders because no one else is in the shop at the moment. Shep recently hooked CeCe up with her very own app, which I have downloaded and use frequently.

It's cool. You can order to-go, earn points toward free coffee, and eventually, when the roastery is in full-swing, you'll be able to order coffee beans and have them delivered to your front door.

"Good morning, King," CeCe coos, walking around the corner with the now-familiar cup in hand. The second he sees her, and the cup, his tail wags so hard it swishes into my skirt and practically lifts it up to my waist.

"Hey!" I exclaim, smoothing my skirt down and relinquishing the leash to CeCe.

She laughs, bending down to let him lick the whipped cream out of the cup. "He's just excited, aren't you, baby? Aunt CeCe has the goods… isn't that right?"

Have I mentioned my dog is spoiled?

Finn keeps telling me he'll be ruined by the time he makes it home. I hate to break it to him, but he's probably right. Actually, it's probably already too late.

"Aunt CeCe baked you some goodies," she says, still kneeling down at King's level, petting his head. "Yummy breakfast goodies… with bacon."

His tail wagging speeds up so fast I think he's going to take flight.

"You're going to make him… fat," I say, whispering the last word so I don't offend.

CeCe stands, smiling wide. "Nah, he's getting all the extra exercise walking to work, he deserves some treats. "And so do you. I packed you both a lunch."

Rolling my eyes, I walk up to the counter and watch as CeCe goes about making my coffee.

When the door opens again, I turn and see Shep walking in, looking like he walked straight out of *GQ Magazine*—a well-tailored suit I know cost a fortune, shoes that shine against the worn floor of the coffee shop, and hair in a perfect state of disarray.

"Good morning, gorgeous," CeCe says, placing my coffee down on the counter in front of me and walking around to greet her husband.

Shep doesn't hold back on my account, kissing CeCe like it might be the last time ever. When he pulls back, he smiles down at her. "That was for leaving me this morning. I hope you think about your transgressions and anticipate your punishment."

Oh, God.

"I can't wait," CeCe says, voice low.

Yep, that's my cue.

"Well," I say with a chuckle. "King and I must be going… there's the, uh, gallery… and work. Ready, King?" I ask, averting my eyes from CeCe and Shep down to my dog who's peering up at me unknowing, just happy to be here.

"Talk to Finn?" Shep asks, turning CeCe until her back is flush with his front… probably to hide an issue with his well-tailored pants.

Stop, Georgette. Oh, God. Just stop.

I feel my cheeks heat up, wishing I could disappear or turn invisible. If I ever get to pick a superpower, that will be it. "Uh, yes," I say, clearing my throat. "We talked last night and again this morning."

"Good to hear Maggie is doing well," he says, relief in his tone. CeCe turns in his arms and hugs his waist. I know this has been hard on him too. With work and all of his business ventures, he hasn't been able to get away to go see her.

I nod. "Yeah, she still has a ways to go, but she's doing so much better."

"We're planning on flying to see her as soon as she's home and recovering," Shep says. "Until then, I'm glad Finley is there taking care of everything."

Smiling, I nod again. It is good. I'm glad he's there with Maggie, but I *really, really* miss him here, with me. "Yeah, it's good."

"He'll be home soon," he says, giving me a reassuring smile.

Home.

I've thought a lot about that word and what it means since moving to New Orleans, and now I know that word means Finley. Finley is home, wherever he is, is where I want to be and I can't wait until he comes back to me.

31

Finley

ANOTHER WEEK AWAY FROM JETTE IS TORTUROUS BUT IT'S also another week in which Maggie has regained a lot of her health and strength. For a while, she wouldn't ask me to do much for her but after explaining time and time again, I wanted to do things for her—needed to do them—and that it would, in turn, help her recover quicker, she finally gave in.

"Finley, dear, can you bring me another pillow from the linen closet?" Maggie calls out from the living room.

"Yes, ma'am. Be right there!" I turn off the kitchen faucet and dry my hands, since I'd been cleaning up after the lunch, and jog down the hall to get the requested pillow and an extra blanket, just in case. Maggie typically falls asleep shortly after lunch due to her meds and I want to make sure she's as comfortable as possible.

After Maggie is situated and dozing in the recliner, I walk quietly to my room and call Shep for my daily check-in.

"Hey, Finn. How's Maggie doing today?" Shep asks, answering the call after the first ring.

"Were you sitting on the phone or something or do you miss the sound of my voice so much you couldn't bear to let your phone ring twice?"

Shep lets out a chuckle. "Very funny, jackass. I already had my phone in my hand when you called. Besides, I know how much you love the sound of *my* voice and I didn't want to make you wait."

"Yeah, you got me." I roll my eyes, laughing with him for a second and it feels good. It also feels good that after all this time, Shep is still there for me... for us. "Maggie's doing great," I tell him. "She's napping now but she's moving around the house more and her appetite is coming back, which is good."

"That's a relief," he says with a sigh. "I can't tell you how thankful I am that you're there taking care of her. I know she's your grandma but she's family to me, too, you know?"

"I know, man." And, I do. Maggie was more of a mother to Shep than his own mom and she was certainly a better example for him. I love how close they are because they're my family and the two most important people in my life, outside of Jette.

Speaking of...

"How's my girl?"

"Why are you asking me?" Shep asks, sounding smug. "Every time I see her she tells me y'all just talked or video chatted or what the fuck ever."

I fight back a smile, but the concern I feel for her is real, so I press further. "Yeah, but what if Jette is only acting like she's okay so I won't worry about her? You'd tell me if something was really wrong, but she wouldn't."

I'm starting to sound ridiculous to my own ears but I just miss her so much.

"Settle down, lover boy. Georgette misses you like crazy but she's surviving. CeCe and I see her a few times a day and make sure she's eating regularly. Plus, she has King to help keep her mind off you. Now that I think about it, you might've already been replaced by the furball."

"You're just full of jokes today, aren't you?"

I've always appreciated this—the way we banter. I only wish we were doing it in person.

"Seriously, though," Shep says, his voice now the one sounding concerned. "How are you holding up? You must be going out of your mind without your music."

"Fuck, man. You don't know the half of it." I pause running a hand through my hair. "I feel like I'm missing a limb or something, not being able to perform or record. I've been writing, though, so that's eased the ache a little, but I miss my sax."

"Dude, if you want me to ship your sax to you, I will. Or, better yet, why don't you go and buy you another one?"

My face contorts into a look of disgust he can't see, but he definitely hears my scoff and audible dismissal. "No way," I tell him and he chuckles. "She can't be replaced." Just like another she that's constantly on my mind. "But thanks for the offer. Besides, I'd rather spend my money on something else, which is what I wanted to talk to you about."

"What's that?" he asks, giving me his full attention.

Letting out a deep breath, I peer out the window and tell him what I've been thinking.

"I'd like to hire a home-health nurse to come and take care of Maggie when I leave. I know Aunt Stella is here but I'd feel better if she was getting actual medical care if she needs it."

There's a pause and for a second, I think he's going to tell me it's a bad idea, but then he says, "I think that's a great idea, but why don't you let me take care of that?"

"No," I tell him, already expecting this argument and fully prepared to win this one. "It should be me; I want it to be me. You and CeCe have done so much for me already and I have money saved up, thanks to my work and the measly rent you two charge me. I need to do this for Maggie. It's the only way I'll be able to leave her."

"Okay, I get that." Shep pauses and I know he's about to give me a counteroffer. It's impossible for him to just accept someone else's idea and move on. "How about this, you pay for Maggie's care and we'll consider what you think you owe us paid in full. We'll be even. Think you can accept that?"

Even.

The way he makes it sound, as if we're the same, is something he's always done for me. Never making me feel like I'm less or beneath him, due to my age or social status. I should've expected this kind of deal from Shep, the generous bastard that he is, but I appreciate him making me feel like his equal.

"Alright, I accept," I tell him, feeling lighter than I have in days. "And, thanks. You know I appreciate you and CeCe so much."

Shep blows off the gratitude, like always, but I know he hears me. "Just keep taking care of Maggie so you can get your ass back down here, deal?"

"You got it." I let out a deep breath, peeking in on Maggie who's still resting peacefully. "Please give Jette my love when you see her."

"Whatever, Finn. I know you'll be talking to her later. You can tell her yourself." And, with that, Shep ends our call.

Later, after dinner, I'm sitting on the couch with Maggie and Aunt Stella watching television, which has become a nightly routine. It's similar to the one I had with Jette before my life got flipped upside down and oddly makes me miss her even more.

Why is it that everything seems worse at night?

"You see that man playing the sax on this talk show, Finley?" Stella asks. "Why don't you do something like that? It'd be so nice to know someone on television, right, Maggie?"

Maggie sighs, adjusting her blanket. "It sure would but he's too busy in New Orleans now, isn't that right, Finley? Which reminds me, how are you able to keep all your jobs while staying here with us?"

I secretly roll my eyes at their passive ways of digging into my life. Either of them could come right out and ask me anything, but they always use each other to get the information they want.

"Well," I say, sighing as I lean forward. "Lola and I speak on a regular basis, she told me not to worry about the studio. My work will be waiting on me when I return. So, that just leaves my corner on Royal St, where I'm my own boss and only really for fun, and to make it easier to see Jette during the day."

Maggie cocks her head, her eyes questioning. "What about that club you were playing at?"

"I actually quit the other day," I admit.

"But, Finley," she says, regret in her tone, which is exactly why I hadn't brought it up, because I didn't want her to be upset. "You loved that job and I'm sure you were great at it. I feel terrible that you had to quit because of me."

Shaking my head, I lean over and place a hand over hers. "Maggie, don't worry about it. Gia was cool with it and told me I can come back anytime I want to. Besides, taking care of you is more important right now."

"Well," she finally says, a hint of sadness on her face. "I know your sweet Georgette must be missing you like crazy…"

Even after a heart attack and open-heart surgery, this woman is still ornery as hell.

"Are you trying to get rid of me?" I ask, only partly joking, but Maggie laughs anyway.

She swats at me, a small smile replacing the frown. "Of course not, silly. I love having you here, you know that, but at some point, you need to go back and start living your life again. Things are going so well for you in New Orleans; I don't want to be the one to hold you back."

About this time, Aunt Stella perks up and sets down her cross-stitching to get in on the conversation. "I want to hear more about this girlfriend of yours. Are you two serious?"

Two old gossips, I swear.

"Yeah, I think we are. I mean, it's been a complicated road getting us to this point," I admit. "But I know she's the one for me. She's my forever."

Maggie and Aunt Stella both sigh and I can't help the smile on my face.

"I always knew you two would make it," Maggie says confidently, like she's somehow responsible for Jette and I being together. "I'm just so happy for you, honey. It sure would make an old woman happy to see you two married soon."

"Good Lord, Maggie," Aunt Stella scoffs, giving her sister a stern look. "Let them live their lives. They're young and have all the time in the world."

Holding her hands up in surrender, Maggie defends herself. "Look, all I know is, life is short. Take it from the old lady who just had open-heart surgery, don't have any regrets, Finley. You marry that lovely lady and continue making people happy with your music but promise me one thing."

I have a feeling she's going to play this open-heart surgery card for a long time to come.

"Anything, Maggie," I say, being completely honest, even though I'm onto her antics.

"Don't marry Georgette until I'm well enough to dance at the wedding."

Letting out a soft chuckle, I lean over and kiss her cheek, so thankful to have this time with her and that's she's finally feeling like herself again.

"We'll wait for you, I promise."

Georgette

"Hey," I say, smiling into the small video screen Cami had delivered last week. She thought we needed video chats for our weekly staff meetings of three—me, her, and Junie. I agreed, because I miss her and I need June to know what my voice sounds like because I have every intention of being her favorite auntie.

Granted, I have stiff competition. For starters, she has two real aunts, plus all of the French Quarter crew... or krewe as I've now started referring to our tight-knit group in my head, because... New Orleans.

Cami holds June up to the camera. "Hello! We just woke up from our afternoon nap."

"We, huh?" I ask. "Did you finally take the advice of everydamnbody and nap?"

Last week, we agreed we can still cuss in front of June because she's too small to know what we're saying. Once she starts babbling, we'll filter. Until then, especially when the older Landry children are running amuck, we speak unfiltered.

"The boys are with Annie and Sam," Cami says, a content, well-rested smile on her face. "Sam stopped by to get them after his shift at Pockets."

"Well, that's good for mama," I tell her, sorting through the last of the paperwork on the desk in front of me. I have some samples I need to show Cami and get her approval on. "How's Deacon?"

Cami sighs. "Honestly, he's been perfect… I know, I know. That sounds cheesy, but he's just so freaking good at this dad thing." There's a dreamy expression on her face as she snuggles June close to her chest. "I mean, I always knew he would be, but he's really blowing this three-kid thing out of the water. Taking a night-time shift, even though he has to get up and manage restaurants and people. He brings home dinner most nights."

"He's a keeper, that's for sure."

She nods, taking a sip of water. "He is. There were some touch-and-go moments during those last few months when I wanted to strangle him for being so overprotective, but in the end, it all balances out."

"Gotta take the good with the bad," I tease.

We spend about half an hour talking business. I give her a financial update and we discuss a new charity project we've been tossing around. Then, I take her on a virtual tour of the gallery, stopping at the new exhibit I've been working on.

"I think their style really adds something to the current pieces," Cami says. "The colors are so vibrant and I'm obsessed with the brush strokes. You said you found them in the Quarter?"

"Yeah," I tell her, walking back over to the desk so I can prop the screen back up and give my arm a rest. "He was set up in front of Jackson Square… I've probably walked by there a hundred times, but last week when I was grabbing beignets from Cafe du Monde, the painting I just showed you jumped out at me. He stopped by earlier this week with a few more samples and they were all so good. I knew we had to have him."

Cami beams. "And you were right… and so was I."

"About what?"

"Hiring you."

I feel a blush creep up on my cheeks at her praise. "Thank you... you have no idea what it means to hear you say that. And you have no idea how much you changed my life by taking a chance on me."

"It wasn't a chance," she says quietly, glancing down at the baby who just downed an entire four ounces of milk. "It was fate."

I couldn't agree more.

After I end the video chat with Cami, I make my usual lap around the gallery—checking all the alcoves and running a dust mop along the edges of the floors. We have a cleaning crew who stops by every Sunday, while we're closed, but I try to stay on top of maintaining it during the week.

"Well, King," I say to my sleeping dog who's curled up on his plush bed under the desk. "I think it's time to call it a day, buddy."

His ears perk up.

"Ready to go home?"

He wags his tail, making me smile.

Leaning down, I rub his ears and dig out his fancy footwear for our walk home. I'm so glad I have him. These past couple of weeks without Finn would've been so much harder without him.

Once he's got his shoes and leash on, we make our way to the front door and I set the alarm before stepping out on the sidewalk.

"Georgette," I hear a familiar voice call out and when I turn, CeCe, Avery, and Carys are walking my way, with Shep trailing closely behind, his phone pressed to his ear.

"What are y'all doing here?" I ask, locking the deadbolt and checking it twice. "If you came to see some art, you're too late... please check back on Monday!" Laughing, I give King's leash a tug and meet them on the sidewalk.

"We came to see you," Avery says, and it's then I realize she's missing my favorite accessory. "Shaw's babysitting, and Shep here." Pausing, she points over her shoulder. "He's agreed to take King home for you so you can join us for dinner."

"Really?" I ask, pleasantly surprised at this turn of events. My only plans for the evening were PB&Js on the couch with King and more reruns of *Friends*.

They all smile and Shep finally finishes his phone call, sliding his phone into a hidden pocket of his suit jacket. "Really," he says, giving me a quick smile and reaching through the group of women to take the leash from me. "Y'all go… chat and do whatever women do."

Leaning over, he places a kiss on CeCe's lips and then dips his head in departure. "Ladies."

Cocking an eyebrow, I wait for a second while Shep and King take off down the sidewalk.

"Is he always that smooth?" I ask.

CeCe sighs, obviously appreciating the view. "Smoothest motherfucker you'll ever meet."

"I don't know," Carys says, shaking her head a little. "I think Maverick gives him a run for his money. Maybe they took a class or something in college."

I snort. "Those two have always been competing for something," I muse.

"I forget you knew Mav and Shep back in the day," CeCe says, walking forward and looping her arm through mine. "I don't even want to think about what they were like back in college."

"It's a small freaking world," I muse.

"That's for sure," CeCe replies.

"Well," Avery says, saddling up on my other side, the four of us taking up the entire width of the sidewalk. "Shaw's roughness definitely balances out their smoothness."

"Oh, he's smooth," CeCe says. "In his own way."

"A dark and mysterious way," Carys adds, her voice a bit dreamy.

We all laugh and it feels good. Even in New York, I didn't have a close group of friends. Most of the people I interacted with were from Sotheby's and we didn't really do anything outside of work together. When Trevor and I would go out, it was always for business—his business.

I realize as we make our way down the street, this was something else I was missing in my life.

"Where are we going?" I ask, realizing we've made it to Canal Street and we're outside our normal realm. I assumed when they said dinner, we'd be eating at Lagniappe.

"Crescent Moon," Avery says, glancing both ways and then leading the group across the street. "We'll take the streetcar."

This excites me. Finley had been planning on taking me into the Garden District to see where Lola's studio is, but we didn't get the chance before Maggie's heart attack. Every time I think about him or her, my heart hurts. It hasn't felt quite right since he left and I'm missing him more today than yesterday… or the day before.

Part of me thought it might get easier as time went on, but it hasn't.

"It's a great little restaurant," Avery says. "I actually used to work there… for a short time."

"Really?" I ask, loving getting little bits and pieces of their history. All of them have a story to tell and it's really fun hearing them.

As we climb onto the streetcar, Avery stops and pays for the four of us and we find a couple of benches in the back to sit. The windows are open and the early March breeze feels nice and we start to move down St. Charles.

"Shaw and I hit a rough patch," Avery says, picking up her story. "I needed a change and some separation."

"They were both being stubborn," CeCe comments, closing her eyes and letting the breeze blow through her dark hair. "I was about to stage an intervention, but they finally figured their shit out."

Carys and I laugh while Avery tries not to smile.

"Kind of like I was getting ready to lock you and Finley in a closet," CeCe says.

I gasp. "What?"

"You heard me," she mutters. "I thought the two of you were never going to admit what's there between you."

"It's really romantic," Carys says dreamily. "And Finley is so sweet... and that sax."

"Don't even get me started on his sax," I say, feeling an immediate heat creep up my cheeks.

"Actually," CeCe says, sitting up. "Do tell."

"God, you're awful."

"You're the one who brought up his sax," CeCe teases and my cheeks heat up even more.

"I can't handle talking about Finley and his sax right now."

They laugh, but all give me understanding, sympathetic nods.

When the streetcar stops, we step off and the cutest little cafe is sitting on the corner across the street with *Crescent Moon* painted on the side of the building.

Walking in, I can tell from the aroma alone this will become a favorite. Then, a man in suspenders and a bowtie steps out from the kitchen with a wide smile on his face.

"Avery!"

"Hey, Wyatt," she replies, meeting him halfway for a hug. "I brought my friends for dinner."

He steps around Avery, grabbing a few menus. "It's about damn time."

"We were just here for Sunday pancakes," she scoffs.

Laughing, he shows us to a corner table, giving us a gorgeous view of the houses and large oak trees that adorn the Garden District. "I meant without that stick-in-the-mud Shaw tagging along," he teases.

"I'll be sure to tell him you said that."

Wyatt gives us a mischievous grin. "Please do."

We let Avery order for us and none of us are disappointed. The food is delicious, not better or worse than Lagniappe, just different. Where Lagniappe has showmanship and flair, Crescent Moon has comfort and casual with added bits of quirkiness.

The bread pudding with rum sauce is to die for.

Avery tells us the story about when she first arrived in New Orleans and came here for a job. Initially, Wyatt sent her to Shaw. He told her later, he just had a feeling—his gut told him to send her there, so he did. Avery says it's, hands down, the best thing that ever happened to her, kind of like when I accepted the job at the gallery.

"Avery?" a woman says, walking up to our table.

She's beautiful. Not like run-of-the-mill beautiful, like striking, stop-you-in-your-tracks beautiful.

I'm as straight as they come and completely in love with Finley Lawson, but if someone was going to make me switch sides, it'd be her. Her sleek, satin-looking black hair and her vibrant green eyes would be enough, but add in she's very tall, there's absolutely no chance she'd pass you by on the street and you wouldn't notice her.

"Ever?" Avery asks, her eyes cutting to us and then back to the woman standing over us with a bright, white smile.

Seriously, there's not one thing about this woman that isn't perfect.

"What are you doing here?" Avery asks, suddenly sounding a bit nervous as she stands and embraces the woman who laughs lightly, hugging her back.

"Well, they do have the best bread pudding in town."

Avery laughs. "That they do." Turning back to the table, she makes introductions. "Guys, this is Everly Davenport. Everly, this is Carys, CeCe, and Georgette," she says, pointing to each of us.

There's a moment of awkwardness that passes before Avery laughs again and then continues. "Everly is a wedding planner."

She lets that marinate for a second, but that's about all it takes. Carys is the first one to make the connection. "Oh, my God. You're finally doing it?"

"Congratulations," CeCe says, standing to hug Avery. "I wondered if you were going to pop out another kid before you finally made it official."

Everly gives Avery an apologetic smile. "Sorry," she says. "I didn't mean to spill the beans."

Avery waves her off. "It's fine. I was actually going to tell them soon anyway."

"This is so exciting," I tell her, standing to get in on the hugs being passed around.

"You should bring them with you to our next planning session," Everly suggests.

Excitement bubbles up inside me. I love weddings. I love love, in general. But there's something magical about weddings, two people pledging their lives to each other.

"That'd be great," Avery agrees. "You know I'm horrible at making decisions. I swear I'm still suffering from pregnancy brain."

"Maybe you're pregnant again," CeCe teases. Although, I'm not sure she's teasing. She's pretty serious about Avery and Shaw having another baby for her to be a godmother to.

Avery groans, tossing her head back. "Why do you keep trying to impregnate me?"

"You make such pretty babies and I love being a godmother."

"Why don't you and Shep make a baby?" I ask, turning the tables.

CeCe grows serious and I'm worried I've hit a nerve or maybe they've been trying without success. Just as I'm afraid I've said something wrong, CeCe finally says, "He just coerced me into marrying him. Let me enjoy this first. I'm sure he'll come up with some reason I need to give him a baby, but for now, I'm enjoying the practice."

We laugh, Everly included. "Well," she says, brushing her long, dark hair over her shoulder. "I can plan baby showers too. And if you're looking for love, I can help with that too." She slips a matte black card out of her bag and lays it on the table between us. There's no logo or address, just a phone number in gold lettering.

"See you next week," Everly says, giving Avery a wink. "Ladies, it was a pleasure."

It's so very secretive and exclusive feeling.

"She's…" Carys starts and we all just nod in agreement.

Intriguing.

Striking.

"She's great," Avery says. "We haven't got too far into planning, but so far, she's been a god-send. Shaw wants to have a big traditional wedding because this is my only wedding… yada, yada, yada. But I don't want that. I know he's not into big crowds and he hates for people to make a fuss. Besides, I don't want that either. I want something small and intimate. Everly has been great at helping us find a happy medium."

"It's going to be great," CeCe says, reaching over and squeezing Avery's hand.

She smiles and Wyatt must've overheard our conversation, because about that time he shows up with a bottle of champagne.

"This is on the house," he says, popping the cork with finesse and then pouring four glasses. "I feel like I should get a commission on this wedding." He winks and Avery smiles, shaking her head as she brings the champagne flute to her lips.

We end up closing down the small restaurant. When it's just the four of us and the waitstaff, who are now cleaning, we take that as our cue to call it a night. Wyatt insists we can stay, but it's late and Shaw has already texted Avery to check on her. Maverick and Shep have each called once. I check my phone, but there's nothing from Finley.

My heart sinks a little at that, but I'm not surprised.

We've been on different schedules since he's been gone and I know he'll text or call when he gets a chance.

After we hop off the streetcar at Canal Street, the walk back to the French Quarter is nice as we enjoy the evening air and make light conversation. When we get close to the Blue Bayou, we stop and say goodnight to Carys.

Maverick is waiting at the corner to walk her home. He waves, calling out his greetings, and then CeCe, Avery, and I continue on the short distance home.

"Goodnight," I call back as I cross the road.

"Goodnight," CeCe and Avery reply, heading into their respective houses.

When I walk up the front steps, I expect King to greet me at the side gate like he always does, but he's not there. "King?" I call out, a hint of worry seeping in.

His bark greets me, but it's not from outside, it's from inside.

Knowing Shep didn't have a key, I'm confused as I turn the key in the lock and open the door.

But then all confusion and worry fade away as Finley and King greet me in the foyer.

Dropping my bag to the floor, I throw myself into Finn's arms. His deep laugh and familiar scent soak into my body, filling every space left vacant due to his absence. "God, I missed you," I tell him, burying my face in his neck and breathing deeply.

"Oh, baby." He sighs, holding tighter as he lifts me off my feet. "You have no fucking idea how much I've missed you… it's been killing me. I've been so torn," he murmurs, stroking my hair with one hand while the other cradles my hips, holding me to him.

Leaning back, our noses brushing, Finn presses his lips to mine. The kiss is slow and savoring, each caress full of intention and unspoken words—*I've missed you, welcome home, never leave me again.*

"Upstairs," I whisper.

Without another word, Finn turns and carries me up the stairs, shutting the door behind him as he steps into the bedroom and we make up for lost time.

Unlike the kisses in the foyer, our actions in the bedroom are hurried and quick. The intense need for each other fills the room. We don't speak, just act, each undressing the other. There will be time for slow and sweet later—I'm hoping for forever—but for now, we obviously both need this—raw and real and *us.*

"Scoot up," Finn instructs, guiding me further up the bed and settling between my thighs. Gripping my hips, his eyes lock with mine as he slides into me. We both sigh.

"Welcome home," I tell him, sliding my hands up his arms and loving the feel of his strong biceps as they flex when he begins to move.

For a few minutes, we watch as he slides in and out, reconnecting our bodies and our hearts.

"I missed this," he says, his breaths starting to come harder and faster as his speed increases. "But most of all, I missed this." Placing a hand over my heart and then guiding it up into my hair, he draws us closer together, our breaths mingling as we inch toward the edge of ecstasy.

33

Finley

"I DON'T WANT TO GET OUT OF BED," JETTE MURMURS, snuggling closer to me, her warm naked body making me want to do anything but what she mentioned.

However, it's not Sunday, so our options are limited.

"If we hurry," I tell her, leaning forward to nip at her ear with my teeth, which causes her to squirm and in turn increases the size of my morning wood. "We can have a quick fuck in the shower."

Rolling over, Jette's eyes go wide in delight. "Race you."

A flash of her breast and amazing ass are all I see before she disappears into the bathroom. When I hear the water turn on, I smile to myself, wondering how I got so damn lucky.

You know what? I'm not going to question that anymore. Instead, I'm just going to appreciate the good stuff in my life, never taking a moment for granted.

"Finn!" she yells.

So impatient.

"I'm coming!" I call back.

"No, you're not… and neither am I!"

Chuckling, I roll out of bed.

Such a smart ass.

Sexiest smart ass I've ever met and the only one I want to spend the rest of my life with.

After the best shower sex I've had since yesterday, Jette and I dress and go about our morning routine—sharing the sink, pouring to-go cups of coffee, feeding King. We've fallen right back into the pattern we'd started before everything got so crazy and messed up.

Something that changed while I was gone?

Our dog now wears shoes and goes to work.

I can't help laughing every morning when Jette slips them on King's feet. He always looks at me like, *can't you help me out here? First, my balls get cut off and now I have to wear these fucking shoes?*

To which I rub his ears, silently telling him we have to pick our battles. And I always slip him an extra treat before we depart for the day.

Since I'm no longer working at Good Times every night, we all have similar schedules. Jette and King spend their days at the gallery and I'm usually at the studio. When I got back from Odessa, Lola had work lined up for me. I'll be busy for the foreseeable future, and according to Lola, for as long as I want it.

She's really become one of my closest friends in New Orleans. She and Bo insist on giving Jette and me season tickets for the New Orleans Revelers season that will be starting in a couple of weeks. After much coercion, I think we're going to take her up on it.

"Good morning," Shep calls out, waving as he slides into his Porsche 911. A lot of things about Shep have changed over the years, but he still loves that car.

Jette waves. "He must have an early morning meeting."

"Yeah," I agree, pulling King's leash tighter as Shep drives by. "He said something yesterday about not being at the coffee shop today."

We've all been meeting up for coffee most mornings.

Most evenings we have an invite for something—dinner, drinks, an art show, concerts. But this weekend, Shaw and his sister, Sarah, have invited everyone to the cooking school for a big Irish feast to celebrate St. Patrick's Day.

"I love you," I say, leaning over to place a kiss on Jette's blonde curls.

She smiles up at me, the day and the moment feeling so ordinary, yet perfect. "I love you too."

34

Georgette

"Welcome," Shaw says, raising a glass as everyone finds a seat at the long table Sarah and Avery have set. It's really beautiful, overflowing with food that smells amazing and all of the familiar faces I've come to know and love since moving to this city.

Shaw smiles down at Avery, who has a sleeping Shae strapped to her chest. The admiration and awe he has on his face every time he looks at her and their baby is so evident.

I want that.

All of it, and more, with Finley.

"We're so happy to have you all here," he says, glancing around the table. "You're friends who've become family and we feel blessed to have you all in our lives." Pausing, he leans down and places a kiss on Avery's temple. "We've brought you all here today to celebrate life and love and a little bit of Irish luck."

He winks and raises his glass. "May the best day of your past be the worst day of your future."

"Sláinte!" Sarah toasts.

We all follow suit, raising our glasses and toasting our friends who've become family, as Shaw so eloquently put it. When someone clinks a knife against a glass at the other end of the table, we all turn.

That's when I see Jules stand. My smile is immediate. It took me a couple of months of being in New Orleans before I finally properly met him, but now that we've been introduced, I'm smitten.

He works at Blue Bayou, but he's also in law school and moonlights at a drag club not too far from here. A true renaissance man and someone I definitely hope to spend more time with.

"If I may," he says, glancing across to Shaw who nods and gives him the floor. Clearing his throat, he gives a saucy smirk before beginning. "A big thank you to Sarah, Shaw, and Avery... which would be so much easier to just say the O'Sullivans, if Shaw would ever make an honest woman out of her..."

"Hey," Shaw says, holding up his hands in defense. "I'm working on it."

"Oh?" Jules asks, turning an ear his way as he holds up a hand to hear better. "Is there an announcement you'd like to make?"

"We set a date," Avery says, beaming and smiling over at me and then to CeCe and Carys. "This summer and you're all invited. Clear your calendars."

Everyone cheers, but Jules quiets the crowd.

"If you need a best man," he says, winking. "Or woman."

"Get on with it," CeCe demands. "We can't let this amazing food get cold."

I glance over to see Sarah, smiling as she basks in the moment. She's a bit reserved, like Shaw, but she's so warm and friendly. I would love to get to know her better. Maybe I'll sign up for a cooking class and add some new, local recipes to my repertoire of grilled cheese and PB&Js.

"Fine," Jules huffs, enjoying his spotlight, as usual. "A toast." Clearing his voice once more for dramatic flair, he pretends to be thinking and starts with, "Money in your pocket, beer in your cup... poke her in the butt, and you won't knock her up."

The group erupts in laughter, Avery hides her face and shields baby Shae's ears, even though he's not quite old enough to know how dirty his Uncle Jules is.

"No, no," Jules says, waving it off. "That's not the one..." Pausing, he thinks some more and then holds a finger in the air. "Got it. Achem... Here's to those we love the best, we love them best when they're undressed."

A few groans echo around the room, but Jules soldiers on, making me laugh and press into Finn's chest as he chuckles. The deep rumble in my ear is almost as soothing as his hand on my waist.

"We love them sitting, standing, lying," Jules continues. "If they had wings, we'd love them flying. And when they're dead, buried, forgotten— we'll dig them up and fuck them rotting!"

"Oh, my god, Jules!" Carys exclaims, pulling on his arm to make him sit down while the entire table loses their shit.

"Wait," he says, fighting Carys off. "This is the real one!"

"It's your last chance," Maverick warns, tears streaming down his face.

"Here's to all my friends and lovers. May all your ups and downs be under the covers!"

"Take his wine away," someone yells.

While everyone at the table gets themselves under control, platters and bowls begin to pass. I glance around, soaking in the moment. A year ago, even six months ago, I couldn't have imagined my life could be this full and content.

I went from craving commitment and a future, to having everything I dreamed of and more.

Now, looking back, I'm so glad Trevor didn't give into my pressure for more. Regardless of his reasons or intentions, I know now it was for good reason. I hope one day a woman sweeps him off his feet and he realizes what he felt for me was never love, not the real kind… the kind that erases every memory of anyone who came before.

It's a beginning, middle, and end kind of love.

The kind I feel for the man sitting next to me—my first and my last and everything in between.

EPILOGUE

Georgette

"COME ON!" CASEY YELLS, STANDING IN FRUSTRATION AS A call on the field doesn't go the way she wants. I love her passion for the game and for the man at-bat.

I glance over to see Lola watching intently, not as vocal as her sister, but just as invested, if not more. It's all in the way she watches the field and her body tenses when Bo swings at the pitches. If she could physically help him knock it out of the park, she would.

"Come on, baby," she mutters, her knee bouncing.

When the ump calls another strike, Casey is on her feet again, yelling so fast I can't keep up with what she's saying. One thing I do notice is she doesn't ever use profanity. Where Lola is letting a few fucks fly under her breath, Casey is more creative in her verbal barrage.

The game is exciting, though.

Before we started being regulars in Bo Bennett's—or should I say Lola Carradine's—box I hadn't ever been to a professional sporting event.

"That was obviously a ball," Finn yells, taking off his ball cap and waving it at the field to emphasize his frustration.

"He fits right in with Casey," Lola says, taking a sip of her drink while Bo walks away from the plate for a second. The count is full, so the pressure is on.

I'm definitely getting better with my baseball knowledge and I appreciate the science of the game. Even though I'm more of a free-thinker, the rules of the sport are fun to learn.

I know one thing for sure, to see someone as well-known and bigger-than-life as Lola Carradine fully-invested in a baseball game—wearing cutoff shorts and a bedazzled Bennett jersey—it's a sight to behold. Her dark hair is hidden under a purple baseball cap and she's not wearing much makeup, so far from the rock goddess she's known to be, but she's still beautiful, maybe even more so than when she graces the pages of a glossy magazine.

Although, she's definitely pulled back from the spotlight since she and Bo started dating.

Dating doesn't even seem like the right word for what they are.

A month or so ago, right after the season started, Bo had a night off and they invited Finley and I over for dinner. I was nervous, at first. But the second we walked in and saw the two of them, along with Lola's sister, Casey, and the Revelers starting pitcher, Ross Davies, goofing around in the kitchen, I felt completely at ease.

It was like one of those articles you see on TMZ, where they show pictures of famous people grocery shopping and pumping gas, showing the world that they're just like everyone else.

And then we all sat down to a meal together and conversation flowed about anything and everything. That's when I really felt like they truly were like anybody else and I understood how Finley became such good friends with them.

Now, I consider them friends too.

Lost in my thoughts, I miss Bo's swing, but hear the crack of the bat.

Lola grabs my arm and slowly stands, her eyes on the field, watching the ball. Collectively, the entire stadium holds its breath as the ball soars into the outfield.

It's going…going…gone!

When it clears the wall in the outfield, the stadium erupts and Lola is jumping up and down, giving high fives to everyone. Finn's strong arms envelop me and he laughs triumphantly in my ear. "Did you see that? Walk-off homerun!"

Fireworks explode over the outfield wall as *Walkin' To New Orleans* by Buckwheat Zydeco blares over the loudspeaker.

After the celebration dies down, we walk out with Casey and Lola, as far as we can go before we'd need passes. Lola said she'd get us some, but Finn and I decline. The box seats are enough and we want to give them time to celebrate, promising to get together for dinner again soon.

"See y'all later," Casey says as we turn to walk away.

"We're going to stop by the gallery soon," Lola adds.

Turning, I smile and wave. "I'll see you then!"

Once Finn and I are out of the stadium, we get an Uber to take us home, but change our minds mid-ride and ask the driver to drop us at Jackson Square. When we step out of the car, the vibe is electric, but it's hot as Hades.

With summer upon us, the intense heat and humidity of New Orleans are on full blast.

"Wanna grab a sno-ball from the French Market?" Finn asks, grabbing my hand as we start down the sidewalk.

"Only if we can get Bahama Mama again," I tell him, pulling my sunglasses off the top of my head and sliding them back into place. The evening sun is still shining bright.

Finn places an arm in front of me, shielding me from a group passing by. "I was thinking Cake Batter."

"Half Bahama Mama, half Cake Batter?" I suggest.

This is a typical conversation for us lately. On evenings we don't have anything to do, we take King out for short walks and usually end up at one of the sno-ball stands around the city. But the one in the French Market is our favorite. Plus, Louisiana Pizza Kitchen is just across the street, and they have a shrimp pizza that's to die for.

"Whatever you want, baby," Finn concedes, kissing the top of my head.

When I glance up at him, I notice he's also wearing shades—an old pair of wayfarers that very well might be the same ones he used to wear in high school, because that's a very Finley thing to do. With the evening sun hitting him just right, he's even more beautiful than usual, if that's possible.

Stopping in the middle of the sidewalk, I reach up and pull him down for a searing kiss.

"What was that for?" he asks, giving me a small chuckle, but then leaning in for a kiss of his own, one that makes my toes curl in my shoes.

Dazed for a moment, it takes me a second to answer. "Because you're beautiful and you're mine."

"I don't know about the beautiful part," Finn says, as we continue walking. "But the being yours part is true… always have been, always will be."

Bringing my hand up to his lips, he kisses it and then holds it close to his chest.

After we get our sno-ball—half Bahama Mama, half Cake Batter—we walk back to Jackson Square and find a patch of grass under one of the trees, close to the cathedral. From here, we can hear different musicians playing. Finn leans back against the tree and I lay my head in his lap, accepting bites of sno-ball and soaking in this perfect day.

One of so many, with promises of more to come.

THE END.

Reading Recommendations

We had the BEST time including characters from our previous works into this book! If you're curious about their origins, we've made an easy to follow list:

If you'd like to read more about Dani and Micah, check out *Finding Focus and Fighting Fire*

If you'd like to read more about Cami and Deacon, check out *Chasing Castles*

If you'd like to read more about Tucker and Piper, check out *Taming Trouble*

In those four books, you also get a healthy dose of Annie and Sam Landry!

If you'd like to read more about Carys and Maverick, check out *Blue Bayou*

If you'd like to read more about Avery and Shaw, check out *Come Again*

If you'd like to read more about CeCe and Shep, check out *Neutral Grounds*

Lastly, if you'd like to read more about Lola and Bo, check out *The Rookie and The Rockstar*

Acknowledgments

Thank you for reading Good Times!

We hope you enjoyed this glimpse into our French Quarter world. Finn and Jette were so much fun to write. Their love story was sweet and warm and we couldn't get enough of them.

As with all of our stories, we have a few people we'd like to thank.

First, we'd like to thank our crazy, awesome families. They give us inspiration and so much grace. We wouldn't be able to do what we do without them.

Second, we'd like to thank our team.

Pamela Stephenson, thank you for being an awesome alpha reader, sounding board, and cheerleader! We appreciate your time and input! Thanks for always sticking with us and being onboard for each new adventure.

Nichole Strauss, thank you for being an amazing editor. Thank you for pushing us to write better and always helping us tell the best story!

Juliana Cabrera, thank you for your creativity and patience and for always working us in when we need you. We appreciate you!

To our proofreader, Janice Owen, thank you for being so meticulous in your work.

And last, but certainly not least, we'd like to thank our super fun and supportive reader group, Jiffy Kate's Southern Belles. Y'all are the best! Thank you for always being there for us and reading our words. You're our favorite corner of the internet.

Much love,

Jiffy Kate

About The Authors

Jiffy Kate is the joint pen name for Jiff Simpson and Jenny Kate Altman. They're co-writing besties who share a brain. They also share a love of cute boys, good coffee, and a fun time.

Together, they've written over twenty stories. Their first published book, Finding Focus, was released in November 2015. Since then, they've continued to write what they know—southern settings full of swoony heroes and strong heroines.

You can find them on most social media outlets at @jiffykate, @jiffykatewrites, or @jiffsimpson and @jennykate77.